Best of Isele

Best of Isele

ANTHOLOGY

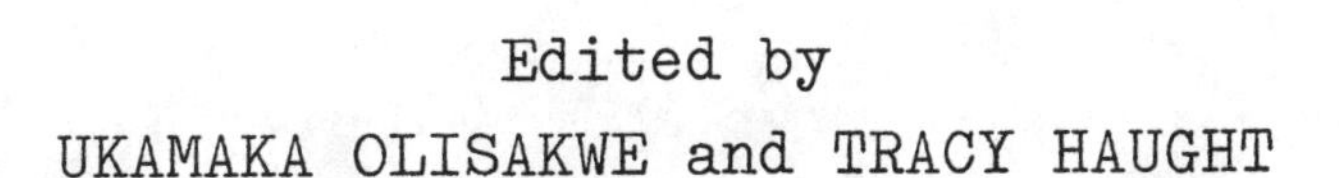

Edited by

UKAMAKA OLISAKWE and TRACY HAUGHT

Published in 2022 by Iskanchi Press
info@iskanchi.com
https://iskanchi.com/
+13852078509

ISBN: 978-1-957810-04-1

Cover Art by Boluwatife Oyediran
Cover design by Akeem Ibrahim

Printed in the United States of America

Contents

Nonfiction

Notable Mentions: Short Stories

Introduction

This inaugural edition of the *Best of Isele Anthology*, which features the excellent works we've published in *Isele Magazine*, despite the impact of the COVID-19 pandemic on our lives, is a distinct and reassuring compilation; more than just a book, it is a vessel of hope.

These stories, poems, and essays appeared in our general and quarterly issues from inception through January 2022. The response to the work we've published has been heartwarming and encouraging—the very validation we needed to continue this journey. Late last year, to show our gratitude to our contributors, we decided to launch The Isele Prizes, an initiative that celebrates the writers who continue to trust us with their work, and who continue to believe in our mission. The prizes are split into three categories—short stories, poetry, and essays; each category is judged by a panel of two judges.

The works we publish at *Isele Magazine* are brilliant and defiant, poignantly exploring themes that defy conventional expectations, which made narrowing down the short stories, poems, and essays for the inaugural longlists a challenge. These works encapsulate our mission: to provide a platform for writers who hold a mirror to our society.

Producing the shortlist was even more difficult. Our judges carefully read each piece, considering them against predetermined criteria relating to our vision for this initiative. Ultimately, it took many months of reading and re-reading before our judges arrived at the winners.

Nora Nneka's deeply moving essay, "Sense of Touch," won the nonfiction category. Nneka uses spellbinding language throughout her piece to explore the relationship between a daughter and her mother, family trauma, grief, and how these experiences shape a woman's narrative arc: her relationship with her body, her journey through pregnancy, and the joy that comes from embracing your own story—stories which define relationship with self and community.

Uche Umezurike's winning poem, "there's more," takes us around the world, gathering stories about people who search for new beginnings despite the dangers that lurk in the deserts and in the seas, dangers that can nip dreams at the bud; our seekers must brave these dangers for their sanity, for a moment away from the despair they are leaving behind. Umezurike's poem is timeless, and we are so lucky he trusted us with his work.

Esther Ifesinachi Okonkwo's winning short story, "The Year of the Sun," explores the difficult conversation about how people love, despite or because of personal and cultural programming, traditions and expectations. With a language that pulses within a tightly controlled structure, "The Year of the Sun," is a masterfully crafted story which fully immerses the reader in setting as Okonkwo builds a world with mathematical precision, so much so that readers, even if they aren't familiar with the period or the culture, are able to see themselves in her characters. This is a story that stays with you.

The exceptional writers in this anthology remind us of the transformative power of stories and the beauty of language. We find succor in their words. Even when it feels like our world is falling apart, we can find healing in the words of these writers who have taken a mirror to our society and showed us new ways to be, to live, and to persevere in the face of what is.

What these works also have in common is their ability to immerse us in different periods and cultures, and to do this with stunning and intelligent language. Some writers respond to ongoing cultural conversations about ways of being, abortion, sexuality, and how we grieve. Others take a keen look at how our interactions during challenging times shape us.

Above all, these works encourage us to remember our duty to care for each other, to nurture an inclusive community where no one feels the pain of discrimination, where no one tramples on the humanity of another. Reading and publishing these stories, especially when we are all still struggling to adapt to a stretched-out pandemic, gave us, and continues to give us, hope.

Included in this anthology are the brilliant works selected by the judges for the notable mention category: Tayler Bunge's "Glowworm," Bono Sigudu's "What it Means to be Free," Desmond Peeples' "GMO," and Boluwatife Oyediran's "The Trial."

Our debut outing of Isele was successful; even though we've experienced financial difficulties, we've found support in our community. And this feat would not have been possible or so successful without the dedication of our editors, who sacrifice their time to the success and mission of this magazine: much gratitude to Kenechi Uzor, Cameron, Finch, Megan Ross, Rebecca Jamieson, and Yvonne Wabai.

We are grateful for all the support we have received, and we are certain that these projects we've launched will continue to flourish, providing a platform for writers who need them.

A heartfelt congratulations to everyone whose work appears in these pages. We will continue to cheer you, support you, and sing your praises at every opportunity. We look forward to seeing more of your work out there in the world. May joy and laughter never stray far from you.

Ukamaka Olisakwe

Tracy Haught

Fiction

Art by Elissa Schappell

The Year Of The Sun

Esther Ifesinachi Okonkwo

It was the year of the sun, the year Agu's body was found in the forest of Amanuke, covered in a mash of red sand and dry blood, the year pythons roamed Akpulu in numbers never before seen, swallowing almost hatched eggs and strangling mother hens until at last, the men of Akpulu trekked the dusty paths of the land in quiet desolation, under the harshness of the midday sun, to Ezemmuo's nkolo, to ask him to ask their gods what was making them angry.

It was a terrible time, and all who had eyes could tell that a knot had loosened. So, the men of Akpulu carried five kegs of palm wine, twelve fat tubers of yam, three heads of sun-dried stock fish, and because the pythons had strangled a considerable number of mother hens, and swallowed a significant number of almost hatched eggs, they could not afford to lose another dead chicken, male or female, so, they added a pregnant goat instead, and went to Ezemmuo's nkolo.

Of all the di okpalas in Akpulu, only one man was missing from the trek. This man's name was Ezuruonye. He had woken up one morning, determined to end the deep, feverish slumber he had fallen into. He had stretched his sleeping bones, looked out of the small, round window of his hut, and saw a python sitting on the stool near the altar his father had built for their family god, Ikenga. It had been two months since he visited his farm, visited anywhere. At the sight of the python, he'd walked back to his bamboo bed, a slow, sad walk, and laid down. He knew that the pythons were a sign that his end was coming. He laid on his bed for a long time, getting up only to urinate and drink water and eat tiny bits from the small bowl of yam pottage or ukwa his neighbor's wife, Adaugo, brought him every evening.

Far from Ezuruonye's hut, near the great river of Idemili, the men of Akpulu sat quietly as they waited for Ezemmuo's figure to emerge from the inside room of the nkolo. They waited apprehensively; they were not eager to hear whatever Ezemmuo was going to tell them.

Ezemmuo finally emerged with his back turned to the men of Akpulu. When he faced them, they rose and said an uncoordinated, "We greet you, eye of the gods," to which Ezemmuo did not reply. His eyes rested on each person. If he noticed that Ezuruonye was not present, his face did not show it. Ezemmuo told the men to come back in three days, that the gods were busy, that the gods do not sit around waiting to be summoned by mere mortals. And though the men of Akpulu knew this was the way of their gods, as they walked back to their huts, they fixed their eyes on the red earth as though returning from a lost war.

Ezuruonye heard about the visit from Adaugo, when she came to his hut with a bowl of yam pottage and dried fish. It was the day after the men of Akpulu visited Ezemmuo's nkolo. She'd usually just drop off the food as her husband, Okugo, asked her to do, but that evening, for the first time, she stood for a while and examined the mass of body before her. Ezuruonye knew she was looking at him even though he kept his gaze on the cane chair next to him. Three months ago, before he killed Agu and left his body in the forest of Amanuke, a woman hovering over him, staring at him like he was a sacrifice to the gods, would have made him uncomfortable. Three months ago, his friend, Okugo, would not have sent his new wife into another man's hut.

"What is it?" he asked.

"Nothing. You are just lying there like a dead man. No matter how much you grieve him, he can't come back."

Ezuruonye was taken aback by this; it stung him, the snarling, scolding tone of this woman who, with her freshly oiled hair and smooth face, looked like she knew nothing about grieving.

"Come, woman, leave me. You have done well by bringing me food all this while. But I no longer need it. I am now well enough to get my own food."

Adaugo arched her eyebrows. "It is not the small portion of yam that bothers me. It is you lying here like the world has ended. It is time for you to carry on. You have mourned him well."

She walked to the other side of the bed and sat down. "When my grandmother died," she said, her voice cracking. "My mother refused to eat for days. She laid on her bed like you for days. And then the days turned to weeks, and the weeks turned to months. Finally, she left me. It is why I continue to bring you food, Ezuruonye. Not because my husband asked me to. I know this kind of pain."

Ezuruonye suddenly felt cold. He remembered his own mother. He remembered the night she had pulled him from his mat and balanced a small load on his head. It was his tenth year on Ani's blessed earth. He could still see the fireflies that adorned the bush as they fled his father's village and walked to Akpulu, his mother's. His father had died of an unnamed illness and his mother was convinced that she could smell him everywhere in the village, taste him even.

"Thank you," he said. "I will heed your advice."

A small smile gathered in Adaugo's eyes and her shoulders relaxed. They sat in silence for a while. Then she began to describe what had happened at Ezemmuo's nkolo the day before. She had heard from Nnedi, her husband's first wife, who had heard from their husband.

"Nnedi told me that Okugo told her that Ezemmuo's eyes were bleeding with both anger and blood. The gods are raging."

Ezuruonye asked her to leave. He was tired, he said. He needed to rest.

"What kind of rest? You have been lying on this bed all day."

"Leave, woman," he said, turning his face to the wall.

Three days after their visit, when the gods had made time for the people of Akpulu and had finally spoken to Ezemmuo, a message was sent to the men of Akpulu, and they all gathered at the nkolo. Ezemmuo sat at the center of the nkolo, singing the song of the spirits, with his legs stretched out before him, and his upper body bent towards the earth. He scattered dirt-stained cowries on the ground, opened one of the kegs of palm wine the people of Akpulu had brought with them on their first visit, filled an Iko halfway, and fed it to the gods. He then drank some himself and passed the Iko, and each man drank, swallowing hard to make certain that every drop was sucked into their stomach. It was the proper thing to do when sharing a drink with the gods. Ezemmuo's nkolo was not the men's wives' hut, so they tucked their agility and ego under their tongues and sat with the humility of soon-to-be-wed-virgins. When Ezemmuo's singing ceased, they stilled their breaths, strained their ears, widened their eyes, tightened their clutches on the knot of their wrappers, and waited for him to say what the gods had told him.

Ezemmuo said nothing. Instead, he stood and danced, circling the cowries scattered on the ground. This time he did not sing; he chanted praises to the gods: "Okaka. The ones who never sleep. The ones who go to war with bare hands. Ekwueme. The ones who see the back and the front at once. Woods impenetrable to termites." Ezemmuo praised the gods with all his might and soul. His body moved with vigor, his feet rising and falling with a swiftness that assured the men of Akpulu that their gods were close by, present maybe.

When Ezemmuo finally spoke, his voice rattled the horns circling the rafters. The horns clinked and clinked, and the air in the nkolo became stiff, so stiff that if one threw a knife from one end of the nkolo to the other, one would have heard the sound of something slicing in two.

The gods spoke of the worst: a man had died at a time the gods had not assigned for him to die. Even they, the gods, had been taken unawares, and it angered them. Worse still was the manner of the death: the man was killed from behind, so he could not fight for his life. And the killer had, at one point, dined with the dead man, eaten from the same soup bowl. Also, the killing was motivated by jealousy. It was not news that if you wanted what someone else had in Akpulu, if you wanted it badly enough, then all you had to do was challenge them to a wrestling match, and if the gods wanted it for you and you win the match, the thing becomes yours.

It then came as a surprise to the men of Akpulu that a coward and murderer lived amongst them. Of the four men who had recently died in Akpulu, two had been old men who died in their sleep. Surely their deaths could not offend the gods so much so that they unleashed the pythons on the people of Akpulu. Of the other two, one had been sick— they had watched him die of a fever that turned his skin red, ate all the hair on his head, and sucked all the flesh off his bones. This left the death of Agu.

The men clucked their tongues and spat on the red mud of the nkolo. They raised their shoulders to their ears and brought them down swiftly. When Agu died, they knew something was not right. How could a man who had the strength of a lion— they even sometimes called him the lion— die in a forest he knew like his palm? When they found Agu's dead body, bloodied and plastered with dry grass and twigs, the people of Akpulu did not know what to make of it. It had been fifty years since someone had been murdered in cold blood in Akpulu, so when they saw the animal marks on Agu's body, they squeezed their noses, shook their heads, and concluded that a wild animal had killed him.

When the men returned to their huts and told their wives what they had heard with their holy ears, the women shook their legs furiously, untied and tied their wrappers, and told their husbands that they knew it, that they felt it under their right breasts, days before the pythons invaded the village, knocking over the clay waterpots of old women, flickering thin tongues at naked, ashy children, curling around the machetes of Akpulu's greatest warriors. The gods' anger was no small matter.

Ezuruonye, again, heard the news from Adaugo. She had continued to bring him food every evening. She came in silence and left in silence, but on the third day after their quarrel, she noticed that he was quivering. She pressed her hand to his neck and screamed: "Chim o."

Ezuruonye was burning. Even with his eyes open, Adaugo was a blur. He did not know when she ran out or when she came back, clutching a clay pot of steaming water, with a rag around her neck and a bag of medicine hanging on her shoulder. What he knew was that he woke a few hours later and his fever had broken.

"Adaugo," he said. "You are still here?" He sat up and rested his back on the wall.

"Rest, Ezuruonye. When I went to gather my mother's medicine for you, I told Okugo you were sick. I have his permission."

"Thank you," he said.

"It is Chukwu that did the work; I only gave you medicine." She looked over at his father's altar. He could tell she was shy and pleased.

"Where are you from?" he asked.

"Umunachi," she stuttered as though she was not expecting the question.

He knew Okugo had married her as a third wife six months ago, but there were many things he did not remember. Many things he was trying not to remember. He imagined that she was very lonely. It was why she came to him. He knew what it felt like to be uprooted from one's furnished life and placed in an empty space, where one had to build, piece by piece, another home. His first days in Akpulu had been difficult. His mother, deep in her grief, was no company. He remembered walking a lot, stick in hand, smacking the leaves that shot out to the roads. It was on one of those walks that he first saw Agu, little Agu, with a smile so big and so whole it caused something insidious and sweet to creep into Ezuruonye's mind. From that second, they became *AguandEzuruonye*. They spent their afternoons chasing each other around the village, wrestling each other, and playing *Ncho*. They spent their evenings with the other village boys.

Adaugo sneezed and made to touch his hand. It was a small move, so small that Ezuruonye would have believed it was in his imagination if she had not clenched her fist, as though restraining herself.

"My co-wife, Nnedi, tells me good things about you," Adaugo said. "Everyone says you are a kind man, and you shouldn't be suffering."

When Ezuruonye didn't reply, she continued: "They say that you loved Agu like a brother. I wish someone would mourn me like this."

Ezuruonye lay still.

"My mother is dead, and my father has forty children, none of whom are from my mother. This is why I am so bothered that I am yet to carry Okugo's child. Who will mourn me when I die?"

"Mourning is not the only thing children are good for," he said.

Adaugo squinted, as though in deep thought. "But is it not important? To have somebody mourn you when you are gone?"

"It is, but it is not the reason to want children. Maybe that is another reason why they have refused to come. They see you planning sorrow for them even before their birth."

"You make me sound like a bad person, Ezuruonye. I am not planning sorrow for them. I just want—" Then she caught the glint in his eyes. "You are making fun of a barren woman."

"You are not a barren woman," he said. "You are just funny."

Adaugo hit the mud floor three times and threw her head back. A growling laughter left her throat. "Nobody has called me funny before."

Ezuruonye liked how unwomanly her laughter sounded. Loud, bursting. It was the laughter of a woman who had grown up without a mother constantly in her ears telling her how to behave. He laughed with her. The sound of his laughter startled them both. It was a low sound, like the gentle bubbling of boiling water. But it was laughter, nonetheless. He didn't know he could still laugh.

Adaugo, radiant, eager to keep the conversation going, narrated the story her husband had told her and her co-wives about what had transpired in Ezemmuo's nkolo. She told him an animated version, intrigued by the suspense of it all, unaware of the violent twitching of Ezuruonye's left foot. She asked if Agu had told him about any enemies? Her questions were met with silence and cold eyes.

Who killed Agu? became a game the children of Akpulu played in the village square, in the silvery moonlight. They flexed thin muscles, beat dry chests, raised bony shoulders, and screamed *I killed Agu* into each other's faces, because, only a strong man could kill a warrior as fine as Agu. The women shook their heads. What did the children know? Had they not heard that whoever killed Agu took him from behind like a coward? Had they not heard that the killer was a ball-less man who could not look another man in the eyes and wrestle him?

But as the women walked to their farms, while the sky birthed the sun, they could not stop talking about Agu's death. They guessed and guessed, each woman taking her turn. Ugodiya, the third wife of Uwabunkeonye, the man whose barn had the most yams in all of Akpulu every harvest season, said it must have been Obidike. Did he not, days before Agu was found dead, accuse him of stealing his land? Ochakomaka, the fairest of the women, whose skin shone like the sun was permanently turned towards her, said she was sure it was Ikechukwu. She had caught him giving Agu the evil eye several times. Ezinne, whose brain worked only half of the year—she spent her bad days roaming Akpulu, muttering to herself, chasing children who sang songs of mockery at her, and her good days with hands deep in clay, molding pots—said it must have been Ezenwa. He had always wanted Agu's chieftaincy title.

The men scratched their machetes on the ground, raised them to the sky, and swore to their gods that justice would be served, that whoever killed Agu like he was an ant would use his eyes to see the back of his head.

They knew what had to be done even before Ezemmuo told them. It had been done fifty years ago when Achebe the albino was found dead with a knife stuck in his neck and the peanut brown of his eyes rolled into his head. Then they did not need the gods to come down from the sky to tell them they were looking at the body of a man who had been murdered. Then, it was Ezemmuo's father who was the mouthpiece of the gods. When the news reached his ears, it was a matter of hours before the whole of Akpulu knew who the killer was.

Ezuruonye heard about the invocation this time from the town crier who went around the village beating his gong. The fever that Adaugo had banished was coming back. Adaugo had come and gone. He was relieved she had gone before the town crier's message. He worried she would pester him with questions about what Agu did and didn't tell him before his death. He would not go for the invocation, he told himself as he reached for his bowl of food. He would wait for them in his hut. But wouldn't his absence emphasize his cowardice? Wasn't attending the invocation the right thing to do? Then again, there was no right thing to do. Everything was wrong, he thought, everything. The air he was breathing was wrong. He cursed the day he had first let Agu touch him. There were many things he had forgotten, but he could not forget that day at Agu's father's farm, when, as they rested under the shade of an orange tree, after hours of uprooting yam, Ezuruonye had turned his head to find Agu watching him with intense want. It was clear; it was unmistakable. They were both sweating. And then Agu had kissed him. It was wet and brief and strange. He did not know he could feel the way he felt, the liquidity and smoothness of this pleasure, the perfection of it. It had turned to a raw roughness when Agu wrapped his palm around him and stroked. Afterward, as they sat a few inches away from each other, grateful that no one had walked into them, Agu had told Ezuruonye he loved him. It was their thirteenth year on Ani's blessed earth, and it was then that everything gradually changed. What he felt for Agu became darker and sweeter. It was a raging and wild thing that had swept into his world that was mostly calm; that mostly revolved around the muteness of his mother. He dropped the bowl of half-eaten yam pottage.

He would go for the invocation. He would look Agu in the eye one last time.

At the crack of dawn on the day Ezemmuo set for the invocation, the people of Akpulu woke up to the sound of flutes preparing the land for the presence of a spirit as powerful as Agu's. A man was as powerful in the spirit land as he was on earth, and Agu's strength was something to marvel at, so they blew their flutes hard, blew it until the veins in their necks threatened to burst.

A frantic, giddy feeling possessed the people of Akpulu. Half of them had not been born when Ezemmuo's father called forth the spirit of Achebe from the land of the dead. They did not see the madness in the nkolo when Achebe's spirit caused a riotous breeze to swirl the light weighted things on the ground of the nkolo. Those who had been there could not explain what it felt like to be in the presence of a tortured spirit. So, it was only normal for the people of Akpulu to have flutters in their stomachs at this coming invocation.

As though the god of the sky was frowning on that day, the sun refused to shine. It peeked from behind tall trees as the people of Akpulu took tense steps towards Ezemmuo's nkolo with pythons slithering behind, beside and in front of them.

At a corner of the nkolo, opposite the staff of Amadioha, sat Agu's four wives: Oriaku, Nnedinma, Adaeze, and Obianujunwa, who now looked like sisters after years of looking into each other's faces. Beside the wives were Agu's sons and daughters, and beside them were Agu's kinsmen. And next to them stood Ezuruonye. They stood nearest to the staff since Agu's spirit would probably possess the body of the person he trusted the most, and that body must not be too far from the staff where the spirit is invoked. The spirit must not be bodyless for longer than necessary.

Ezemmuo fixed his eyes on the half-formed sun, waiting for it to dip into the shrubs that circled the hills of Akpulu. It was the sun that would tell him when the link between the land of the living and that of the dead was at its weakest. When the moment came, he began calling Agu by his praise names. He gyrated, and dust rose from his feet. He twirled and twirled, giving his body to his father, and his father's father. The people of Akpulu would, for many years to come, be unable to say what they saw when the staff of Ani split in two and birthed a surge of wind that disappeared into Oriaku, Agu's first wife. Oriaku swelled in an instant: her gait became Agu's, her eyes became Agu's, her arms became Agu's, and when she spoke, her voice became Agu's, a roar that left a tingling in the ears of all who heard it.

As Oriaku opened her mouth, the nkolo fell silent. Even babies balanced on the hips of their mothers were transfixed; they watched with big eyes and drooling mouths, fat fingers entwined around the sweaty thumbs of their mothers'. A chill settled upon the nkolo, and as was normal in the presence of a spirit, the people of Akpulu felt the hair on their bodies kink, and a heaviness engulf their heads.

Agu's eyes darted around the nkolo, taking everything and everyone in as if to assert his presence, as if to say: I see you. His eyes finally rested on Ezemmuo, who, already, was no longer himself. His skin had become a pale shade of white, and a subtle glow flickered in the blackness of his eyes. Agu walked up and down the nkolo and then stopped in front of Ujunwa, the fifth wife of Ikedieze the palm wine tapper. His eyes rested on her flat belly adorned with colored waist beads and asked her if she knew she was pregnant. Ujunwa nodded no and smiled, and did a little dance of thanksgiving to the gods. Agu stopped beside Mbaka, a man whose yam seedling had refused, year after year, to produce yam good enough to sell at the market square. Agu told him he was farming on land that wasn't his to farm. The story of how Mbaka's father had snatched the land from his late brother's wife would later be told, but at that moment, the people stared at one another in confusion. The air grew compact. To have a spirit see what everyone wanted to hide made the people anxious. Whose secrets was he going to tell? Whose wrongdoings was he going to air? Everyone knew they had something to hide.

At last, Agu stopped in front of Ezuruonye.

"Why?" he asked. He was a spirit who knew everything, but he still asked, not to know, but to understand, because, indeed, there was a difference between knowing and understanding.

"Why?" he asked again. Ezuruonye did not speak.

Agu looked at Ezemmuo, pointed to Ezuruonye, and said: "He killed me. He took a knife to my heart from the back, a person I call my person." He turned his head to face his family and smiled, and then he disappeared.

Oriaku's body lay on the ground, empty. Her co-wives bent over her, praying that her spirit found its way back to her body. Ezuruonye still could not speak or move. The people of Akpulu wanted to ask him the same question Agu had asked: Why? Why kill a man you call brother? Ezemmuo, now himself, did not know what to make of the new information. Of course, a man who killed another had to pay with his life, but the men were best friends. Oriaku sneezed, and her co-wives breathed in relief. Now Ezemmuo could concentrate on the problem in front of him. He moved towards Ezuruonye, who towered over him by a good foot. He looked him straight in the eyes and then spat on the ground. "As you have killed so shall you be killed," he said, and the whole village chorused, "So shall he be killed."

That night, after the invocation, as Ezuruonye lay on his bed, he wondered why he had never thought to build a bigger hut. He had the means. His barn was not the biggest, but his farm produced good yams. The hut had become too small for him a long time ago; or, rather, he had become too big for the hut. He remembered building the hut, smoothening the roughness of the wall with red soil. He had spent days drawing shapes and patterns with white chalk on the wall inside and outside. He would look out of his window occasionally and catch the admiration in the eyes of people as they walked past. It used to please him. He stood up from his bed and walked to his water pot. The hut was aglow with light from the firewood Adaugo had brought him. He stared into the pot. He kicked it and the impact sent a sharp pain to his head. It was Agu's pot. Agu had given it to him as a gift after his mother died. He had continued to stay in this small hut because it used to make him feel closer to Agu. They had spent many nights in this hut making love, making promises. He shouldn't have gone to the invocation, he thought. He should have waited for them, in his hut, as he had planned. He was not thirsty. What did he come to get? He walked back to his bamboo bed and sat down. He thought of quenching the fire and lying in the darkness. He thought of Adaugo. She wouldn't bring him food now that she knew what he was. He wasn't even hungry anyway. He adjusted his loin cloth. He had thought seeing Agu again would thrust him deeper into the black hole he had made his home the past months, but, strangely, he felt awake, as if he had been moving in the world half asleep and now, suddenly, he could feel everything. He swatted a mosquito that perched on his shoulder. He knew they would kill him. He missed the mosquito; it was now buzzing in his ears. He laid down and closed his eyes. Agu's face glided in the darkness behind his lids. He wasn't shocked at Agu's reaction at the invocation. 'Why? Why?' He had said, as though he did not know. It was just like him to act ignorant. To do as he liked and expect no consequences.

He did not know Adaugo was there until she cleared her throat.

"What are you doing here?" he asked. It was not the question he meant to ask.

"What I have been doing here for the past months is what I am doing here today. Bringing you food."

"Thank you, Adaugo. I was not expecting you."

She set the bowl on the floor and walked to the door. She stood for a few seconds and then turned back and sat beside his bed. "I feel great pity for you, Ezuruonye," she said, "I have never seen a person as sad as you."

Ezuruonye had not noticed, until then, how beautiful she was. She was a short woman with the features of a tall person. Her hands and legs were long and slender. She had full pointy lips that reddened at the middle, where the upper lip met the lower lip. He imagined he could cup the whole of her face in his palms.

"I am sad, Adaugo. As you now know, I have committed an abomination."

"Why is my heart telling me that you did not do it?" Her eyes grew small.

"It is because you have a good heart."

"But you don't look like a person who can kill another, especially his best friend."

Anger rose in him. "He was not my best friend."

"But everyone says you were inseparable from childhood."

"Please leave. I am tired." He rolled to the other edge of the bed, away from her.

"I do not believe that you are a bad person. I know that the gods are angry and want you to pay for what you have done, but if you say why you did what you did, we can appease the gods."

He turned to her. "Did you not hear what I said, woman? Leave. What is wrong with you? Is this how the women in your village behave?"

"Between the both of us, who is acting like something is wrong with them? Am I the one who killed my friend? Am I the one who has been lying on the bed for months like a lazy fool? Am I the one who did not even move his body when his friend pointed at him and called him a murderer? Am I the one?" She was now standing, her head thrust forward, her hands on her hips, as though really expecting answers to her questions. "Open your mouth and talk."

The room grew dimmer, the firewood was burning out.

"Go home," he said. "Please, just go."

"No, I will not. I will only go if you tell me what happened."

Ezuruonye closed his eyes. He would ignore her until she got tired and left.

"I know that good people do bad things. I have not known you for long. I am a newcomer to this village, but I have only heard good things about you. Mama Nkechi told me how you brought tubers of yam to her house every three moons after her husband died. She said everyone forgot about her except you." Her voice was calm, pleading.

"I didn't give him the chance to fight for his life," Ezuruonye said. "I just took him from the back."

The biting sound of nightlife had gone quiet. The mosquito no longer buzzed. He felt as though his heart was forcing itself up his throat.

"Please go, Adaugo. Please just go."

The next day, the people gathered to decide on how Ezuruonye would go. They sat underneath the Udala tree at the center of the market square, where, when the sun had retreated and given way for the moon, children danced to songs about the greed of the tortoise and the poise of the lion; where women dipped their hands into the rebellious curls of each other's hair and tamed them into fat braids and gossiped in measured tones about the latest happenings in the village; where men sat with legs ajar, and kegs of palm wine an inch away from their big toes, and bragged about their new achievements. This time, the men did not sit ajar; there was no palm wine or laughter. They sat stiffly, with heads turned up to the sky as if questioning the gods. Their minds flashed back to their peculiar and identical experiences of Ezuruonye. They thought of his gaze that lingered on their faces so steadily yet so daintily, as though he was in no hurry, as though he could sit with them all day, listening to everything that made their hearts heavy. They thought about his calming quietness, how he spoke only to comfort, to soothe. They thought about how he noiselessly made space for everyone without shrinking himself. And though he had killed Agu, whom they envied for his strength, who did not look them in the eyes, whose agility discomforted them, who chipped at the stony hardness of their egos and flamed their insecurities, they felt killing Ezuruonye was like crushing a blooming flower.

It was Dimkpa, the hunter, who suggested they summon Ezuruonye to ask him why he killed Agu. If they could hear the wickedness in his voice, they would steel themselves.

Four men marched to Ezuruonye's hut to summon him. They found him standing beside the coconut tree that shaded his hut. He stood akimbo, his eyes turned up to where tiny coconuts clustered under the canopy of the dull green leaves. He seemed in deep, sorrowful thought.

A lizard scuttled past the four men as they spoke. Ezuruonye nodded a stiff yes. His eyes did not linger on their faces or meet their eyes. He entered his hut and came out with a straw hat on his head.

"Let's go," he said.

The men wondered at how he could have an axe dangling over his head and still walk with lightness in his feet. While they walked to fetch Ezuruonye, they had talked about his mysteriousness, this man that had neither wife nor children. It was, perhaps, for the best. Now that he was going to die such a shameful death, he would leave no one behind to mourn him, or to carry the shame which he would leave after his death. But as they walked to the market square with feet browned by dust and cracked by many treks to farmlands and villages far from Akpulu, the men said nothing.

Ezuruonye stood at the center of the half-moon shape the men of Akpulu had formed. He folded his hands just below his breast, his body slightly slanted backward. There was something soft about the way he did not glare at the men, or lean towards them, something that could have seemed like remorse if his eyes did not hold a kind of certitude; he deserved to stand where he was standing, deserved to breathe the air he was breathing, deserved to fold his hands how he was folding them.

The men told him why they had summoned him: to know why he killed Agu. Ezuruonye told the men of Akpulu he had no answer for them, that he had accepted his death and he was ready to die on the date they set for him, and if all they called him here for was to ask about his reason for killing Agu, they had better let him return to his hut and spend his remaining hours on earth asking the gods to cleanse his spirit.

The men looked at each other, then at Ezuruonye, then at each other. There was no contempt in Ezuruonye's voice, his tone was soft and smooth, devoid of stuttering and cracks. They had summoned him so he could harden their hearts against him, but here he was, ready to give what he had taken. He did not beg or ask for lighter punishment. He did not make up a fabulous, pitiful story about a wrong meted on him by the late Agu who could not defend himself. They let him go.

However much they guessed, the people of Akpulu could not agree on why Ezuruonye killed Agu. They became tired of guessing, of thinking about death and talking about it, of pythons circling things that should not be circled, so they set a date for Ezuruonye's execution.

"I will tell you what happened," Ezuruonye said to Adaugo

as she walked into his hut. He did not understand why she continued bringing him food. He did not understand why Okugo let her.

Adaugo tried to hide her excitement but failed. "You will tell me? Me, a barren, ordinary woman. You will tell me what you have refused to tell important people?"

She said she had heard how he latched on to silence at the village square earlier that day.

"But you will tell no one," Ezuruonye said.

She nodded. "I swear on my mother's grave. May Amadioha strike me dead if I ever say a word about this to anyone."

Ezuruonye breathed deeply. "I don't know where to start."

Adaugo sat stiffly, unmoving, breathing softly, as though trying to become invisible. "Start from the beginning."

The moon was not out that night. A startling blackness covered Akpulu's sky. Ezuruonye could hear the piercing sound of a baby's cry from a close-by hut, and then the soft, oil-like voice of a woman singing: '*Onye tiri nwa n'eba kwa...*'

"I don't know where the beginning is," he said.

"Start from when the pain began, when it started to hurt."

It was an odd, precise response, and for a moment he wondered about Adaugo, about her life before now, and he wished he had a chance to know her well.

When it started to hurt? In their seventeenth year on Ani's blessed earth, when he saw Agu and Oriaku, arm in arm, laughing, touching, gazing. It slashed into him. When Agu visited his hut later that night, he'd said nothing. He'd let Agu touch him, but each touch felt like a thousand pins. It was then clear that his mother's muteness was now his. He'd said nothing as Agu went from Oriaku to Nnedinma, and then to two other wives and six other concubines. He said nothing as Agu visited his hut whenever he liked, with a mouth that held an equal amount of lies and promises. For some people desire burned out, flickered and died off under such pressure; Ezuruonye's raged on and on, from boyhood to manhood, till all he was left with was hardness, like a fruit sucked of all its flesh and juice and sweetness. But he didn't tell Adaugo this, he told her about a certain kind of clarity that eludes a person in torture, only to reveal itself afterward. And it was that clarity that came upon him on their twenty-fifth year on Ani's blessed earth, when Agu stopped coming to his hut entirely. He saw that he had shaped his life around the unsteady curve of Agu's. He had bottled up himself. Lived his life in a daze. Until, one night, while walking to the village square to sit with Okugo and his other kinsmen, he saw Agu entering the bush. He followed him, walking carefully on the dried leaves. It was there he saw Agu's hands wrapped around the waist of a boy, a stranger. As though mocking him, the moon, which had been hidden the last three nights, was full and blinding. It painted Agu's dark skin a glittering silver.

He realized he was crying when Adaugo wrapped her arms around him. "Ozugo," she said, "It is okay." She gathered the edge of her wrapper and wiped the tears on his face.

"I don't need to hear the rest," she said.

He did not want to tell the rest. He did not want to tell that what truly broke him open was that Agu had stayed behind when the boy left. It was what he and Agu used to do when they still made love in the bush. He would leave first; Agu would leave a few minutes later. It was a dance they had danced so many times, a performance that was completely theirs, and Agu had so easily given the boy Ezuruonye's part.

"Ozugo," Adaugo said. "What has happened has happened. Let it be."

He wondered what would have happened if he hadn't packed a knife in his bag, alongside oranges which he planned to peel and lick at the village square. Would his rage had dwindled the next day? Would Agu still be alive?

She placed his head on her lap and stroked his hair. Ezuruonye knew then what he must do.

The day of Ezuruonye's execution, everything appeared to be happening slowly. The day would not break. The people of Akpulu stirred on their bamboo beds and raffia mats, dozing in and out of sleep, peering into the dark night and wondering when the sun would rise. When it finally did, the women made breakfast of boiled yam and salted palm oil, swallow with the ofe oha of the day before, ukwa with dried fish and roasted bushmeat. The children knew that an important event was to take place and they behaved properly. They did not let their mothers ask them twice to go to the Kalawa river to fetch water. They did not play as they walked to and from the river, did not whistle, did not run, did not say anything provocative to each other. The men dragged their feet and spent more time than usual pouring libation to the gods, praying that they watch the backs of their humble servants.

That afternoon, the sun was at its awful best. It beat the people so mercilessly they had to fan themselves. When it was time, they gathered at the home of Ike, the executioner, a position most of the children of Akpulu did not know existed. Ezuruonye was going to die exactly how he killed Agu, with a knife to his back. But unlike Agu, he had wide-eyed spectators, people whom he had dined with, laughed with, sang with, danced with. Old women who he had lifted heavy loads for; young girls who had given him the eye that meant he could have them however he wanted; full chested boys at the peak of their youth, whom he had taught to wrestle, to let their feet be one with the ground, because a wrestler's strength is in that balance, the balance of the feet on the ground.

Everyone had arrived, even the little children who could not be left at home because no one was willing to miss out on the execution. Everyone except Ezuruonye. They knew he was a murderer, that he had killed someone who trusted him. They knew he was the reason the gods had unleashed pythons on them, but knowing that wasn't enough to erase their memory of the goodness he had shown them, or the sunniness in his eyes, so they did not hound him, did not think he might try to escape the punishment he had wholeheartedly accepted.

But when their legs became restless from waiting, and they saw pythons everywhere, on tops of trees, on the thatches of huts, on the benches left outside huts for evening catch-ups, and laying on small carpets of grass, as though, in the few last minutes, they had suddenly multiplied, fear rose inside them, and they sent another group of four men to fetch Ezuruonye.

This group of four men found Ezuruonye beneath the same tree where the other group had met him. The coconut tree, speckled with the green hue of algae, with leaves that shivered in the soft evening breeze, held Ezuruonye's body dangling from a thick brown rope. His feet were neat, a scrubbed-clean neatness. The men imagined him, hours before his death, scrubbing the thick, dried calluses off his heels, the rope around his neck and his death plan laid out before him.

The men shuddered, shook their heads like they could shake away the reality in front of them. Two men stayed behind, and the other two sprinted to the executioner's hut to say what their eyes had seen. Soon, the people gathered. Women and children wailed, and men tried but failed to hold the tears that welled behind their tightly shut lids. But no one cried harder than Adaugo. She rolled on the ground and cursed the gods in a language that was understood by her alone. Though the people of Akpulu knew that the pythons would disappear, and the gods would no longer be angry, they were not relieved. The gods were always right, always right, but they couldn't stop thinking that, hanging there, dead in the worst possible way, was a good man.

About the author:
Esther Ifesinachi Okonkwo is a graduate of the Iowa Writers' Workshop. She's currently pursuing a PhD in Creative Writing at Florida State University. A 2021 recipient of the Elizabeth George Foundation Grant, her fiction has appeared in *Isele Magazine*, *Guernica*, and *Catapult*. She is at work on her debut novel.

Today She Will

Saratu Abiola

Stop smoking. Not because she believed it was such a terrible habit, but because of how she started. It was a small thing, really. She merely saw the cigarette packet on a table, slipped one out of the pack, and began smoking it. Just like that. That was how she did most things. Her marriage, for example. She doesn't know why she married her husband. She had met a tall, handsome banker at a dinner party her sister threw for a PR consultancy firm. He had said hello, poured her a drink. When he spoke, she heard a Nigerian accent smoothed over by years abroad as though with sandpaper. He seemed nice enough, smart enough. *Enough.* Why wouldn't she let him take her out a few times then, to parties where she had nothing to do but smile politely and listen to him drone on about Nigerian politics while hoping to get a contract? He was perfect; everyone thought so. When her sister saw him talking to her that first time, it was as though someone had blindfolded her and put her on a one-way express train to somewhere she had always wanted to go but had not yet packed for or learned any of the languages. Six months later, he had asked her to marry him and she had said yes. There was no reason not to. When asked about how they got married, she'd always laugh and say, "It all happened so fast!" She thought of everything in her life that way—her marriage, her child, her not going out to get a job. She did not know how any of those came to be so permanent, so *there*.

She had only traveled to the UK three times, each time

with her husband, but this last trip was different. This time, over the novelty of London and bored of being at home waiting for her husband's sister to take her out, she went on long walks on her own. Sometimes, she would even hop on the train and purposely get lost, find herself in Bayswater or Kilburn or Canary Wharf, walking the packed streets aimlessly, pretending that she had come to London by herself, on her own terms. One day, she chose not to go straight to the train station a block away from her sister-in-law's apartment, opposite the newsagent she often guiltily bought tubs of Haagen-Dasz and Maltesers. She instead planned to walk to the next station over but first, have lunch at the chip shop down the road. That was how she met Eric.

Eric was not as tall as her husband, but his broad shoulders and toned arms made him look strong and athletic. He had a wide, gap-toothed smile, a short afro like Samuel L. Jackson in *Pulp Fiction*, and an easy manner. He took her order and, hearing her accent, asked if she was Nigerian. She confirmed that she was. Well, he was, too.

A Nigerian named Eric? Was he serious?

Yes, he had said, laughing. His mom and dad just liked the name.

She made her order and stood to the side, and he told her he was studying for his undergraduate degree at a small university in London. She smiled, amused that he would tell her that without her asking, even more amused that he found her worth the quick attempt at respectability. He was Nigerian after all.

While she waited for her fish and chips, he asked her what her name was. He asked her where exactly she was from. When he had to attend to another customer, he asked if she could wait, and she did. She liked watching him with the customers, leaning over the counter as though they were telling him a secret, smiling when he bantered with the customers, first the heavyset ruddy-faced man with gold-rimmed glasses and a Kangol cap, then the petite girl with a blond bob. She liked how differently he sounded with these people, how much more British. It made her think that she reminded him of home.

She was not the type of person to harbor secrets. Perhaps her husband was more the type. She did not know anything about his private life before they met and later married. Indeed, she had never thought it her place to ask or try to find out. Her husband had always played his part while holding himself apart, but that was normal. Aren't men *always*, in the real sense of it, single? Her husband was so solitary that when he would go to meet business partners or friends after work and she never went along, nobody thought it strange. So she began to make a habit of stopping by the chip shop to talk with Eric on his lunch break, until a week passed and she saw him every day since their first meeting. Nobody suspected a thing. When she said she was going shopping all by herself, that she wanted to wander and get lost in Central London, nobody batted an eyelid. When she would go out on long walks with Eric and tell her husband and his sister that she went to dinner in a Greek restaurant then off to catch a jazz show, everyone assumed she was by herself. On these walks, they talked about everything—her Lagos, so different from the one he left five years ago; his London, as full as it was with studying and work. *There's nothing fun in my world,* he often said. *All I do is work. London is where I work. Like, the entire city is a job.*

But nothing was supposed to come of this. She had just wanted a secret thing to curl her fingers around in her pocket, something that only she knew was there.

That one day when her husband went to Manchester to see old friends from university and his sister spent much of the day at the law firm where she worked, she and Eric spent the whole day together. They took the train to Central London to walk around the Tate Modern, then linger by the riverbank before having lunch at Wagamama's. They were like natives to each other, sitting and laughing over green tea and noodles from their table by the restaurant window, watching the tourists pass. He teased her about liking green tea (*it tastes like the agbo my mom used to force-feed me when I had stomach trouble as a kid*). She made fun of him not liking football (*So your name is Eric and you don't like football. Next thing now, you'll say you don't like pepper"*). The air was cool, the sun was out, and the river just off the broad walk shone like new leather. She felt herself carried along by the conversation, their easy laughter, the ease with which she walked in step with him. She could feel herself committing to something she could not yet name, something almost tangible, something that she actually wanted.

They took the train southeast to his apartment, a three-bedroom on the fourth floor of a beige-colored ten-storey block. The interior was more welcoming than the building's exterior, if sparsely decorated; all the living room had was a green corduroy-looking sofa and a shaggy black rug in front of the large flatscreen television set. Beneath the crisp air wafting in through the windows was just the hint of cigarette smoke and, from the tiny kitchen that she did not enter, warmth as if someone had just been cooking.

"We try to keep it clean, but you know how it is," he said offhandedly, as though it were something he felt like he had to say, as he closed the door and draped his jacket over the sofa.

There was a pounding in her ears and her hands shook a little. She sat down slowly, as though afraid the ground beneath her might shift. She knew what she was about to do. He sat on the couch and offered her a bottle of Newcastle. She took a long swig, savoring the bitter even though she had only ever finished a bottle of beer once (aged seventeen, on a dare). When he spoke, it was to say how happy he was that she was there with him. He wrapped an arm around her and stroked her shoulders, and she leaned into him, breathing him in, thinking how strong he felt, how solid. He kissed her easily, without hesitation. Her fingers reached for the back of his neck and crept into his hair, and thinking how different his short afro felt beneath her fingers from her husband's closely-cropped hair. She closed her eyes and willed herself to forget the apartment, this couch so comfortable it was almost as if it were folding them in, the entire world beyond Eric's front door. She thought, instead, of the fingers lazily tracing their way down her back, the pleasant roughness of his stubble against her skin when he kissed her neck, her surprise at how much she wanted him. When his hands slipped between her thighs with an ease that surprised her, she did not push them away. When he laid her on the couch and pressed against her, she ran eager hands up his back, into his thick hair, arched her back, pulled him even closer. When he finally began to undress her, she did not protest that she was married, claim that she had to leave, give him any reason at all to stop.

She did not linger afterward. He remained on the couch

while she got dressed, looking away from him in an effort not to admire his naked body. All he did was ask if she was leaving, and she said yes. He did not ask where she was going. He did not ask her any questions. When she was dressed, he got up from the couch, still naked, to wrap his arms around her and kiss her lips gently. He must have known that she would not go back to see him at the chip shop. She found that she could not look at his face. When he withdrew from her, she left his apartment. On the way out of his apartment, there was a packet of Dunhill cigarettes and a lighter on the wooden table by the front door, and she took them. She walked to the train station with a cigarette burning between her lips.

That was when she started smoking. And she really ought to stop.

Refrain from buying a ticket to London to see him. It's not like she's in love or anything. It's just that she just noticed an ad in the paper for return tickets to London and the thought—the delicious, thrilling thought—ambled through her mind. But as she drove to and from the market for shopping, came home and cooked lunch and dinner, she realized the thought wasn't fleeting at all. It stayed in her brain, lodged there like a stubborn tenant, refusing to budge. Go. Go. Go.

She was surprised at who she had become with Eric, how easy it had been to simply shove her life into a dark corner in the room of her mind, how calmly she conducted herself when she went back home. She had said she went sightseeing at Trafalgar Square, took a long walk, then had some tiramisu at an Italian restaurant somewhere on Edgeware Road. She had lost track of time, and it was wonderful. Yes, her husband did not seem happy she had simply drifted off by herself, but he did not say so. He did not have to, and she'd have hated to pretend as though she cared. He let it rest, and so did she.

She imagined turning up at Eric's door with a huge, genuine smile on her face. He would wrap his arms around her and whisper something about how he was scared he'd never see her again. And they would pick up where they left off, as though the distance and the intervening weeks had never happened. They would have their easy conversations, walks around London streets, holding hands. She would forget herself, forget the weight of all that Lagos bears, and be someone other than herself, someone closer to who she wanted to be.

Fail miserably at refraining from buying a ticket to see him. This was far from the plan. Whatever her issues with her marriage, buying a ticket to London to see a man who could not even be aptly named a lover triggered too many moral tripwires in her mind. But the travel agency's name was below the advert. Go Well Travels, Ltd. Enquire Within. So she did. The ticket was for Royal Air Maroc, which meant a stopover in Casablanca before the onward journey to London. She had also taken a peek at her bank account, the personal bank account that her husband knew existed but probably didn't think much was in it. She did have enough for the ticket. So why not check?

"This ticket would be available for another five days, Ma, but not for longer than that. If I may advise, Ma, I think you should buy it before then." She could almost hear the slight smile on the agent's face, the slight nod of the head as though urging a sale by sheer will. The agent's name was Abosede. Her voice was friendly and soothing, like the vocal equivalent of a pat on the hand. She wondered how old Abosede was.

"OK, so I have to buy it very soon, ehn? Send me the ticket details...."

"Yes, Ma."

"... time of the flight and all that. I should decide within the week whether or not I'm interested."

"Yes, Ma. I'll send you the ticket right away. Once again, the quote in the email would be valid for five days, after which the ticket deal would no longer be available."

"I understand."

"OK, Ma. I will send the ticket now, Ma. Have a nice day."

She waited by her laptop, the internet modem still running, waiting for the email. She thought of how her husband merely informed her of his actions, never even imagining that she may raise an objection. When she opened her email and saw the ticket in her inbox, she felt the smile spread slowly, unbidden across her face. She felt a tingle in her body so small but so powerful that she could not tell where it came from. She could go. She took a cigarette from her bag, lit it, and took a deep drag.

She had five days.

Waver. She bought the ticket two days ago, and it gave her private pleasure. It was like a door left ajar, a private jet at her beck and call, something liberating and reassuring by its mere existence. But she woke up that morning and saw an email reminder about the ticket. Abosede, friendly and reassuring Abosede, was politely reminding her that she had three days to buy the ticket.

She wondered how well she had hidden her delight from her husband these past two days, if he was baffled by the strangeness of her countenance, indeed if he had noticed a change in her countenance at all.

That evening, he came home at eight. She set the dining table with a plate of jollof rice and moin-moin and a piece of chicken, and smiled as she did this; her husband did not like meat with moin-moin. She sat with him but did not eat.

"You're not eating with me?"

"No, I've had dinner already."

"Do you want my chicken? You know I don't like meat with moin-moin."

She didn't answer. She, in fact, hadn't had dinner, and had begun to regret this plan. Her husband ate hungrily, and the jollof rice smelled spicy and good.

Fork and knife scrape plate. He reached for a glass of water and downed it in one go. "*Omo mi nko*?"

"Your daughter is at my mother's."

He laughed heartily. She's always loved his laugh, how unfettered it was, how much it always sounds like he meant it. *"My daughter, ehn?"*

She looked away, waiting to see if he'd notice that she wasn't laughing with him. Suddenly annoyed with herself, she got up from the dining table and walked to the living room to watch the news. She felt his eyes on her back but refused to turn to look at him.

"Everything alright?"

"Yes, why wouldn't it be?"

Now she turned to him, willing him to somehow reach behind her eyes and drag her thoughts out into the open.

But he didn't. He just carried on eating.

She kept her eyes forward, squelching the sudden urge for

a cigarette. She heard him get up from the table, his footsteps when he walked to the kitchen, the soft crash of dishes in the sink, the hissing of water from the tap. His footsteps grew closer until he was right behind her, and he squeezed her shoulder and pressed a lingering kiss on her forehead. *"Thanks for dinner, baby."*

She wanted to speak, to tell her husband that she wanted to go away for a while, to tell him that she needed to be away from him, from this house, from her life, that she wanted to be someone else and return—she'll promise to return—but her tongue felt heavy and her mouth felt dry, and nothing she wanted to say would pass her lips.

Leave the house an hour before her husband is due to return home. She saw the subject line of another reminder email from Abosede the day before the ticket would expire, but she did not open it. Instead, she lay on the couch, hoping to still her restless mind. The room was too cold, but she did not reach for the AC controls on the table in front of her. At that moment, there was nowhere she wanted to be less than in that house.

Drive to Bar Beach. She could think of nowhere else to go. Lagos traffic from her mainland home to the island knew better than to stop her. The road was an open mouth. She weaved her way past the 7-Up manufacturing plant, through Third Mainland Bridge, past Tafawa Balewa Square, all the way through until she passed Eko Hotel and found a place to park her car.

The night had fallen quickly. She found a seat by the man

selling grilled fish at the charcoal grill along the dirty white plastic chairs, close enough to the crowd of drinking people but far enough away from the prostitutes. The roasting fish was a mere side-dish to the chatter and beer, even though it dominated the air; over and above the ocean, the weed, the cigarettes, the cars belching exhaust from the main road just by the beach. She sat at a vacant table and immediately looked for a lighter to light her cigarette.

A man sitting across the table from her called out, *"Ah, sister! Na by yourself you come?"*

She looked up at him. The darkness hid most of his features. She could only tell that he had a white smile and was not alone. Judging by the beers on his table, and a quick assessment of his company, he did not need her money. Nigerians who don't mind their own business can be charming, but not tonight. She ignored him.

"Leave her alone, jor," the woman sitting beside him said, laughter in her voice. *"You don't know somebody, you want to start bothering them."*

"Which kin' bother am I bothering her? This woman, leave me! Sister!" He called to her again. *"You want to join us?"*

She found herself smiling at him. *"No, thank you. I'm waiting for somebody."*

"You can join us if you'd like," the woman called to her. The other friend, a slim, tall-looking man, nodded agreeing.

Why not? She got up and joined them. A cool, salty breeze greeted her as she sat on the white plastic chair. Someone was playing a Nigerian pop song she'd heard on the radio recently, something dancehall-influenced, something young that managed to reduce the blaring car horns on the main road just off the beach to a more distant sound, like a phone ringing from afar.

She got a better look at her company. The other tall-seeming man was young-looking and handsome, with razor bumps on his face, and light-skinned. His white shirt almost glowed in the night. His friend, the man who called her over, was pudgy and bald, with a friendly smile. He wore a black shirt with Fela drawn on it in white.

"You like my shirt?" He asked her when he saw her look at it. *"I bought it at the Afrikan Shrine. Did you ever see Fela perform? Ah! The man was a madman! Once, in the middle of one of his shows, he pulled one of his dancers to the ground and had sex with her right there! In front of everybody!"*

"You too dey tell that story, mehn," the other man said, dismissing his friend with a wave of his beer bottle. His voice was a surprise, a deep elderly-sounding baritone from such a youthful face. *"He was mad o, but he won't just fuck somebody in front of everybody, jor."*

"But he did! I'm telling you!"

"So he just pulled his trouser down and started fucking her there, abi?"

"Yes!"

"On stage? In front of everybody? Iro e ti poju."

"So I'm a liar now, abi? My sister," he turned to her, *"what kind of person does not believe his friend when he tells him something?"*

"You see this man?" The light-skinned guy gesticulated to the friend with his now-empty bottle. A wide smile creased his thin, leathery face like an old napkin. *"This man is a godforsaken liar. Back in the olden days, Sango would have struck him dead."*

She leaned back in her chair and allowed herself a smile. All three laughed.

What little light there was from the beach bar gave the green bottles of beer on the table an eerie glow. A cool wind blew. The night felt good against her skin. She breathed in the warm, spicy air. A group of young men walked past the table smelling heavily of weed, stumbling. She brought out a cigarette. The tall, light-skinned man extended his arm with a lighter.

Smoke another cigarette. Because, well, fuck it, right? You have a right to want what you want, even if you have no right to want it, even if you can only want it when no one else is around. She smiled her "thank you." He smiled his "you're welcome." The woman leaned against the pudgy man's arm and sighed deeply, as though she had relieved herself of a heavy load, and both men carried on talking about Fela and sex and whatever else fly-papered across their minds as friends do. She let their conversation pass her by and they let her, without demanding anything of her, not her name, not why she was there. They seemed to understand, at least the tall one seemed to, that her being there with them was enough. Besides the smile in her direction, and her smile back, and her laugh, they expected nothing. For the first time since she returned from her trip, her presence was enough. The dull ache in her chest, the longing to be elsewhere throbbed at a distance. A phantom pain.

Ignore the phone calls. Because she could. She knew who was calling anyway, and it felt fitting not to answer. It was a call reminding her of what she left, of what she was to return to, a call she was not ready to answer. So she didn't. She just leaned back against the chair, lit a cigarette, took a deep drag.

Stay. Breathe. Watch the sky darken. Listen to drunken conversation. Allow herself to smoke the joint when it was passed her way. Give in when they asked to buy her another drink. She would go home eventually, but not now. Just a while longer.

About the Author:

Saratu Abiola is a freelance writer based in Abuja, Nigeria, and Amsterdam, Netherlands. She's been published in *Guardian Nigeria*, *Quartz Africa*, *Open Democracy*, among other places. She also writes a monthly pop culture newsletter themonthlythree. Substack.com.

Right

Rilla Askew

She is sixteen and her mother puts her on a bus at the Trailways station in Fresno and sends her to Oklahoma to live with relatives for the summer and maybe forever because her mother's new boyfriend keeps walking in on her in the bathroom when she's taking a shower and he won't fix the bathroom door lock no matter how her mother yells, and her mother needs the new boyfriend more than she needs her, so: what are you so miserable about? her mother says, straighten up that sour face, for god's sake, it'll be fun.

Yes, she thinks. Fun. She is sixteen, and it is 1972 and you can still smoke in the back of the bus. She slots her dwindling stash of quarters into the vending machines in the piss-smelling bus stations at Barstow and Flagstaff and Albuquerque, chink, chink, push the knob in, pull it out, down the chute into the metal tray plops a soft red pack of Winstons. She taps the pack on the heel of her hand like a grownup.

On the bus she sprawls across two seats beneath her spread-open jean jacket, lighting one cig off the smoldering butt of the other, so that by the time her aunt and uncle pick her up at the bus station in Tulsa, she is green with nausea and her aunt pulls away from her, good lord, child, you smell like an ashtray, what have you been doing? it's an hour's drive home, we'll have to ride with the windows open.

Her aunt and uncle live in a housing addition on the outskirts of a middling sized town fifty miles north of nowhere.

Her uncle is an accountant and her aunt is a housewife and her girl cousin, who is older, lifeguards at the public pool in town and stays gone all day, and her boy cousin, who is younger, has a paper route and mows lawns and snaps her bra strap through the back of her blouse when he passes her in the dim hallway. She is sixteen, and it is summertime, and there is not one fucking thing to do but the chores her aunt lays out for her: vacuuming, dusting, sorting the laundry, putting away the groceries, and she never can do it right. In the evenings she hears her aunt and uncle talking in the front room in low voices: what are we going to do with her, it's two months till school starts, I can't have her laying around the house all summer. Well, it's your flaky sister won't raise her own kid, you're the one said she could come. Can't you find her a job, Jim? A carhop or office girl or something?

They think she doesn't hear, but she hears, and she thinks about running away, but where? and how? she doesn't even know how to get to the highway.

Her uncle gets her a job taking inventory in a dark, oily-smelling auto parts warehouse downtown. He drops her off on his way to work and picks her up on his way home, and for a week she edges through the dusty aisles with her clipboard, pulling out boxes of screws and metal clamps and hoses and counting and writing down numbers, until the afternoon the boss catches her making out with the stock boy in the back office and fires her or, as he says, with his mouth pursed and eyes tight, lets her go.

So now she goes absolutely fucking nowhere, except to the grocery store with her aunt, who has her pushing the cart through the aisles and gathering produce and toilet paper and cans of Chef Boyardee. At the house she puts the groceries away—wrong again: No, dear, the new milk goes behind the old milk, like this, see?

Okay, she says, and walks down the hall to her cousin's girly room and lies on the rollaway cot and stares at the ceiling. She puts a hand on one breast. Then the other. Something is wrong. Something is really not right. She comes out of the room, finds her aunt in the kitchen and tells her she's going for a walk and her aunt says, it's a hundred degrees out there, dear, why don't you go in the front room and watch TV?

Just around the block, the girl says, I won't be gone a minute, and she lights a Winston as soon as she gets around the corner, but the cigarette makes her want to throw up. She smokes it down to the filter anyway and drops it in the gutter and walks back to her aunt's house smelling like sweat and smoke and she goes to the hall bathroom and throws up in the toilet, running the faucet full throttle to cover the sound; then she takes a bath, washes her hair with White Rain, the smell makes her gag, that oversweet smell, so now she's getting an idea about something, and she's scared. She tries to think back to her last period, but she can't remember. Before school was out, probably. For sure before the two-day bus ride. She's always irregular, her cramps have always been hellacious, and her mom says her own periods were like that, too, till she…got pregnant.

Right.

The girl puts on her t-shirt and cutoffs and goes to her cousin's room, sits at the vanity combing out her wet hair. Her aunt calls her to come set the table, but the girl sits staring at her own face. Nothing is changed. She looks just the same. Maybe it's not even true. If she doesn't smoke any more cigarettes, maybe she won't get sick again. She reaches a hand under her shirt, touches her swollen, tender breasts. No, she thinks. It's true.

She tells herself she knows who, and where, and when: the end-of-school kegger out by the river, the skinny blond kid always trying to fit in, and she was drunk, and he was drunk, and they were both there—*she* was there, when she was almost never anywhere. And she didn't want to go home. Then everybody started pairing up, drifting away from the fire, everybody but her and the skinny blond kid and a couple of skeezy dudes even weirder than him. So, when he said, let's go over there, she did. And when he said, you wanna lay down? she did, and when he crept his hand under her shorts, she did, and she did, and she did…

And now she's sixteen and in trouble, and it is 1972, and she does not know what to do.

This is a thing making her body change without her will, like it changed when she was twelve and started growing breasts, like the pimples she gets when it's time for her period, but she has no pimples now. Just these waves of nausea sometimes, spit filling her mouth, but she doesn't throw up, not very often. She volunteers to Ajax the bathroom and runs the water hard and flushes the toilet, and her aunt says, when you're finished in there, come on out to the dining room, I've got a little job for you, and the aunt sets her to polishing silverware or sorting tea towels, made-up jobs, the girl knows, but she does everything willingly, obediently, without her sour face, as if being good could eject the thing growing inside her, and the aunt tries to smile and calls her dear and shows her how to do these made-up jobs right, and she tries. The girl tries. But it's hard to do stupid things right. When the aunt runs out of busy work, she tells her to go watch TV, and the girl sits in the front room watching *The*

Young and the Restless, surreptitiously reaching up a hand to see if the tenderness in her swollen breasts has subsided. But, of course, it has not.

What the girl does not tell herself is that it could be her mother's new boyfriend, what he does, has done, did do, almost since he first moved in, coming to her room at night, his flat hand on her mouth, you know it would kill your mom, he says, if you tell her, you'd better not tell her, you know I'm the one she'd believe. And she does know that, and she does not tell, and she pretends in the daylight that it does not happen in the night, and he wears a rubber, he's very careful for that, taking time to tear open the wrapper with his teeth, and the first time it hurt like hell, and it still hurts, in her gut it hurts, and in her heart, so she clamps it down, pushes it away, tells herself it does not happen, did not happen, tells herself it's the skinny blond kid from the kegger who got her like this. She tells herself she cannot tell her aunt because her aunt would send her back to Fresno and then her mother would know, and she cannot tell her girl cousin, because her cousin would tell the aunt, and the aunt would send her back to Fresno, and her mother would know.

So the girl starts walking every morning to the neighborhood grade school, closed now for summer, and she does jumping jacks in the heat next to the building so nobody from the street will see, and she swings on the kiddie swings, high and fast and hard, jumps out and lands with a great jarring thump, a shudder from her feet to her chest; then she turns and climbs back on the swing and does it again, again and again, but she can't shake the thing loose. She's heard that horseback riding can do it. But where can she go horseback riding? To even bring up the words to her aunt and uncle would be weird.

If she starves herself, would that help?

But no. Starving herself does not help.

Every day the sense of fullness and portent swells larger.

There's one thing she's heard of. A coat hanger. But how would a person even do that? She tries to think it through. She tries to imagine. On a Monday when her aunt gathers her pocketbook and grocery list and car keys, the girl begs off. She says she is sick. It is the only time she has refused any of the jobs her aunt makes for her, and the aunt comes to her, frowning, puts a hand to the girl's forehead. You do feel warm. Go lie down, dear. You can help me put the groceries away when I get back.

And the aunt leaves, and the girl goes into the bathroom and locks the door. She scrubs the wire coat hanger with soap and water. She knows at least to do that. She takes off her clothes and sits in the tub. She untwists the wire hook, and untwists it, and untwists it, until the hook breaks off. She bends the hanger into a long, looped probe, the broken end with its jagged edge in her hand, the other end looped small. She lies down, puts the blunted, looped end inside her. It is cold, hard, foreign, and she pushes it deeper, tries to push it deeper, but goddamn, it hurts! She stops. Lies still, breathing shallow breaths. While she waits, she thinks about everything, her mother, her mother's boyfriend, the kids at school, her girl cousin, her boy cousin, her aunt; she thinks about what will happen to her, about how much it hurts to have a baby, people talk about that all the time, how much it hurts, and she thinks, worse than this? Probably. Probably it does.

She tries again. Deeper, harder, her body resists the cold wire, her uterus cramps, a great pinching, rolling paroxysm, worse than any period cramp she's ever had in her life, but the girl grits her teeth, pushes a little deeper; it feels like an iron bar probing her, a tire tool, an axe—ah fuck, she feels it now, the warm rush of blood, oh thank god, relief! like finally getting your period after days and days of bloated weight and waiting, but it cramps, and it cramps, and shit, it hurts!

The girl pulls out the hanger, blood covered; it makes a small ticking clatter when she drops it against the bottom of the tub, and the cramps clamp down worse, wave after wave, and the blood pours. The warm blood is flowing, gushing now, hard throbbing pulses, and she is afraid her aunt will come home before she's finished, before she has time to clean up. She thinks about turning on the tub faucet to wash the blood away, but the cramps are too stabbing, too relentless, and she's too tired right now. She cuts her eyes to the Ajax can perched on the closed toilet seat beside her. The soft blue sponge on top of it. The girl closes her eyes, lets herself drift. The pain is bad, and she's so tired. In a minute, she tells herself, she'll sit up and turn on the faucet. She'll scrub out the bathtub, wrap the coat hanger in a piece of newspaper and take it outside to the trash. She'll remember to put the Ajax can back under the counter. It's a stupid job, but she wants to do it right.

About the Author:

Rilla Askew is the author of four novels, a book of stories, and a collection of creative nonfiction. Askew received a 2009 Arts and Letters Award from the American Academy of Arts and Letters. Her essays and short stories have appeared in *AGNI, Tin House*, *World Literature Today, Nimrod*, *Prize Stories: The O. Henry Awards,* and elsewhere. Her novel, *Prize for the Fire,* about the Early Modern English martyr Anne Askew, will be published in 2022.

Witch Hazel

Gabriela Denise Frank

The death of Briony's parents left her, at sixteen, to run their homestead alone. Decades later, the townsfolk still whispered about the car accident that killed her folks—not because it was unusual, but as a means of gossiping about Briony. *No wonder the girl turned out weird.* She had shunned college, marriage, and children, yet through some strange alchemy, transformed her parents' struggling dirt farm into a prosperous honeybee ranch.

Briony's bees grazed on barrel cactus flowers that bloomed two weeks a year. Only magic could explain how her bees produced enough honey to fill the large mother-well on her property. She never apprenticed with a beekeeper or earned a master's degree—how could she know what she was doing? Her powers were *unnatural.*

Despite their slights, the townsfolk were addicted to Briony's succulent-flower honey. They traded twenty dollars for each hexagonal glass jar of gold, calling her *Witch Hazel* behind her back. It was Briony's self-respect, rather than poor hearing, that held her chin high. Growing up, her mother had taught her to ignore their petty, stinging chatter.

Briony inherited the land in the '70s before the cancer of master-planned homes and manicured golf courses spread across the Valley. Briony's homestead was situated in the foothills off a long dirt road far west of Phoenix—a pine cabin hewn by her father's hands. Her parents first used the cabin for weekend retreats, then moved in permanently when Briony was in grade school. Her family's distancing from society is what started everyone whispering. *They're jealous of how freely we live*, her mother, a former professor, explained.

A sturdy girl, Briony picked up where her parents left off, tending fields of parched agriculture, until she realized what thrived best in the hot, gravelly earth wasn't corn or wheat but indigenous barrel cactus. Her parents had considered them a weed amongst their crops, but Briony observed the candy-colored blossoms attracted fat honeybees who made the sweetest honey she'd ever tasted. She cultivated the cactus in neat rows, designed a label and sold her first jars of honey from a card table at the Saturday farmers market, winning fans with free tastes. As demand grew, she negotiated a permanent shelf for her honey at the general store.

Briony's magic brew was said to cure colds, flu, burns and cuts—in addition to tasting damned good. The townsfolk picked Briony's Magic Barrel Cactus Honey four-to-one over the national brands. They sweetened their tea and porridge with it and made honey sandwiches, spreading it thick over grainy slabs of bread, closing their eyes and murmuring, *Mmmm*. Drunk on her sweet elixir, the townsfolk joked they were under Witch Hazel's spell.

It was true what they said: after high school, Briony found no reason to attend the local college. What would she learn there that she couldn't from her mother's books on botany, biology, chemistry, philosophy, physics, and woodcraft? Briony taught herself to raise the knee-high barrel cactus, build bee boxes, and nurture healthy colonies. It wasn't witchcraft, it was educated diligence. *Elbow grease*, her father would have called it.

Tending to the bees became Briony's life. Her so-called

magic cactus bloomed during the full moon each spring and fall, feeding rumors of her honey's otherworldliness. Her witchy reputation was a back-handed compliment, seeing how the ridiculous buzz drove sales. She fed tactical morsels of scuttlebutt to the owner of the general store, like how she tiptoed through the prickly rows at night, singing to the sherbet-hued blossoms. Yellow, pink, and orange, the flowers opened in her wake, as if Briony was their sun. *Maybe she does have magical powers*, he whispered to his wife who spread word of Briony's sorcery through town, thick and golden as the profit it yielded.

One afternoon, Briony returned home late from tending her bee boxes, having fallen under the soothing hum of the hives. She schlepped two buckets of fresh honey, one strapped to each shoulder with thick swatches of leather, singing to herself beneath the brim-shade of her straw hat. She nodded at her noble saguaro, its lone green arm raised to say, *Hello*. She distracted herself from the pre-thunderstorm swelter by daydreaming of the handsome newcomer in town. Hale and broad-shouldered, James was a ranch hand at the neighboring spread. He shopped in town on Saturdays, his brindled cattle dog, Blue, trotting at his ankles. A well-mannered fifty-something bachelor of few words, James kept to himself. Even Blue, a rabid barker, was anesthetized by James's aura of calm. Briony's heart swelled to see his grocery basket always contained a jar of her honey.

Though people called her a witch, Briony was hardly old or ugly. Her long brown hair hadn't a filament of gray nor had her waist grown thick with middle age. She wondered what—or if—James thought of her. Was he threatened by her entrepreneurship, like the rest? Or might a forty-six-year-old businesswoman be the sort to turn his head? A hardworking man of unstirred passion, James had thick salt-and-pepper hair. She fantasized plunging her fingers through it.

The previous week, James spoke to her.

When she passed him in the aisle at the general store, James raised a jar of her honey, ignoring the high school girls who elbowed each other at their exchange. He smiled and drawled, "Mighty fine." Heat rose in her cheeks. Did he praise Briony—or her honey?

"Th—Thank you," she sputtered.

Briony replayed the compliment in James's deep voice—*Mighty fine*—as she opened and closed the wooden gate with a clunk. If she had stayed to talk with him, would he have asked her out? Lost in daydreams, Briony pulled up short at the sight of her front yard.

In the clean, raked dirt, someone had scratched *BITCH HAZEL* with an arm broken off her ocotillo. The young barrel cacti straddling the footpath had been defiled—twelve tender fontanelles bashed in like baby skulls. Briony gasped when she saw the real damage: the vandals had plundered her honey.

Choking back sobs, she recalled her mother's counsel: *Never let their cruelty make you cry.* She couldn't help but despair at the sight: globs of gold ran down the sides of the ceramic mother-well and pooled on the concrete slab, drawing swarms of insects who became trapped in an orgy of consumption. Their bodies created a sticky carpet of thoraxes, wings, antennae, and legs, some still twitching. Half a year's honey crop ruined.

It took Briony hours to clean and secure the well, to hose down the cement pad until it was free of death and destruction. Who could hate her enough to threaten the delicate livelihood of a single professional woman living alone?

Before she went inside, Briony noticed marks carved into the wood of her home, which her father had cut and sealed and secured by hand. Two initials—*H* and *G*—scarred into the pine, along with sticky bite marks from two jaws. This was the handiwork of the town's hooligans, the Twins of Terror they called themselves—children of the Sheriff who wrote off their vandalism to high spirits: Hansel and Gretel. Their obsession for destruction had fueled them to ride their bikes twenty miles out of town in grueling heat to reach her place, to ruin her honey, knowing they would get away with it. Somewhere, they were cackling at her, their bellies bloated with honey. They had marked their territory and would return to finish the job—that's how they operated, feeding on their victims' fear even more than property damage.

Briony's blood boiled. She would teach the vile children a lesson.

The next morning, she set out her most precious stock: pure, glistening honeycomb she usually saved for the holidays when it fetched a higher price. She set small, neat hillocks on white plates, the first in view of the mother-well. A line of plates with honeycomb led around back and down into the cellar, which her father had blasted into the caliche.

Briony made a show of locking the front door, slinging her harvest wells over her shoulders, and striding out through the gate. She felt Hansel and Gretel lurking in the brush. *Bitch Hazel,* she imagined them snickering from the tall sunburnt grasses. She walked to the outfield, trying not to glance back at the house. All day she was distracted, wondering whether the Twins of Terror had triggered her trap.

Briony returned at dusk to find her homestead undisturbed.

A quail trilled *coo-coo.* All else lay still. She tried to stride confidently into her yard, but her assurance was cracked. She hunched protectively like the witch they said she was, wincing glances left and right, expecting the children to jump out of hiding and beat her with ocotillo arms. Hands trembling, she set down her vessels of honey near the mother-well. There, she spied the first empty white plate. Someone had found the honeycomb.

She picked up the plate and walked to the second, also empty. And the third. She turned the corner to discover a series of empty plates leading to the cellar. The wooden doors lay closed. Cries rose from inside, muffled by another sound. She threw open the cellar doors and leaped backwards in surprise. A dark, buzzing cloud of bees swarmed skyward. On the dirt floor, a carpet of yellow-and-black corpses. Briony had set the lock to trap the children inside—she planned only to scare them—but the bees must have followed them in, attacking them for the honeycomb. The Twins of Terror writhed in the dirt, their fists wrapped stubbornly around the sticky, glistening bits. Drones proceeded to sting them and drop to the floor, dying.

"Help," Gretel, a blond waif with cerulean eyes, moaned. Her pale skin was pocked with angry welts.

"I can't believe you sicced killer bees on us, you bitch-witch," spat Hansel, knobby-kneed and freckled. His eyes were swollen shut with stings.

Briony wept. Not for the children, for the hate seething inside her.

"It'zzz what you wanted, yez?"

Briony spun around.

"Lazzzt night. You zaid you wizhed zomeone would punizh them."

Briony *had* said that, sobbing to herself as she cleaned the mess. In wondering what she would do to make up for the lost revenue, she muttered a wish that someone would smite the wicked children.

The most regal of Briony's queens flew to her shoulder, a tinkle of laughter next to her ear. "You were right—theeze are terrible children!"

Briony paled, realizing what her wishing had set into motion.

Hansel and Gretel gagged down in the cellar, choking in anaphylactic shock.

"They'll die," Briony whispered to the Queen. "What should we do?"

"What'z the world minuz two hooliganz?" the Queen shrugged.

"Anybody home?" a voice called.

Briony skittered to the front yard to find James pondering the carrier wells she had abandoned.

"For a second, I thought the rumors were true," he chuckled. Blue circled her legs madly until James lifted his hand. The dog settled at her feet, gazing up at her, his tongue lolling from his pink maw. "I saw the honey," he nodded at the wells, "and wondered if you'd disappeared, like magic—*poof!*"

Briony smoothed her work shirt, darting a look over her shoulder, wishing she had closed the cellar doors. "Nope, it's plain old me."

"Have—you been crying?"

"Oh no," she sighed, wiping beneath her damp eyes. "Just tired after a long day."

James nodded. The brim of his sable gray Stetson shadowed

his face. "I love my job, but by God, my body's tired at the end of the day. I figured yours was, too—you don't have any help out here—so I brought dinner," he said, raising a picnic basket. "If you're interested."

Briony's head swam. First, her honey, then the children—now this? She needed to think. "Why don't you come in," she said, relieved that he couldn't hear the children's moans. She wasn't sure how she would keep James from discovering Hansel and Gretel. Getting him and Blue inside was step one. He pulled up short behind her as she unlocked the front door.

"What's that?" he said.

"Huh?"

"I hear… buzzing."

"Oh—ha!—it must be the bees out for a late afternoon stroll." She ushered him inside.

James unloaded the picnic basket, explaining how he had moved to town from the Midwest where farm work had evaporated. Normally, she would have hung on his every word, but Briony's attention crept back to Hansel and Gretel dying in her cellar.

"What about you?" James said, slicing the steak thin. "How did you end up out here making Briony's Magic Barrel Cactus Honey?" His green eyes twinkled at the creases when he said, *Magic*.

"I'm sure folks in town told you."

"I don't put much stock in gossip," he said. "Why don't you tell me."

Briony couldn't recall the last person who asked her more than, *How are you?* except the occasional grad student she slept with. Their version was, *How's this?* (or was it, *How do you like this?)* No one cared enough to heed her answers.

"My parents died when I was sixteen. In a car accident. This was our home."

James shook his head. "Hard on you, losing them so young. What happened?"

It was a question Briony never had to answer. Everyone in town knew.

"Tr—truck driver. Fell asleep and crossed the double yellow. Hit them head-on. They were driving home late from the State Fair."

Here, Briony paused. What the townsfolk did not know was the truth. The real reason she tended her parents' homestead for thirty years, alone.

"We had an argument that morning. I said I didn't want to grow up to be a hippy farmer like them. I was going to have a *career* in town." Briony darted a glance at James. He nodded for her to continue. "My dad said it embarrassed him to have a snob for a daughter. He told me to stay home. He'd sooner show a prize hog than a sullen girl amongst hard-working people he respected. Mama could barely look at me, she was so disappointed."

Briony swallowed, summoning the grit to say what weighed on her mind for decades.

"I was supposed to be with them," she breathed. "Their punishment saved my life."

James set down the knife and wiped his hands on the dish towel. He lay his callused palms, cool and moist, on the sides of her face, tipping up her gaze. She tried to smile, to be agreeable, something she was never good at. Instead, she sobbed into his chest. James held her, petting her head the way her father used to. Blue bumped gently against her calves. Briony felt herself take too much comfort from the stranger's arms. She drew away from him, watching while he finished making dinner. James drizzled a zee of blue cheese dressing across the steak salad, which he had plated on fresh butter lettuce from the farm. James was kind of a dream.

"So that's how you inherited the bees," he said. He sat across from her at the table she once shared with her parents. He poured them each a glass of red wine.

"No," she said. "The bees came later."

She would never tell that story to anyone.

After the accident, Briony sat out back on the covered porch, crying, wondering how she would support herself. She had no other family, no income beyond her parents' meager savings. A Queen Bee, seeing her distress landed on her shoulder. *Let her sting me. Maybe I'll die,* Briony thought. Instead, the Queen crawled up her cheek and sipped the salty sadness that fell from her eyes. Sipped and sipped until tears flowed no more. She couldn't explain it: after the Queen feasted on her despair, Briony felt better.

"What elze can I do for you, dear?" the Queen asked.

"Never leave me."

And she hadn't. Eight more Queen Bees came to join their sister, setting up colonies in the white boxes Briony built. The drones gathered pollen from throughout the desert (if the town was foolish enough to believe otherwise, so be it), and the Queens drank Briony's tears. In reality, it wasn't the barrel cactus that made her honey potent and flavorful, it was Briony's well of grief and guilt, the royal jelly that fed them all.

The deception that secured her survival never bothered Briony. Better to be labeled a witch than starve, she decided.

Now, with those dying brats in the basement and a man whose affection could save her from isolation, she questioned her dignity, as her mother once had, even if the truth could ruin her.

James gathered the dirty dinner plates and washed them by hand, setting them onto the rack to dry. He plated two thick hunks of spongy angel food cake garnished with tart, juicy blackberries and drizzled Briony's special reserve of lavender-infused honey on top. Briony's sadness, sweet and golden atop the cake, was dizzying.

After dessert, she poured them each two fingers of bourbon, then two more.

Briony described her childhood growing up on the ranch. James confided tales of his youth on the rodeo circuit. At midnight, he pulled himself up from the table.

"I ought to go," he drawled, beaming a moony grin. "This has been the best evening in recent memory." He wobbled, then righted himself on the back of her chair. An echo of fate sounded: James would be driving home in the dark of night. Like her parents.

"It's late," Briony said. She curled her fingers through his belt loops, pulling his body to hers. "You should…stay."

Blue's ear twitched where he snoozed beneath the table.

"Imagine those wagging tongues in town," James teased as she led him to her bedroom. "Briony and that handsome rancher spending the night together on the first date."

That's exactly what they'd say. The hens would cluck their jealous tongues, begrudging her the freedom to sleep with whomever she wanted because they were mired in dull marriages.

"Yeah," she murmured, brushing her nose against his, "but they'd call me Witch Hazel."

She unbuttoned his shirt, admiring his lean muscles in the moonlight that shone through her bedroom window. A life of farm work kept James in good shape. She ran her hands along his chest, deliciously carpeted in thick hair. Briony kissed his neck, stubbly beneath the jawline, and worked her way down. There was not a spare ounce on him. She undid his belt buckle, a thick slab of silver with a rearing horse in the center, and drew his belt off the loops. She snapped the leather and cackled.

James growled and drew the belt away to the floor with a thud. He undid the snaps of Briony's work shirt, sliding it off her shoulders, followed by her camisole bra. She shivered at James's mouth on her neck, across the bones of her clavicles, down to her breasts, nuzzling her nipples and the swelling curves beneath, down to her belly, then he worked his way back up, slowly. "Mmmm," she growled into his ear.

He crushed her to his chest, skin to skin, and kissed her with urgency—my God, what a good kisser he was—stoking her desire, slow and low and aching across the floor of her pelvis. James unzipped her jeans, and she unzipped his, tugging them down and off. She was delighted to find that the skin of his back and butt were creamy smooth despite his woolly chest. He peeled away her jeans from her ankles, one, then the other, and pulled her onto the bed. She ran her hands over the flesh of his legs, his back, his butt, his perfectly respectable six-inch cock.

Mighty fine, she smiled to herself.

He rolled her on her back, his hands clasped with hers overhead, and pinned her to the bed with the gentle shift of his body on top of hers, kissing her neck, her breastbone, down past her belly, her navel, down, down, and finally, gloriously, in between her thighs. He was as skilled a kisser there as he had been mouth-to-mouth, his tongue gliding over the secret purple folds of her flesh. When she came, white-hot bottle rockets exploded behind her eyelids. She lay in the thudding luxury of the moment, feeling James—not the random college student who didn't know her sad story, but a man of character—entwined with her, naked, under her spell.

He took his time working his way back up, kissing her belly, her breasts, her elbows, her wrists. "What about you?" she sighed. He kissed her throat, her jaw, her swollen lips.

"Better to start with you one ahead," he winked.

She pulled him on top of her and kissed him deeply, pleased to feel him at attention between her thighs, neither too big, nor too small, but just right. She guided him inside herself and thought, *There's nothing better than the weight of a wanted man*. An amber well of desire stirred deep inside her; she had forgotten she possessed it. Passion. Unlike her college boys, Briony was delighted that James knew—exactly—where her clit was. He made her come again, a second little death that shook her core.

In between snoozing and making love, Briony forgot Hansel and Gretel in her cellar.

After a rushed breakfast of fried eggs, toast and coffee—James and Blue started work at six—Briony embraced him at the door.

"Would it be too soon to see you tonight?" he said, hugging her tight to his chest.

"No," she gulped.

That would give her ten hours to adios the children.

Blue chased James to his truck, hopping up into the cab. After the sound of tires on the dirt road faded, Briony scurried out back and gritted her teeth, eying the storm cellar doors, open as she left them. She had never wanted kids—potential orphans she would over-nurture, abandon, or accidentally kill—and these children, dead or alive, were more responsibility than she could bear. She strode to the edge of the cellar—she would fix this, somehow—and gasped. In place of Hansel and Gretel, swollen and stung, lay two skeletons.

"You zeemed aggrieved, girl," the Queen Bee buzzed, "zo I called in a favor."

"Huh?"

"Dermestez maculatuz," the Queen said. "Flezh eaterz."

"Happy to help," burped a voice. It came from a brown beetle the size of a dime. "Aloysius," he said. "At your service."

The Queen mad dogged her until Briony realized her rudeness.

"Thank you," she said. "Aloysius."

The beetle fiddled grit off the ends of his antennae. It must have taken thousands of beetles to clean the children's carcasses overnight.

"What do we do now?"

"Disposal is your business, ma'am; eating 'em is ours," the beetle belched. "You could bury the bones—although, if you boiled them, they'd make a nice stock."

Briony shuddered.

She filled an old canvas sack with the bones of her enemies and interred them at the bottom of a nearby arroyo. What else could she do—call the Sheriff? She couldn't explain what had happened to his children and expect *not* to be arrested for murder. She piled shovelfuls of sandy dirt onto the remains, wiping sweat from her forehead with a faded red handkerchief. The children's cruelty—the fact that they, the Twins of Terror, brought her to this—would bite each time she eyed their vicious teeth marks in the beams of her father's house.

The following weekend, a thunderstorm ripped through town.

Purple-white lightning crackled through the cumulonimbus clouds, the metallic smell of water hung in the air, drones buzzed in the fields. While Briony and James made love, a flash flood barreled down the dry riverbed, loosening the silty bottom of the arroyo—and unearthing the green canvas sack. Meanwhile, missing posters for Hansel and Gretel flapped from every telephone pole in town. It was the Sheriff's deputy, out on patrol, who discovered the sack of bones. The flood washed them to the roadside. The Sheriff rushed DNA tests of the skeletons, their identity soon confirmed as his missing children.

The road where the bones were found was close to Briony's ranch. Though he had no hard evidence against her, the Sheriff called her into the precinct for questioning. Everyone knew Witch Hazel hated children. It was one thing the Sheriff could control in an investigation that was quickly escaping him.

The Sheriff questioned Briony for hours in a stuffy, windowless room. He enjoyed watching the spinster's knees knock. Why shouldn't he lean on that high-horse-riding Mary Tyler Moore? Her perspiration, her quavering made him feel strong, especially when he pressed an alibi out of her for the night of the twins' disappearance. She had been with that rancher fellow, *doing it*. "Turns out old Witch Hazel is a hellcat in the sack," he cackled to his deputy.

The rancher's testimony confirmed it.

Oh, the delight of Briony's shame—the Sheriff told her he had spoken with James, that he *knew* what they had been up to. She was off the hook, for the time being. He advised her not to leave town, like she had anywhere to go, and felt satisfied knowing he could squeeze her dirty little secret whenever he wanted to. The townsfolk clucked about her affair with James, goaded by the Sheriff's colorful commentary. *That poor rancher's got no idea what trouble he's into with old Witch Hazel. One day we'll find him turned into a frog!*

Briony held her chin high and went on collecting her honey money. The prattle raised to peak levels when she and James shopped together into town. Oh, the gall of the fools who underestimated her. They were more interested in gossiping about her sex life than her capability of committing a double murder. Briony felt so furious she nearly confessed, though she didn't technically kill the children, she reminded herself. Nature finished off what nature had begun. Besides, those brats started it.

The Sheriff clucked his tongue at Briony when their paths met. His eyes feasted on parts of her he found pleasing, evidence of the Jezebel he always suspected she was, cloaked beneath dusty work clothes. Her breasts swelled beneath her button-down shirts, her hips curved inside her dirt-scarred denim. She avoided his gaze, set her jaw and stuck her nose in the air, like she had in high school. This uncoiled an ancient resentment inside the Sheriff. He once dreamed of unloosening that auburn witch-hair of hers from its demure bun. He despised her false purity. *Bitch* Hazel. She and her hippy communist parents thought themselves too good for everyone.

Neither the Sheriff nor his deputy could pick up the murderer's trail. The suspects were few, the crime well executed. The MISSING posters bearing the twins' faces weathered and frayed, eventually disintegrating into fragments. That fall, Hansel and Gretel's bones were interred in the family crypt; by Christmas, the police file was stamped in red, UNSOLVED.

Briony, again, had been saved.

"Good day," the Queen tinkled at Briony, out in the field. She wondered what she owed the Queen, and when the bill would come due. James, too, was a gift, for without the honey they would never have met. Rumors of her bedevilment of James drove demand of the honey, which the town bought as fast as she could harvest and bottle it. Briony's magic honey was rumored to be an aphrodisiac that could cure infertility, too. Several couples confided in the maternity ward nurse that they had used Briony's honey during lovemaking and—*poof!*—they got pregnant. Upon hearing this, Briony shook her head, the magic of gossip both her savior and undoing.

On the humid August anniversary of their first date, James brought the same dinner in the same picnic basket: steak salad, spongy angel food cake, cabernet. Briony came three times that night, remaining one orgasm ahead as always. The next morning, James left at daybreak for work, Blue trotting at his feet.

Briony leaned against the doorway, a mug of steaming, strong coffee in hand. She waved goodbye to James, the yolky fingers of dawn curling over the jagged hump of Camelback Mountain. Sex with him remained lovely—*Mighty fine,* she teased when he spooned her afterward—and James's company was something she looked forward to in the evenings. She appreciated his acumen, his humor, his support of her business. Some nights, they read books from her mother's library in bed. She shared almost everything with him.

Given her affection for him, it amused Briony how relieved she felt when the house became hers again. It surprised her, the mindfuckery of middle age. Briony no longer wished to change her past, her present circumstances, or even herself. Was this resignation or maturity? The power of being loved? *If only things could remain this way,* she thought, but no magic power could trap the universe in amber. At least, none she would wish aloud for.

It was ironic, wasn't it, that old Witch Hazel wouldn't use magic to alter things, not even a little, not even if she could? She replanted twelve baby barrels to replace the ones the Twins of Terror pummeled to death in her front yard. She stepped back from her work, her lower back aching, part satisfaction, part pain, the scales offset and far from perfect.

About the Author:
Gabriela Denise Frank is a Pacific Northwest writer, editor, and creative writing instructor. Her writing has appeared in *True Story, DIAGRAM, Hunger Mountain, HAD, Poetry Northwest, Bayou, Baltimore Review, The Rumpus*, and elsewhere. She serves as the creative nonfiction editor of *Crab Creek Review*. www.gabrieladenisefrank.com

Souvenir

Roseline Mgbodichinma

Prayer

My body went missing when I started to touch myself. It disappeared totally into the brim of darkness with my shadows fighting to be seen. It was before men knew me, even before I knew myself. I was mining my way through everything I could not tell Uzo. I found a cure for my loneliness on the atlas of my body.

My sheets smelt of saliva and raw emotions. I only washed them when my Chi sent molds as a reminder that my prayers would choke before they reached the heavens. It was important to me that God answered my prayers. I did not pound my fist on the floor and ask God to kill every obstacle and provide a good life as Uzo did. That prayer point was the reason she tried to abort me seven times and failed. Unlike hers, my method was more solemn and sensual, reciting proverbs as I engulfed the fullness of my chestnuts. I asked God to protect the children I had turned to blood, then I bit my lips hard in *amen*. There is an old figurine beside my bed. It is the only legacy I have of my grandmother. When she was alive, she polished it with oil and potash, massaging every nook and cranny with what was left of her index finger. Her turban always sat firmly on her skull, her waist bent from carrying boys who returned to their ancestors at the taste of her breast milk. Women in my lineage had ill-luck with keeping men from fleeing. She did not speak or see. Too bad her last hearing memories were sounds of moaning from my sacrilegious body entanglements.

Stench

When one of Uzo's husbands first came to my room, he said he could smell death. He said I should take down the picture of my grandfather that hung loosely on the wall and dispose of the basket of rotten onions growing stems beneath my bed.

He was a short, bearded man shrunken by lust and alcohol. I imagined him on top of my mother, how his small frame would be invisible when it met with the vastness of her hips. He thought it disrespectful that I called my mother by her name, but I liked to think that I had earned that right. I had tasted the things she'd tasted and fought battles she could not even imagine. I was the reason men did not come to her for leftovers.

Uzo complained of slow sales, but she had enough money to pay her bus fare to Lagos every weekend for parties. I would have asked her to save up the money and send me back to the community school, but the children there mocked me. Plus, Uzo always brought souvenirs from her trip. Some of them I liked, while others forced themselves on me. After all, children were a gift from God, and if my mother gave her blessing, who was I?

Unknown

I never knew my father because my mother never knew him. She said she was drunk, upset. My grandfather had just died in an accident, and that day she was angry; she just wanted to fuck out her emotions, never cared for the man's face. Auntie Julie said she saw Uzo leave with the bartender that night.

I was still pale and pink when I was brought to him. He said nobody in his lineage had dark spots, and none of his forefathers were light-skinned. He said my mother would have to do a DNA test with all the men in the area to figure out my paternity. She did not argue. We had similar traits, me and Uzo. We wear our baggage like a silver lining; the woman I know as my mother can spread her legs for anything with a tail to pass through. My father could be any man.

Pepper

The first time it happened, I had gone to buy bread across the street. It was normal for men to catcall women on our street. Nobody complained about it. If anything, it was motivation for your bum to jiggle more at their wagging tongues. People stared at me weirdly, like I was both an eyesore and a sight to behold.

Izu was the first man to grab me. He took me to the side of a rickety bus and asked me to bend over, and I obeyed. It was polite of him to ask. Uzo's souvenirs did not ask her anything, they ripped off her wrapper at the door and just banged.

Izu paid for my bread, and I thanked him. I became a regular customer at his workshop, allowing his apprentices to work on me like a spoilt Benz. They took turns on me, and gave me boli, fish, egusi and assorted meat, in return. My mother said I marked my territory in her womb for a reason, that she knew my star would bring her good fortune. She never asked me how I got the delicacies. She only devoured the meat, her eyes wide, allowing condiments to splash into her pupils as atonement for what she dreaded had been done to me.

As she chewed, I understood what it meant to starve on a full stomach. She looked at me like she was trying to convince me that swallowing the heaviness that came with the meat was better than opening her heart to the inevitable truth. She told me to boil water, put it in an iron bucket, sit on it and allow the steam to make its way into my womanhood. I did not ask why.

The Visit

I should have known that my mother's sudden interest in the mansion was not without cause. She bantered with Aunty Julie over how it was only *ndi Malay*—people from Malaysia that had the money to build and paint a mansion white. She went there every evening to beg for water, even though it was the rainy season and our well had not dried.

It was not long before this pale man, Ahmed, fair, with a well-structured face and pointed nose, started sleeping over at our house. There was something about him that was not foreign. He told us he had been in Nigeria for three weeks because of a contract and was traveling back abroad soon. This man swallowed *akpu* like Mother Nature had him in mind when she blessed the earth with cassava. He devoured peppery Jollof like it was garri and sugar, and he knew how to haggle like a seasoned businessman. He promised Uzo that they would fly to Kuala Lumpur after the wedding.

My name was never in the plan. An unwanted seed should not be allowed to cross countries. I cannot say how they agreed on a date to travel, or if Ahmed agreed he was from Malaysia, all I know is that Uzo is very impulsive, a master at finishing people's sentences and trusting penises more than her God-given instinct.

The Present

Aunty Julie was nothing like Uzo. Julie was petite and very busty with a smile that made her head look too heavy for her short neck. She met my mother at the club, and that is as far as I know. Uzo teases that God was hell-bent on finishing the work in front and got exhausted when he came to the back, so he abandoned it. Julie was a simple woman, worked in a government office and made a decent living. She did not have any children.

When Uzo gave all the savings she made from her sales to Ahmed for the processing of papers, Aunty Julie was there. She was still there when my mother knocked at the white mansion and the owners told her that there was no one named Ahmed. That it was Malik, their former housekeeper, and he had finally returned to his family in Sudan after serving them for ten years. While my mother was moving mad with Ahmed and planning to leave me behind, I was catching up on her old flings: Mike, Akpan, Jide, Cole and other nameless men that had a feel of my mother. I got testimonials from them on how I *knacked* better than Uzo. It became my guilty pleasure to swallow substances and use a hanger to poke half-formed things in my vagina. They said my mother could not bear any more children because of the complications she encountered at my birth. I wondered when my time would come, when I would have my own complications and my body would refuse to house any more bodies. If Uzo said she did not know that my skin had become a dumping ground for men to release all the emotions they could not confront, then she is a liar, and God will spit her out like lukewarm water.

Oblivion

She knew that when Ike had complained of the smell of death and onions in my room, he was only trying to make the room more conducive for him to enjoy an extension of her. She was old wine, and I was the new wineskin. Men liked to pour themselves in, new and raw.

Ike became my stepfather the same night he unlocked my womanhood. I was fourteen. He said I did not look my age and many men must want me now. I needed to be wanted because it was something my mother did not have. She was not wanted; she was always taken. Everyday someone took a part of her, and she let them chew on it like kola.

Ike said children like me could not handle cash, and each time he had me, he would give extra money to Uzo, it was part of his fatherly duties. I was not mature enough to handle money, but I was ripe enough to feel his warmth. Aunty Julie walked in on him trying to climb into my pants one time. The air felt smaller when she barged in. She was fuming and staring at Ike like he was a *suck-away* poop. Ike sheepishly picked up his shirt and walked out of the room; that was the last we saw of him. If Julie told my mother what she saw, it didn't matter. That night, Uzo came to my room with an iron pail to ask if I still wanted to sit on hot water, and I nodded.

Nameless

I pretend that my skin is not a problem, and I am good at it. Uzo made me aware of my curse when she mixed charcoal with kernel oil and asked me to apply it as lotion every morning. Our conversations were always a thin line between hot water and charcoal, so I didn't tell her the boys said that I was bad luck and should stop coming to the workshop. The treasure under my skirt had suddenly become trash.

Uzo was ashamed of me. One day, she told me not to leave the house except if it was very important. She made up a story about area boys looking for Albinos for rituals. I stayed put.

I have never seen my birth certificate. I didn't have a christening. Aunty Julie wanted to give me a name, she thought Ifechi would be good—*God's thing,* but it was not her place to name another woman's child. Uzo did not call me anything. She spoke her piece whenever she needed to. Her tongue spiralled into sentences, and I had to decipher which one was intended for me mid-air. I mastered her tone. I understood her silences. Whenever she spoke into the void of her room, I knew which words were mine. She called God with a shameful temerity as though she was sure he owed her everything, yet she was unworthy to receive it. With me, she started loosely, her voice sounding like water, slippery. I was always attentive, waiting to hear that there was food in the kitchen or that she had a special visitor and Julie was coming to get me.

Outré

If Julie wanted to get married, she would have done it. A lot of men would pay anything for the space in-between her breasts. Her house was clear; nothing clogged my spirit like it did in my mother's house. She even used white bed sheets. She cared for me like I was her child, and even though she had questions, she saved me the trauma of answering them. I wanted her to ask me about the time she saw me leaving the mansion with Ahmed, or the number of children I had removed from my body, and how many of them belonged to the men who slipped from my mother's thighs. I would answer that one.

Julie's eyes were watery and full of assumptions I could not refute. She kept me company till she was sure my mother had finished her escapades. She was not a coward like the men in our lives who took flight at the sight of our baggage. Nothing was too much for her to handle; my mother was broken, and she was balm. I wished she would just leave and forget that Uzo and I existed.

Burn

It had been a while since I said a prayer. I cleaned my room and anointed my body with lantern oil. This time, I let my fists pound mercilessly on the hard concrete and I laid down without my clothes, ready to go up like incense.

Heaven would reject this offering. It was not sweet smelling like grandmother described from the Bible before she became mute. There was foulness associated with my life and I embraced it more when I saw Uzo kissing Auntie Julie. It was not a sisterly kiss. It is the type of kiss you give to show openness, to welcome your lover. They made unforgiving noises in the living room, and I watched their butterflies dance all over the house till they died at the entrance of my room. It was unfair that Uzo got something she did not need to work hard to keep.

I lay on my bed and stared numbly at my grandfather's portrait. I massaged my body with lantern oil and I lit the matches. The pain was not excruciating because my whole life had been both fire and ice. I would be burnt crisp before Uzo and Julie could try to quench anything. My spirit was leaving, and because of that, something in Uzo dies. I know Auntie Julie will try to save it, but this damage is permanent.

For once my skin turned brown without a darkening cream or charcoal. Uzo would like this new tone.

About the Author:
Roseline Mgbodichinma is a Nigerian writer, blogger, and poet whose works have appeared or are forthcoming in *The Hellebore Press, Serotonin Poetry, Down River Road, Blue Marbel Review, Kalahari Review, X-ray Lit Mag, Native Skin* and elsewhere. She is a poetry mentor & Alumna at SprinNG, an NF2W scholar in poetry, and a fiction contributing editor for *Barren magazine*. Roseline won the audience favorite award for the Union Bank Campus Writing Challenge—Okada books. She is the third prize winner for the PIN food poetry contest. You can reach her on her blog: www.mgbodichi.com

The Children of No. 39 Faulks Street

Innocent Chizaram Ilo

The first thing you should know about No. 39 Faulks Street is that it does not really exist, at least not to the folks who live on Faulks Street or in Selemku. Popular town gossip has it that a woman—squeaky shoes, holes in a pink shawl that hugged her shoulders, and chewed out, crooked fingernails—once came to the Mayor's office to buy a house number. In all the years since Ani threw a grain of sand into River Bambu and formed Selemku, no one has seen or heard of anyone buying just a house number. The mayor did not bother to ask the reason for her strange request, iyaasikwa! Instead, he stroked his jelly-belly chin and demanded the price of a house and a plot of land just to dissuade the woman. But the strange woman paid in full, with real gold coins. She did not even haggle with the mayor. They said she even tucked extra coins between the many folds of the mayor's neck. So now, there is No. 38 Faulks Street next to No. 40 Faulks Street. This is how much the townsfolk know. What they do not know is that when their children play *In-Out* in the sandpit between No. 38 Faulks Street and No. 40 Faulks Street, the roof of No. 39 Faulks Street, buried underground, creaks under the stumping of their puny feet.

I know what you are thinking now, that Faulks Street and Selemku is happy-happy because you hear me mention sandpit, playing children, and puny feet. Odikwaegwu! The story Selemku does not like to tell itself is that ten years ago, a woman was accused of witchcraft and dragged out to the city-gate to face the guillotine. Her name was Nwanyi Kà. Strange meaning that name has, the Greeting Woman. You would think the people of Selemku will remember all their foremothers taught them about how people with strange names come from strange places and should be let be. Nwanyi Kà did not want to give the jeering crowd the satisfaction they sought, asi-asi! Before the executioner lowered the serrated blade that shimmered in the warm afternoon light, the woman cursed herself to burst open and her many pieces possessed the nearest bodies they could find.

The townsfolk went home delighted in their minuscule minds that they have purged Selemku of this filth called witchcraft. Many months later, the women of Selemku started giving birth to unusual babies: babies with white pupils, with aluminum fingernails, with thorns in place of eyebrows, babies with seven toes on each feet, babies with spinning heads, babies that sweated blood, babies with hairs on their palms and soles, and babies who exhaled fire. Ngwa-ngwa, the townsfolk sought Ani's face at Ekan Hill as they always do when their lives begin to spiral out of control. They pitched their tent at the summit of the hill—every man, woman, and child—and kept vigil for four long nights until Ani finally spoke. Or, they believed she did. No one could tell because one minute they were straining their ears to hear Ani's voice filter through the crater at the top of the hill, the next, Anyanzu, Ani's priest, was screaming that he could feel Ani's voice in his bones.

"The Great Goddess has instructed that all the unusual babies be dumped into Gworo Pit before tomorrow becomes memory."

Sunrise. Mothers wrapped their babies in little purple

clothes and did as Ani commanded. The babies cried. At first, they thought the cries were just babies yearning for their mothers, but the crying continued, shrill, searing, causing people's ears to bleed. And then mornings became too bright and nights took an extra layer of pitch. The townsfolk stuffed their ears with wool and reeds and anything that could block out the cries, avoided going out in the mornings because the sun's scorch could peel skin, and carried lanterns around all night so they wouldn't bump into each other. Selemku remained like this until the day after the strange woman bought a house number. The crying stopped and Gworo Pit was empty. All the unusual babies were gone.

This is where the story ends for the townsfolk and begins for the children of No. 39 Faulks Street.

Madam Principal built No. 39 Faulks Street with the help of her friends: Stool, Flower Vase, Illumination, Coffee Mug, Bell, Ceiling, Zinc, Floor, Sewing Machine, Roster, and Armchair. Illumination is not really Madam Principal's friend-friend, she does not live in the house like everybody else, comes only in the mornings, does not even wait for most lunches, and lurks behind the windows like she is scared of entering the house.

In this house, Madam Principal gave us new lives and new names. She told us how our mothers left us to die at Gworo Pit while our fathers downed bottles of Ogogoro at Quidi Bar. Every day she reminds us that nobody wants us, that we are forever indebted to her generosity, and that we are stuck with her forever. She feeds us. Clothes us. In return, we go for night-rounds. Sometimes the night-rounds can be fun, like when you are told to raid the baker's shop for bread or steal golden necklaces from the dancers at Lasisi Disco hall. Other times, they are not so fun because you could fall into a pot of boiling okra soup or have your limbs forever maimed by a glue-mat. When one of us becomes too much trouble, Madam Principal expels him or her.

Tonight, Madam Principal will expel Ogobuchukwuonye. Although she has not announced it yet, we know because Ogobuchukwuonye tried to use magic on her during breakfast. Madam Principal had just caught Tobi slipping extra bacon into the back pocket of his shorts and was about to scold the pimple-faced boy when Flower Vase flew above her, missing her head by a quarter-inch. It was easy to tell it was Ogobuchukwuonye because her eyes were still locked on Stool, where Madam Principal keeps Flower Vase so her roses will catch Illumination. The rest of us shuddered at the dining table.

Nobody is allowed to use magic while we are at No. 39 Faulks Street, not to talk of using it on Madam Principal!

"Ogo, upstairs, now," Madam Principal had said. "The rest of you go and study or practice some spells. Just do something that will not make me see your faces until evening."

All day, we hear heavy thuds upstairs, from Madam Principal's bedroom. Our voices thin into whispers because we do not want to untangle the gauze of uncertainty wrapped around No. 39 Faulks Street. We scatter around the house like the lupines in the back garden. Some of us mill around the doorways, the kitchen, and the verandah, while the rest of us go back to our rooms. I do not know what made Ogobuchukwuonye try to smash Flower Vase on Madam Principal's head. She has always been Madam Principal's favorite. Ogobuchukwuonye who Madam Principal called a *shining example*. Ogobuchukwuonye who had the keys to Madam Principal's room. Ogobuchukwuonye who could slip into houses through keyholes, drainpipes, air vents, wall cracks, and all the tiny places you can think of. Ogobuchukwuonye who rubbed shame-powder on our faces when we failed to complete our night-rounds. If anyone will throw anything at Madam Principal, it should not be Ogobuchukwuonye.

"Maobi, what are you doing?" A voice asks as I close the kitchen door. The voice grows hands and starts pulling me along the dark hallway. And before I can protest, it has grown eyes, dim blue eyes, that are now peering into mine.

"You're trying to steal food."

"No. I just went to drink water, I swear."

"Open your mouth lemme smell it…uhmmm…hmmppp…that stinks. When last did you brush?"

The voice transforms into a giggle. I can tell who it belongs to now, Ifiok, but this does not stop my stomach from doing cartwheels or my legs pressing together to calm the pee threatening to burst. Everybody feels this way when Ifiok holds them. There is no denying No. 39 Faulks Street is a house filled with shape-shifters, spell-casters, dream-conjurers, and astral-travelers. Still, we all think Ifiok is weird. She sits by herself most of the time, staring into space, smiling to herself, and talking to people we cannot see. Even Madam Principal says *something is a bit off with that girl*.

"Ifiok!"

"You should have seen your face. Scaredy-dooduu-bambam."

"Pfft, I wasn't scared. Not one bit."

"Tell that to your rotten breath."

I hiss and make my way out of the hallway. Ifiok never stops talking and the longer anyone talks with her, the spookier she gets.

"I can tell what you are thinking." Ifiok's voice dangles between threat and matter-of-fact.

"Good luck with that."

"You want to know why Ogobuchukwuonye did it?"

"Don't pride yourself for reading my mind. We all want to know why Ogobuchukwuonye did what she did."

"But nobody knows it's because she refused to do Madam Principal's bidding."

This is crazy talk. Nobody dares to disobey Madam Principal.

"It's not crazy talk. That's why she tried to smash Madam Principal's head with Flower Vase."

"Get out of my head evil spawn!"

Maybe it was a mistake. Ogobuchukwuonye should know better not to…

"If it was just a mistake, why will Madam Principal expel her tonight?" Ifiok asks.

"We don't know if she will be expelled. Wait, what?"

"You know it." The girl cocks her head at me in an *ehn* stance.

"How do you know I know it?"

"Because I read people's…"

"Shut up already!" My voice rings across the hallway and echoes throughout the house.

"What are you all standing and looking at?" Madam

Principal's voice towers above us. She is standing on the top stair, her right arm slant on the banister for support. She glares at Ifiok and me with her bad eye, the left one that drips cloudy jelly, until we pretend to be minding our business. Madam Principal goes back into her bedroom to continue whatever she is doing with Ogobuchukwuonye.

"Does my truth scare you?" Ifiok asks me.

"Your big mouth will get us all into trouble."

Evening. We now know for sure Ogobuchukwuonye will be expelled. Madam Principal gathers us in the dining room. Bell rings and the Ceremony of Expulsion begins.

Madam Principal lays Ogobuchukwuonye on Stool. Stool is so small, Ogobuchukwuonye's legs and arms jut out at her edges. Madam Principal does not pause to catch her breath or flinch when a globular of sweat runs down her nose or blink even though Ceiling is sprinkling sawdust into her eyes. You cannot really blame Ceiling; he has been telling Madam Principal to change his boards for so long because age has caught up with him and he can hold sawdust no more. Madam Principal wrenches Ogobuchukwuonye by the neck and begins to peel the girl's skin, carefully lifting each coffee-stain-on-yellow layer of flesh with a knife. Floor does not complain when the strips of Ogobuchukwuonye's skin fall on her. Yes, she knows the drops of congealed blood will cause molds to grow on her and make the kitchen rats gnaw at her newly polished surface. No, she will not complain or she will face whatever it is she is sure Madam Principal will do to Ceiling for sprinkling sawdust into her eyes.

When she is done peeling Ogobuchukwuonye's skin, Madam Principal plucks out Ogobuchukwuonye's bones and crushes them in a mortar. She pours the powdered bones into a cauldron and lets them boil for some time before scooping the white paste into a bowl. Sewing Machine helps stitch Ogobuchukwuonye's skin together while Madam Principal remolds Ogobuchukwuonye's bones. Madam Principal fits the new bones into the stitched-up skin and seals it as if nothing happened.

Ogobuchukwuonye lifts her body off the table and starts walking towards the door. We trail behind her, Madam Principal in front. The girl squeezing the doorknob is Ogobuchukwuonye, but not Ogobuchukwuonye-Ogobuchukwuonye because all her magic is gone. Just like Rukus, Nati, and Zimo; the other children Madam Principal has expelled from No. 39 Faulks Street. They all walked out of the door and we never saw them again.

"Are we going to stand here all night looking at a lost soul?" Madam Principal barks. "Go, get ready for your night-rounds." The corners of her lips fold into a sly smile.

We trudge to our rooms, ninety-six pairs of feet lined with lead.

Bell rings again at midnight.

We shuffle out of our rooms and form a single file in front of Madam Principal's room. Roster yawns before climbing atop Stool. He spreads his brown pages and starts calling out our names in pairs. As Roster calls each pair of names, Madam Principal tells them what they are going to do for the night-round. Tobi and Ramut will mismatch all the drug labels at the pharmacy down the street. Okem and Ajayi will steal fresh bread from the baker's. Iyanle and Otuba are to chew off the mayor's signature on all the documents at Town Council Hall.

Unoma and Obong will unclog the water pipes at No. 40 Faulks Street so that our above-the-ground neighbors will stop digging a new borehole. Kelem and Ifenem will gnaw at the feet of the children who peed in the sandpit during the day. Madam Principal says the children's screams when water touches the sores will be soothing and compensate for the stench of their pee that hung all over the house.

"Now, make sure you're back before dawn so I can turn you back into your human forms. Trust me, you don't want to be stuck in a rat's body," Madam Principal says as she gives each child a shape-shfting potion to drink.

"Maobi and Ifiok," Roster says.

Only Ifiok steps forward.

"Maobi and Ifiok," Roster calls again. This time he slams shut, scattering the dust clinging to his dog-eared pages. It is now I realize he has been calling my name.

Madam Principal whacks the center of my head with her knuckle when I stand beside Ifiok. "Where is your mind drifting to, Maobi? You should always listen with–"

"–rapt attention," I say.

"The two of you will steal *The Book of Things Locked In Shadows* from the library. It's in the restricted section."

The library! With Death Claws, the library cat, manning the shelves and waiting to pounce on any rodent sniffing around. I have never gone for a risky night-round before, unless you count the night Mama Risi of No. 40 Faulks Street nearly bashed Tobi's and my skull with a spatula when Madam Principal sent us to steal her pancakes.

My body takes time to adjust to its new form after I drink the shape-shifting potion. Ifiok looks comical. Her rat-nose seems as if someone glued it on her face in a hurry and her tail is stiffened at its end and curved like a walking stick.

It is dark-dark when Ifiok and I crawl onto the surface of Faulks Street. The shops are all closed, save for the blacksmith's.

"Hey, you know we've not been paired before for night-rounds," Ifiok says as she wallops my back with her tail.

The pain bites into my skin and I try to whip her back but my tail swooshes above her head. Ifiok giggles. She leaps on top of an old toolbox lying beside the gutter, picks up a bolt and hurls it at me. The bolt bounces against the left side of my belly and spirals into a nearby pothole. I ignore her. A night-round becomes a different kind of hell when Madam Principal pairs you with Ifiok. Determined not to be ignored, Ifiok sinks her teeth into my left hind limb.

"Ouch! What did you do that for?"

She lets out a fulfilled sigh. "You kinda have tasty blood. Just the right amount of salty."

"Just stop. We have to get going if we ever want to complete our night-round, or we'll face the shame-powder tomorrow."

"Chill out. Ogobuchukwuonye is no longer around so Madam Principal may as well forget about the shame-powder. Why are you gloomy tonight? Lemme read your mind. Emmm... because she expelled Ogobuchukwuonye."

"Easy guess."

"Snap out of it," Ifiok nudges me. "Not that you were even friends or anything. I never really really really liked that girl. People like her, with long names, I find hard to trust. What kind of name is Ogobuchukwuonye? My chest does back-flips just pronouncing it."

We burst into an almost synced laughter. I have never seen Ifiok laugh before. Her default face is blank. We continue laughing until we reach the library. There, our laughter dies in our throats. The thought of Death Claws resurfaces. We peer through the front window to see if we can catch any sight of the cat before we sneak in. Madam Principal told us that the restricted section is fifteen bookshelves away from the entrance.

Ifiok and I crouch from shelf to shelf until we get to the fifteenth shelf marked **RESTRICTED AREA**. *The Book of Things Locked In Shadows* is the first book on the top compartment. In haste to grab the book and head home, my right hind limb kicks another book off the shelf.

The book lands on the floor with a dead thud.

Don't breathe, I say to myself, don't freak out.

Paracetamol.

Aracetamol.

Racetamol.

Acetamol.

Cetamol.

Etamol.

Tamol.

Amol.

Mol.

Ol.

L.

I look around to see if the noise roused the cat. It didn't. We climb down the shelf and make for the exit.

A pair of green eyes looms above us when we get to the third bookshelf. The eyes also have a pink tongue licking a hairy, black face. By now, our eyes are accustomed to the darkness and we can see Death Claws forming an arc around us with his body. He meow-yawns, revealing a set of jagged fangs, and pokes our sides with his claws.

"When I bite his paw, we'll make for the window." I cannot tell if it is my voice or Ifiok's.

The things I am seeing now are warped. My eyes are spinning as if someone hoisted them on a conveyor belt. Death Claws growls. Ifiok runs towards the window. I slip under a bookshelf but the cat grabs my tail. He pulls me out and throws me into his mouth. I scratch and tear at his tongue, his lower and upper palate. Death Claws spits me out. He bares his teeth and leaps toward me. As I dodge, the tail of my left eye catches Ifiok grappling the cat's ear. Death Claws whips his head backward. This sends Ifiok sailing through the air. She bashes her head against the curtain rail and falls on the floor. A faint wince. She does not move.

The last thing I remember is Death Claws's paw pummeling my skull.

"He's awake."

"No, he's not."

"Shhhh!"

"His eyes are twitching."

"Let the boy rest."

"But time…"

"I know."

The words cut my insides like sickles slashing at rice stalks. Everything is bleak. Some monster is playing jamba-jamba inside my head. This should be inside Death Claws's belly. But the voices…

I slip into soothing darkness.

A soft pair of eyes, with an aquamarine gleam and square pupils, is the first thing I see when I open mine. I am lying on a bed, a strange bed that is doing a rupu-rupu sensation on my back. The room is as large as my tired eyes can go. It is also well-lit; you'd think Illumination lives here all day. The wall is painted the color of water; tiny pictures of children building sandcastles hang on it. A table at the far end of the room overlooks the window and the floor is spread with a raffia-woven mat. Someone coughs. It is the pair of soft eyes and she has taken the form of a woman. A blue gown wraps her body, clingy, like it does not want to let go. Her face. Her face looks so much like Madam Principal's.

"Where am I? Where is Ifiok?"

Scrambled scenes from the library flash across my mind. I try to get off the bed but I cannot move.

"Lie still. You are going to slow the healing process," the woman says in a voice that shares a fierce semblance with the pulled strings of a cello and a violin and a lyre. I don't know why, but I am smiling now.

"I know you must have questions, Maobi, but time is running out."

"How do you know my name? Who are you?"

"Ifiok told me your name. I'm Nwanyi Kà."

"That can't be true, the story says you did katabom-bom and died."

"Yes. But we witches always have a way of dealing with situations like that," Nwanyi Kà says and pulls up a stool beside the bed.

"Wait," I reach for my tail but grasp air. "You changed me back into my human form?"

"Yes. Your head wounds will heal faster this way."

"Where is Ifiok?"

"Ah, your friend. She is eating breakfast. You took so much time to heal. The cat almost ground your head to pulp. Glad I came in when I did."

There is a scuffle behind the door.

"What's that?"

"Not what, who. They are your expelled brothers and sisters; Rukus, Nati, Zimo, and Ogobuchukwuonye."

"Why are they here?"

"I took them in after Madam Principal expelled them."

"Can I talk to them?"

"No, not yet. We don't have time for that."

"You look so much like Madam Principal."

She pauses as though gathering her thoughts. "Yes but that's beside the point. You have to go back to No. 39 Faulks Street."

"Where is *The Book of Things Locked in Shadows*?"

"Ifiok has it. She will tell you everything you need to know."

Nwanyi Kà gives Ifiok and me a shape-shifting potion to drink before we leave her house. "May the good spirits guide you," she tells us at the front door and pecks us goodbye.

Because it is well into the morning, Ifiok and I take the sleazy street corners, sewer lines, dark tunnels, and gutters to No. 39 Faulks Street. We do not want the town folks going about their daily business to see two rats talking to each other on the street.

"Many years ago, Nwanyi Kà lived in Awada; a town at the tip of the Great Volcano," Ifiok begins. "She was the daughter of a great wizard-chief and an enchantress. Many years after her parents died, Nwanyi Kà became bored with her life. She wanted something else besides living in a castle filled with magic and gold."

"I won't mind living in a castle filled with magic and gold."

"Ahhh, let me finish!" Ifiok glares at me and continues. "She left Awada and came to Selemku."

"To do what?"

"I don't know. She didn't tell me but she told me it was in this place that she met a man, Nkem. They got married and brought a son into this world. One night, Nkem walked into the room and saw Nwanyi Kà strangling their son. He raised an alarm but she turned into a bat and flew away. But the child was dead already."

"Nwanyi Kà, killed her own child?"

"She didn't do it, stupid."

"Who did it then?"

"Madam Principal."

"Madam Principal?"

"Yes. When Nwanyi Kà left Awada, her spirit split into two: the part that wanted to leave and the part that swore to continue her family's bloodline. Madam Principal is that latter part who would haunt Nwanyi Kà until she decides to come back home."

"It doesn't make sense."

"I know."

"So Nwanyi Kà is the good spirit and Madam Principal is like the bad one?"

"Neither of them is good nor bad, they're both acting under justified volitions."

"What does that even mean?"

"I can't think for you."

"But.."

"So back to the story. Nkem raised an alarm that his wife had killed their son. When the neighbors gathered, a sleeping Nwanyi Kà was dragged out of bed to Town Council Hall where she would face–"

"– the guillotine."

"Maobi, I am the one telling the story!"

We are at the library now. Death Claws is licking a bowl of sugar beside the window. He bares his teeth when he sees us walk past.

Ifiok scoffs to draw back my attention momentarily stolen by Death Claws.

"Nwanyi Kà started a quiet life at the outskirts of Selemku after what happened. You know, her bursting into pieces, the birth and disappearance of the unusual babies. She still comes into town to make sure we are all safe during our night-rounds, like last night when she saved us from Death Claws. We still contain pieces of her inside us. And she took the children Madam Principal expelled. You should have seen Ogobuchukwuonye this morning when she served me tea; she was all flowers and candy."

"Did she tell you why she wanted to smash Flower Vase on Madam Principal's head?"

"Yes. Madam Principal had sent Ogobuchukwuonye to burn her original parents' house at No. 10 but she refused."

I find it hard to believe Ifiok so I move on to my next question. "What does she want us to do?"

"To go home and pretend as if nothing happened."

"Just that, do nothing?"

"Yes. Sometimes doing nothing is the hardest thing to do." Ifiok stops to catch her breath. "Nwanyi Kà has been looking for Madam Principal for all these years. Rukus, Nati, Zimo, and Ogobuchukwuonye couldn't tell her about No. 39 Faulks Street because Madam Principal wiped their memories about where the house is. But now she knows about the house and will come by to make things right with Madam Principal."

"You told her about the house?"

"Yes, as a return gesture. She saved us from Death Claws, remember? You want to know what Nwanyi Kà will do when she visits?"

It's as if Ifiok yanked the thought right out of my head. "I thought you forgot this mind-reading thing when Death Claws bashed your head against the wall?"

"Because they're fragments of the same being, if Nwanyi Kà touches Madam Principal, time will rewind." Ifiok sidesteps a puddle of urine. *The Book of Counted Shadows* on her back is weighing her down so she has to double her pace to keep up with me.

"To when?"

"To the night Madam Principal killed Nwanyi Kà's son. Nwanyi Kà will be awake by then to stop her. So none of these things would happen."

"What will happen to us? Will we still exist?"

"Of course, but without our magical powers."

"We won't be able to do cool stuff like fly or shape-shift?"

"Yes, but we'll have a real family like other children in Selemku and stop sneaking around street corners, doing night-rounds for Madam Principal."

"What about the other children?"

"Not a word to any of them. They're too scared of Madam Principal, they'll spill the beans."

"What if they don't want to lose their powers? You know it's also their life?"

"Maobi, the life is ours but the magic belongs to Nwanyi Kà and she has decided to take it back."

Madam Principal is prancing up and down the stairs when we get home.

"What kept you so long?" She snatches the book off Ifiok's back, runs her fingers along the book's spine, and takes a long sniff.

"We had to wait for the library cat to sleep before we could get in," Ifiok answers.

I almost heaved a sigh of relief. My head is still wrapped around Ifiok's story that I did not remember to cook up a lie for Madam Principal.

Madam Principal gives us the shape-shifting potion and tells us to go in and join the others for breakfast. I cannot concentrate on my plate of corn porridge and fish sauce because Ceiling is whimpering. I excuse myself from the breakfast table to talk to Ceiling. He says Madam Principal bore holes on him with a hot rod and that Madam Principal promised to repeat *the gesture* if he tells anyone what happened.

The morning drags along like it does not want to pass. But night comes and the next day and another day and another, still nothing happens.

It's midday, exactly two weeks after the incident at the library. Madam Principal summons Ifiok and me upstairs, to her bedroom.

"Ah, come in. Lock the door behind you," she says to a shuddering Ifiok and me.

I am certain we are called in because Madam Principal now knows for certain what happened that night. Any moment from now we will be expelled.

"You know how Ogobuchukwuonye was special to me," Madam Principal begins. "But you've brought me something even more special."

She picks up *The Book Of Counted Shadows* from the dressing table and runs her fingers along its spine. "This book," she says, flipping through the moldy brown pages, "is a cut-and-join diary of a woman who was haunted so much by the Mirror Witch she drowned herself and her daughter at Eucalyptus Ridge." She buries her nose in the middle of the book and inhales the musk. "At least that's what the townsfolk know, what they don't know is that Nkem journeyed to Awele to find her lover. Long story, you won't understand."

We stand there gaping at Madam Principal.

"Hey, every time my favorite child errs and I have them expelled, I send two of you to the library to get me a book. After they've succeeded in getting the book, I choose my new favorite child from the pair. That's how I chose Nati, Zimo, and Ogobuchukwuonye. Books help me forget to stop wondering what is happening to them as they walk alone in this dangerous world. But you see, I've rid them of magic so the townsfolk will show them mercy, even it's just a weeny bit." Madam Principal gathers the loose ends of her lappah, drops the book on the table, and faces us. "Funny thing, Ifiok has always been among the pair I send to the library but she never gets chosen as my fave. Weird child, let's see if your luck changes today."

Someone raps on the door.

"How many times do I have to tell you all not to bother me,

especially when I'm in the bedroom!" Madam Principal bawls. "Maobi get the door. Wait, lemme get it myself and smack that little rascal right in the forehead."

"So long, stranger," someone says as Madam Principal opens the door. She hastens to slam the door close but the door slams against an obstructing foot. Madam Principal loses her balance and sprawls on the bedroom's floor.

Nwanyi Kà walks into the room.

"Don't touch me." Madam Principal manages to voice over her pain; she probably bruised or sprained something falling.

"It's time for this to stop. You can't hold me hostage in Awada forever."

"What about your duty to your parents; The Great Wizard and Enchantress?"

"A duty I didn't choose myself."

"You told her about this place," Madam Principal says as she points at Ifiok and I. "Maobi, I knew she put you up to this…"

Nwanyi Kà wraps her palms around Madam Principal's wrists and everything starts dissolving into air or phantom, I cannot say for sure. I become formless, although I can still see and hear things. A tiny room appears where a little boy is sleeping in a metal cot. The window creaks open and the rushing night wind blows out the candle. A woman is standing above the cot, looking at the child. The little boy stirs awake and begins to cry. Another woman enters the room and shuts the door. It is a bit confusing now because the two women look alike. There is shouting and rage and fighting and thunder and lightning and blood inside the room.

The little boy continues to cry as this air or phantom I have become disappears.

This body I am in now feels strange. It's small and bathed with talcum. I am in a room that smells of egusi and uziza. A woman scoops me up and nuzzles my chin. Her eyelids are sagged and her hands are shaky. Someone calls her Nwanyi Kà. The other women around are all telling the story of how a thunderbolt nearly killed Nwanyi Kà's son three weeks back. A woman comes into the room and takes me from Nwanyi Kà's hands.

"We're running late already," the woman says, "but still carry him, Mama Chikwerendu has not finished rubbing otanjele on my eyes."

"That's your mother," Nwanyi Kà whispers to me. "Don't worry, you'll forget everything once the naming rite is over. A new name. A new you."

We are going somewhere. Men, women, and children are walking behind my mother. We stop at a shed where a man in shiny loincloth puts me in a basket.

"His name is Unoanyierika; our house is numerous." The man in shiny loincloth says and holds me out to the sun.

There are other women carrying babies waiting to be named. I feel like I know all the babies from somewhere. I want to talk to them, to ask them if they feel queasy in this form but it's only gibberish that comes from my mouth.

About the author:

Innocent Chizaram Ilo is Igbo. They are the winner of the 2020 Commonwealth Short Story Prize (African Region) and the 2021 Nommo Award for Best African Speculative Short Story. They are also a finalist of the Gerald Kraak, Short Story

Africa, Ignyte, and Author of Tomorrow prizes. Their works have appeared in *Isele*, *Lolwe*, *Granta*, *Catapult*, *BBC Culture*, *The Guardian UK*, *Strange Horizons*, *Fireside*, *F&SF Magazine*, and elsewhere. They live in Lagos and write to make sense of the world around them.

The Only One I Have Not Lost

Dennis Mugaa

She closes her restaurant early and asks the one waiter she has employed to come later than usual the next day. His face lifts in surprise. "It's only tomorrow," she assures him. Outside, dusk settles on Eastleigh's First Avenue like brown dust reclaiming space on a roadside stall. Walking out of the restaurant, she quickly adjusts her hijab to shield herself against the wind as she rushes to find her son. His life is in danger. She'd tried to tell him about the police officer on the phone earlier, but she couldn't find the words. The old shoe shiner waves at her from his chair, but she doesn't wave back. Instead, she feels the hairlines behind her neck constrict and her heart starts to beat faster; she has been afraid for her son before, but never like this.

Drivers hoot in traffic. A pushcart is dragged on the wrong side of the road. Dust whirls up from the street as a cold wind blows. Hearing the adhan, she realizes she'll miss maghrib prayer. The sound of brakes screeching sends an irritable electric rush down her spine. It reminds her of her madrassa in Mogadishu when ill-mannered children scratched the blackboard with their nails. She passes a fruit seller cutting pineapple into thin long slices, and a young man selling roasted maize beside uncollected garbage. As she nears the butchery where she buys her meat, she hopes Abdi, the owner, doesn't see her. He always wants to talk, even when there is nothing to say, and today she does not have the time. She clasps her face in her hands as if to yawn and walks past quickly. At the junction where she crosses into Pangani, she leans into a wall to evade an overlapping matatu.

There are election campaign posters everywhere: on walls, on electric poles, and on some street stalls she passes. There are potholes on the road. Some recent, some old, and she knows the ones filled with mud where cars get stuck when it rains.

She arrives at Pangani Liberty Hall at seven. At the entrance, she meets a group of women who she realizes from their T-shirts, are mothers and widows who have lost someone to police shootings. Her son, Yusuf, is moving between them, hugging them. She wants to shout to draw his attention, but the women pull him aside and kiss him on the cheek; the men embrace him as if he were their son. His gait is confident and proud, and she is ashamed that as his mother, she has never noticed this before. But how could she? How could she have ever known that her son, scared of the slightest confrontation as a child and often tormented by other children, would have grown up to be like this? And yet it is she who made countless duas for him as he grew, teaching him how to walk like that, albeit with varying degrees of failure. "Yus, chin up, shoulders straight, and look someone in the eye when you talk to them." She would cane him with a ruler or a bathroom slipper when he didn't do one of these.

She doesn't go inside, not yet. She watches her son's sporadic reappearances: consoling a mother, comforting a friend. Her fear is replaced by jealousy as if each person Yusuf speaks to is given a piece of him that is somehow removed from her.

"Ingia," someone ushers her in. She doesn't know most of the people here. Her social circle is small, mostly composed of Mogadishu Somalis who like to talk about the past. Although she knows an old Eritrean who works at Asmara Restaurant—she speaks to him in Italian as if it were a secret language between them.

Inside, people are holding candles and wearing T-shirts that say, "Our Lives Matter". It's a vigil for Yusuf's friend. The sad story of his death is well known. He'd been playing football with friends. Night had fallen and the city was slowing down. A police car pulled up in front of them. The police officer asked where they were coming from; they told him. The officer told them they were lying and accused them of being in a gang. He then asked how much money they had. All of them, except Yusuf's friend, had money. The others were let go. His body was found the next day with a gunshot wound to his temple.

"Hooyo," her son says.

She places her palms on his face, noticing he has cut his hair in the style her husband had when they first met. In those days, Xamar was defined by light. The light washed over the sea, the streets, and it reflected off buildings. It was everywhere. She remembers that day when her husband walked into her family's restaurant, he had all the light of Xamar in his eyes. He was twenty-three, in his final year at the Somali National University; he was with two exchange students from La Sapienza. They'd come from the beach, having seen her restaurant as they soaked in the sun. "Ciao," he'd said to her, and then he ordered three cappuccinos in Italian. His voice was so sweet, like the smell of rosewater. And she, nineteen years of age and wanting to impress him, had replied in even better Italian that she would not serve him unless he promised to come back the next day.

"Are you alright?" her son asks. She nods, and before she can say anything else, Yusuf is called to the front of the hall.

Everyone sits. She goes to the front because she wants to be the first person to reach him when the vigil is over. Yusuf's friends from the social justice center appear on the podium. They place large black and white photographs of Thomas Sankara and Che Guevara, and a large, framed quote ascribed to Frantz Fanon: "In these poor, under-developed countries, where the rule is that the greatest wealth is surrounded by the greatest poverty, the army and the police constitute the pillars of the regime…"

Minutes later, they give speeches condemning the shooting.

When her son approaches the podium, everyone applauds. A drum sounds. The hall lights are dimmed, and the room becomes silent. It is mystical: the simultaneous silence of several people.

"The police in Kenya are destroying lives! They know it, and they do not care!" He goes on, saying he spends his free time at the social justice center cataloguing sadness. He says that what happens in their neighborhoods is the same thing the police are doing to young black people in Brazil, the United States, and France. "Here, it's because of where we live." He mentions his friend who was shot, tears filling his eyes. Perhaps this is why they loved her son: he felt what they felt but wasn't afraid to show it. "I wrote a poem for my friend," he says. She'd taught him buraanbur because she didn't have a daughter to pass it on to, so at least even though his poetry is different, she knows it comes from her.

"An Elegy for Those who Remain."

& sometimes our souls form rivulets / to bind us in different worlds / our hearts burn the color of rage / tunasema kwaheri Allah amepata malaika / here a thousand candles are lined to form your name / we cry & try to do the impossible to bring you back.

She tells him at night after they've finished eating dinner. She is washing the plates, her hands in a bowl of warm soapy water.

"A police officer came to see me. He said you should stop what you're doing or you're next." She says it in Somali, so he knows it's serious.

"Stop what I'm doing?" he responds, baffled. "I'm collecting funds to organize for a court case Hooyo. The police should not kill people because people are poor." His Somali isn't fluent, it is sprinkled with Swahili and Sheng, like white rice cooked with onions and carrots.

He goes to the living room. She follows, stands over him, folding her arms. Behind him, on the wall, is a verse from the Quran. Beside it is a red arabesque carpet, sold to her five years earlier by a merchant in transit. Its middle contains a map of Mogadishu in the mid-eighties, and to her, it is a cartography of memory—the places destroyed in the civil war reappear there.

She tells him about the officer, the same one who killed his friend. "Listen to me Yusuf, it's not your fight, we are not from here."

"Hooyo, I was born here. It is my fight."

She claps her hands and folds them again. If her son were younger, she would beat him into obedience. She can't quarrel with him because she knows he is right. And he is a good son, a dutiful son: he bought a new couch for their apartment, and he helps at the restaurant when she complains of tiredness. But he has been arrested twice. Once in 2013, after terrorists attacked Westgate, and two years later when they attacked Garissa University. Each time, the police said he looked like Al Shabaab and he didn't have identification to prove otherwise. After the second time, she forged documents for him and spent half her life savings in bribes to get him a Kenyan identity card and passport.

"What would Aabo have done?"

She wonders why he speaks of his father as if he has met him before; he only knows his father as a collection of memories she has passed on to him. She does know what his father would have done. Her husband was loyal to Siad Barre, and he was from the Darood clan. He was a rising government official. He believed the Somalia he grew up in would always be the same. He did not say a word when Hargeisa was bombed even though he felt it was wrong. And three years later when the civil war forced them to flee, he held onto hope that it wouldn't be long before the government restored control. Her husband would not have stood up against authority. But she does not mention this to her son, because she'd once told him that his father was a brave man.

Yusuf leaves the room. She knows he no longer listens to her. He has not listened to her since he started reading. Some mornings, when he was not teaching at the orphanage, he'd wake early to go to the national library in Buruburu, only leaving when it was closing. He read everything. She has seen books on Politics, Economics, Law, Philosophy, and Literature. In his early days, he used to pay the daily charge of twenty shillings, but now the librarians allow him entry without charge. Often, he talked about the books he read. She liked to listen even though she didn't always remember what he said.

She suspects him of something else too. She has seen a new graffiti tag in the neighbourhood with the words *Flossin Mauwano*. She knows he draws when he is bored and she has seen spray cans in his bedroom; but more so, she suspects him because he is the only one who knows what it means. "It represents police who kill people without consequences," he'd told her, speaking like the books he read. When she asked him about the spray cans, he told her it was for the children he taught at the orphanage.

She is unable to sleep, but she likes the intermittent stillness. From time to time, on the street overlooking their apartment, a vehicle passes. The intervals are consistent enough to pass for sea waves. Back when she was hired to cater events at the Croce del Sud Hotel, she would ask her husband to join her in the evening. They would walk along the shoreline as the sun set and the sea felt like the romance films she watched at Cinema Xamar, the scene where the lovers promised each other they would be together forever.

Restless, she remembers her last days in Xamar when everyone was leaving. They left for Italy, the United Kingdom, the United States, Ethiopia, and some crossed the Kenyan border into a new refugee camp called Daadab. She and her husband left on one of the last flights to Nairobi after his extended family was killed by the rebels. She remembers when they first arrived in Nairobi twenty-six years ago. It was so cold. Kenya was Anglophone, and there was the Swahili she couldn't speak at the time. She spoke Somali, Arabic, Italian and, importantly, English because of her restaurant clients in Mogadishu. Her husband did not speak English and so she became his translator in this new world. When they arrived, they registered with the UNHCR in Gigiri. For her, Nairobi was supposed to be a transit point. She wanted to leave Kenya as soon as possible and applied to have them resettled. But her husband refused, saying they would go back to his beloved Somalia when peace returned. So, they rented a place in Garissa Lodge, and it seemed as if Somalia followed them there. Soon the lodge turned into shops, and the shops turned into malls selling everything: clothes, jewellery, curtains, shoes, and perfumes.

In those earlier, happier days, when her husband believed they could return home only after a few months, they were grateful to have each other. Her husband never spoke of his family, but he grew quiet, and once, he had cried.

They would go to Uhuru Park in the mornings. It was often cold. They would take boat rides on the lake. In the boat, she would place her hand lightly in the water so that when it moved through her fingers, it formed soft forks. One day they met a photographer who took a photograph of them as they stood on the Nyayo Monument. On the LOVE sign, she stood beside the L, and he stood on the E.

Their settlement papers dragged, and the Kenyan government told them they had to go to refugee camps, otherwise, they would be declared illegal aliens. Suddenly, they found themselves not wanted in a country they didn't want to be in. But why would they go to the camps? Go to the camp and wait for aid? She and her husband were not beggars, they had only lost a country.

"Foolish jareers," her husband said whenever he had to bribe police officers enforcing the encampment policy. Then he started having chest pains, which seemed to follow the violence of the civil war. When she became pregnant two years later, she no longer wanted to leave Nairobi. However, it was different for her husband. He said he wanted his child to be born in the hospital near their home in Mogadishu. He died from a fatal heart attack the day Yusuf was born as if he couldn't exist in a world where he shared a different identity from his son.

It's the morning of Eid-al-Fitr and she and her son alight from the matatu in the city's central district. The clouds hang low, but she knows it will not rain because of the patches of sky between them. Several shops' shutters are closed. There aren't many cars on the road. She decided that they should go to Jamia Mosque for Eid prayers even though they haven't spoken much since they argued. She is wearing a black buibui with yellow embroidery, while Yusuf is in a cream kanzu and kofia, an outfit he reserves for special occasions. At the zebra crossing, they don't wait for the light to turn green. It's a feature, she learnt of Nairobi: to disregard the traffic lights.

"Eid Mubarak! Eid Mubarak!" A street child rushes towards them holding out his hands. Yusuf gives the child a twenty-shilling coin. Two more street children come towards him.

"You shouldn't give anything. When you give one, more come," she says.

He doesn't say anything. It surprises her how different her son is from her, how naïve he can be sometimes.

She sees the mosque's green minaret. As they walk past Al Yusra Restaurant, they are met by a long line of worshippers. Some of the women are wearing such beautiful buibuis; she promises herself that she will buy herself one once she saves enough money. At the entrance, her son says: "I'm organizing a protest against the police on election day."

Her mouth drops but before she can say anything, a man she knows appears and greets her: "Saalam Alaikum." As she replies, her son disappears into the crowd of worshippers.

She is at her restaurant making breakfast for a few customers. Her restaurant smells of dough, masala, and camel-milk tea. She adds cardamon to the sambusas and checks on the sabaayad. For lunch, she will make bariis iskukaris. Every morning when she arrives, she writes down the meals of the day on a blackboard outside in multicolored chalk. It's simpler this way: taking away from the customer multiple choices of what to eat. She realized this when she worked in her family's restaurant. It was mostly frequented by tourists, and they would ask what type of meals were on the menu and then still take her recommendations. Sometimes she makes canjeero, baasto, maraq digaag, and kalun iyo bariis. When she caters weddings, she makes xalwo for the guests.

A politician's caravan outside causes fatigue to envelop her. During election season, they always promise the eviction of illegal immigrants in Eastleigh. And the police respond with force. She knows people who have been arrested and transferred to refugee camps. But those are the ones who couldn't pay the bribes. She survived on bribes. Whenever a police officer comes to her restaurant and asks for her registration papers, she shows them (she bribed the City Council officials to get them), but when they ask for her identity card, which she doesn't have, she must bribe them. They often accuse her of being a beneficiary of piracy on the Somali coast. She has learnt to wear a cloak of invisibility. When a police officer or government official looks at her, she avoids eye contact. And when confronted, she does not question them at all.

She wishes she had a family to tell her troubles to. When she first came to Nairobi, she went to a payphone and dialled the phone numbers she knew. She called an uncle who had fought in Ogaden; she called a cousin who had worked at the fish market; and she called an aunt who had fled to Baidoa when the rebels announced on Radio Mogadishu that they had taken over. No one answered. Sometimes, when she replaced the receiver into its cradle, she thought maybe the telephone lines had been cut, so she sent letters, but still no word. When new arrivals came to Eastleigh from Mogadishu, she asked them about her extended family but there was nothing. It was as if the earth had opened up and swallowed them.

Five years ago, when the Transitional Federal Government was formed, she had the idea of going back; she knew of some people who had returned. Her son introduced her to the internet, and they searched online for places she knew but she didn't recognize them anymore. All she saw was loss. The pictures of the coastline showed it didn't curve in the places she remembered. Her memory felt like a nostalgia time capsule opened in a destroyed city. She cried knowing she couldn't go back. What was there to go back to? The problem with exile was longing, longing for a place as it was before, longing for people as they were.

Her restaurant is small; when she first started it, she installed mirrors on opposite walls to make the space appear bigger. But, when she served customers, she kept running into herself. The effect stunned her, made her afraid; her image recurred as if splintered. She saw how fractured she had become. She saw the sadness in her eyes, her developing wrinkles, and the secret places her husband touched that he never would again. It reminded her of what she'd lost, a mist that would never turn into water. And she thought of her customers, who were mainly refugees searching for their identity in her food, and how devastating it was for them to look in the mirror: an intrusion into a part they would prefer to keep hidden. The next day, she called a carpenter who removed the mirrors and replaced them with brown tiles.

She's in the kitchen when she hears the commotion; she raises her head and sees the waiter scampering towards her. The customers have turned their heads towards a tall imposing man. Outside, beside the shoe shiner's chair, is a police car. There are other police officers, but she knows the one inside her restaurant, even though he is not in uniform.

"Waria! Nilikuambia!" He points a finger at her. "Your son anatusumbua." She bows her head and leads him to an unoccupied table, feeling a burning in her throat against this man who has proclaimed himself her son's juror; and at the same time, she is engulfed by fear. She must be as polite as possible. She wants to shout at him, to slap him, but she cannot.

The officer picks up a toothpick from the table and places it in his mouth.

She walks to the cashier box, comes back, and shakes his hand, handing him all she has made so far in the morning.

"Because you're my friend, I'll give you one more chance."

"Afande, wallahi. I'll talk to him. I'll talk to him."

When the officers leave, she instructs the waiter to take charge of the restaurant. She rushes to the orphanage where her son teaches. Here, the houses transform into shanties that dip into a valley, separated by the green sludge of Mathare River. As she walks, she is struck by a memory of herself and Yusuf walking there when he was little. He was about six years old, and his baby teeth were starting to fall out. She was contemplating taking him out of madrassa and enrolling him in the orphanage since the headmaster had offered her free schooling in exchange for free meals for himself at her restaurant. She was holding Yusuf's hand. He'd learned a few hadiths, but overall, she felt the ustadh wasn't doing a good job. Obviously, her son was a smart boy: she'd taught him to recite his lineage through several generations. The afternoon was filled with sun and a few clouds. She asked him to recite the numbers in Arabic.

"Wahid, ithnan, thalaatha, arba, khamsa, sita, saba ..."

"Go on. What comes after?"

"Eight."

"No, in Arabic. What comes after?"

He stood in the middle of the road and placed a finger on his mouth, thinking.

"Yus, what comes after seven?"

"The end of the world," he said, laughing, and then he made the sound of an explosion.

At the orphanage, children play hopscotch and kati in the play area. At the end closest to her, some girls skip rope. They sing:

Public Van, Public Van, Number 28. I went for a ride but I stepped on the break. Blue band by zero, zero point zero is a round, around is a round, a round and a round. These are the actions I must do...

She finds Yusuf's class. His lesson is on the verge of chaos. Hands fly up in the air, students scream out answers while Yusuf screams back disobeyed commands for order. She stands outside of the class trying to find the right words. Some of the children ask to go to the bathroom—but then stay out to play. When Yusuf sits to mark assignments, they swarm around him like fireflies at starlight. At the back where manila paper charts are pinned, two children make paper planes and throw them to the front. She realizes this is Yusuf's problem: he has a soft heart.

She knocks. Yusuf sees her and tells the class to stay seated as he walks to the door.

"Hooyo, what's wrong?"

She says a silent bismillah and then holds his hands. "You have to stop Yusuf, they are going to—"

"Hooyo, calm down." He places a hand on her shoulder.

"You need to stop with the protest," she says, and, when he is about to open his mouth, she doesn't give him a chance to speak. "Promise me."

When she looks up at him, she sees her whole life. Not her life as she had dreamt about when she was a little girl in Xamar, but her whole life in the sum of what has been taken from her for him to be here. Does he not see what she has sacrificed?

She cries openly. Yusuf's students move to the door, some jut their heads to look at him. She brushes the tears away with the back of her palms.

"Hooyo macaan, I promise. I'll stop."

"I can't lose you, Yus," she pauses, looks him in the eyes. "Don't you see, you are the only one I have not lost".

They watch as the election results are about to be announced. Yusuf did not go ahead with the protest; he is still alive. She wants him to leave the country. It is the only way her heart will calm down further. She's been researching immigration into Europe. On the internet, she saw photographs of African migrant boats arriving in Lampedusa, and on the Sicilian coast, in Palermo. She saw capsized boats on the Mediterranean Sea and migrants drowning with their dreams. The ones who reached Rome spent nights on streets outside Termini Station. On the journey to Europe, some were swindled and sold off into slave markets in Libya. So she opted for the Middle East, but when she saw the kafala system there, she closed her browser immediately. She cannot believe she wanted him to migrate illegally, cannot believe that exile has corrupted her so much that she didn't bother to check legal and safe means for him to migrate. She will ask him to apply for scholarship programs, to study, he likes to read after all, and he will be safe.

"Would you like to leave Kenya?" she asks him.

"No. Why?"

She doesn't say anything. On the news, the president wins a second term. The opposition party says the election was rigged. It says it will move to the Supreme Court to challenge the election results.

A dawn to dusk curfew is announced in Eastleigh, Mathare, Kibera, and Kayole.

"Why don't they ever announce the curfew in rich neighborhoods?" Yusuf says as she goes to the kitchen. Outside the window, as the sun sets, several police vehicles move past. Opposition supporters are holding a protest against the results of the election. She hears gunshots. They come and go, similar to her final months in Mogadishu. She feels a familiar tingle in her spine. The country is coming undone, and they are at its seams.

As she is finishing making dinner, her son's phone rings. As he speaks, he frowns, and then his face is full of anger. "What? What! No! No!" he shouts. She rushes to him.

Yusuf looks at her and says: "The police have killed a girl I teach."

The shooting makes newspaper and television headlines. The girl had wandered out of the orphanage as the opposition party supporters protested. A police officer knelt, took aim, and fired at her. She was nine years old.

She cannot stop her son now. He goes to the orphanage every day and comes back with stories of grief. She knows he doesn't have classes to teach, but he still goes. Days later, he comes to her restaurant and finds her preparing rice. He comes in with dusty shoes, and even before he speaks, she complains. "Yus, your shoes. There's a shoe shiner—"

"Have you heard?" This is the first time she has seen him smile in days. He opens the browser on his phone and shows her a news page: *The Supreme Court has nullified the election of Uhuru Muigai Kenyatta as President citing irregularities with the voting. IEBC now must hold a fresh election …*

"Hooyo, we will hold our protest on election day, inshallah."

So many things are happening at the same time. The ground shifts every day. The neighborhood feels on edge, the anger visible, almost bursting. Whenever she walks anywhere, the air is thin; she feels as if a choking wind is encircling her. She closes her restaurant early because the curfew has been extended indefinitely. She is home by six, watching her son organize the protest.

The police raided and ransacked the social justice center so he can no longer go there. He designs and prints posters for the protests. Most of them are black or red and have a fist raised to the heavens. He makes phone calls to his friends. Everyone gives her renewed respect when they see her walking with Yusuf. "Mama Yusuf. Mama wa mtoto wetu," they say. On Fridays, when they go to the mosque, she holds his hand tightly as if he were still the child who couldn't count past saba. Yet, she still feels him slipping, like dry sand through fingers.

One day, on her way home, beside a construction site, she sees a police car with its windows smashed. A charred Molotov cocktail lays on the driver's seat. On the car's side, scrawled in white are the words *Flossin Mauwano*. An empty tear gas canister rolls into her feet and she kicks it away. Around the neighborhood, graffiti portraits of the murdered nine-year-old girl mushroom and claim the space of green moss and peeling paint on old buildings. On the shanties, near the orphanage, they also serve as decoration. The girl has become a martyr: her face a symbol of police oppression. And still, the government responds by bringing more police officers in. Deep inside, her fear rises with each passing day.

The morning of the protest is a ripple, strumming somewhere in the middle of the sea. She seems to exist someplace else, in a past she has lost and a present she is losing. She doesn't see her son when he leaves at dawn to the protest meeting point. She cannot eat. She tries to watch the news, but she cannot. She is afraid she will see him lying in a pool of blood.

She needs to find something to do.

She goes to her restaurant and opens it, tearing down a printed sign which said *closed*, and tunes her portable radio to the news.

From a distance, a group of people are queuing up to vote. There aren't many voters: the opposition party decided to boycott the vote, citing the electoral commission was compromised. An electoral official in a green reflector ushers them into a polling booth. Clothes hang outside on the building opposite her restaurant. She watches water drip down from them in soapy droplets. A customer comes in. From his henna-dyed beard, she recognizes him immediately. It is Abdi, the butcher.

"Mama Yusuf, kwani hauogopi leo?" he asks, laughing at his joke. She does not answer. She is there precisely because she is afraid. She serves him his usual camel milk tea and sambusa. She listens to his stories; they make her laugh, but they do not ease her worry. The portable radio breaks into a live broadcast. It is the Interior and Security Minister:

Fellow Kenyans, I want to appeal to all of you to maintain peace. We have dispatched the police, the military, and other security personnel to hotspot areas. An election is not an excuse for violence. Kindly vote co-operate or you will blame yourself.

He then issues a directive shutting down all media outlets except the state-owned one. The radio goes dead after the broadcast. Silence reigns. A deceptive silence, as if it is pawing the air before it rips into chaos. She slaps the radio and turns the tuning knob to resurrect it. It doesn't. She takes out the batteries, chews on them and places them back. Still, nothing.

"Are you alright?" Abdi asks.

When she looks at him, she doesn't see him, but rather sees outside. She notices the old shoe shiner isn't there. And she sees how bright the kiwi shoe polish logo is without him.

"How is Yusuf?" Abdi asks.

Again, she doesn't speak. How is her son? She doesn't know. There is no way to know. What if she loses him and she is the last to know? The thought makes her lose balance and she holds onto a chair. She feels as if she is losing everything. She has lost a country, a husband, a family; and now, her son?

She leaves Abdi baffled and hurries to the protest's meeting point.

She runs and runs and runs until she sees the protesters marching. There are hundreds of them. They are wearing "March for Our Lives" t-shirts. There are placards: "End Police Brutality", "Haki Yetu", and "Protect Our Children".

Her son's voice booms from a megaphone at the front: "The police do not maintain law and order, they maintain those in power!" The protesters roar in agreement. Their passion merging with Yusuf's. They raise fists and punch the air.

"Yus! Yusuf! Yusuf!" she calls to her son. She can't get through the moving crowd. Suddenly, they all stop. They are face to face with the police.

There's an armored riot truck ahead of them. Its green gleams from the sun. Its side is meshed like a prison fence. In front of it are police officers in helmets, bulletproof vests, riot shields and guns. Around it are more police vehicles. An officer with no helmet issues instructions; as he turns around, she recognizes him.

Suddenly she is shoving her way through the bodies in front of her. She has never been so strong. As she reaches the front, her hijab unravels. The wind carries it off and it tangles around the wheel of the armored truck.

"Hooyo," her son says to her.

She stands in front of him and stretches out her arms. The police raise their guns. She closes her eyes and hears a memory belonging to her and her son.

Yus, what comes after seven?

The end of the world.

About the Author:

Dennis Mugaa is a writer from Meru, Kenya. He was longlisted for the Afritondo Short Story Prize and was a finalist for the Black Warrior Review Fiction Contest. His work has appeared or is forthcoming in *Jalada, Lolwe, Isele* and *Washington Square Review.* He is currently studying for an MA in Creative Writing at the University of East Anglia where he is a Miles Morland Scholar.

Poetry

To the FUTURE: Eternal yolk. Knots
unwound. Unwounded. Salved and saved.
God, help me to see She. Through caves
of clay and blood and ashes. And trust.
Mud and fire and salt. Stardust.

"Unbridled" by Jennifer Purling-Baker

Three Poems

Uchechukwu Peter Umezurike

there's more

i.
your day begins

coffee   croissant   a kiss at the door
hunch over the keyboard   lost in the landscape of your head

ii.
but there is more

a family flees Mogadishu in a truck   in Nador   a man skirts
the muezzin's call
a woman soothes the heart of her man in Juba   a boy tells his
dad about   motley lights beyond Awka
a girl quits the plains of Asmara   a horseman   ferries his
woman through the dunes of Dirkou
each blinded by   the shimmering across the sea   the
shimmer of Spain

iii.
from the rooftop a son   maps the stars   longing for what's
across the sea
he's dreamt of plenty   he's dreamt of   what's on the other
side where   the plums look redder

than the sun   within reach any hand   could reach out &
pluck   the giant tender sun its redness
in the face of the sea   across the sea he's been told   there is
more   there's more plums
for one mouth & plums rot   plums rot in plenty   & he's
dreamt his mouth brim
with juices of a different plum

iv.
in the doorway a daughter   measures   the hours in her
mother's breaths   how much longer
she prods the wind   dreaming of peers   charmed to the
other side where   the apples look redder
than the sun   within reach any hand   could reach out &
pluck   the giant tender sun its redness
in the face of the sea   across the sea she's been told   there is
more   there's more apples
for one mouth & apples rot   apples rot in plenty   & she's
dreamt her mouth brim
with juices of a different apple

v.
one brother pawns his family's amber   the shadows bear
the slink of his steps across the medina
the twenty-four years he's known a blur   one sister slips out
the hedges   the naira warm
between her breasts   like her twin sister she thinks   it's best
her father   is best left by himself

vi.

in Garabulli   bodies bloat on the beach   some drift into
Tarifa where
pink carnations   await odd remains   the surf of Trafalgar
has washed away   the shapes
of love in the sands   washes afresh   what's left of a three-
year-old   whose parents
no one can retrieve   but an old lady drops   lilies at its
blistered feet   in Bodrum a girl looks asleep
in the sand   face sunk an inch   half of it gnawed by fish
only her parents   know the span of agony

vii.

under the low sun of Karpas   the gleam and shale of dusk
a boat bobs empty   next to a body
by a buoy   another body has seaweed in its mouth   one has
froth between its eyelids
a photographer steadies his hands   framing in a lens the mess
crabs & shrimps   have made of flesh
the image   may not rouse boys & girls   stamping down
the city hall   a beachcomber
dawdles before him & says   *a shell holds a memory of water*
but the sea is sanctuary for some

viii.

an uncle in Zarzis   who's known the heart of the sea   the
dark belly laugh of water
lays out headstones   behind a grove of olives   a tourist car
trundles by   a boy says

mira papa hay un cementerio   his dad stuns him with an eye
from the front seat
an aunt unmoved   by the loops of gulls above   speaks of
children of a time lost
the echoes of distant waves

ix.
half-risen from fatigue   a coastguard lists at the liquid edge
his mind
a funnel of last week's exhibit   of coffins bare of bodies
close by a nun chokes her dream
of mermaids & their stash of bones   stumbles shoeless
through driftwood   touching a rosary to her lips

x.
on a cliff in Lesbos   a priest stands & chants
Lampedusa is a path of bones   *(Sweet Mother of God)*
Lampedusa is a path of bones   *(Sweet Mother of God)*
& the Middle Sea builds   the Middle Sea builds
its own body of bones
its own city of bones.

Summer is gone

with its conceit and cheer
        open arms and clear laughter
            desire on squirrel feet
and the gooseflesh of thrill

the bloom behind oaks and sumacs
turns the sky into butter
slivered with plums
cherries and oranges

to be young and labile
hear nothing urgent in the earth's groan
what's gone mad
in the waters or at the borders
lands scarred by oil cobalt or local egos

what's left of *us* anyway?

should we trace
dandelion dust on bare limbs
uncounted gold of pollen and rust
in the field where we sit?

inside of us
warmth losing its bite
you—wanting more
me—wanting to keep
what's out and spent
loss we have no name for   and longing
like petals sucked dry of sugar

above our heads
a bee is an idea
see it turning
quicksilver:

are we to tail its buzz
or not
wherever it leads
gleaning joy
like fuzz along the way?

but in the air   winter
is closing in   quiet heavy with purpose.

In My Father's Shoes

I.

His face is the memory of my father. I start from his form,
a fish ebbed out of the water of sleep. *Are you...?*

His voice is a knife's tip, as was my father's:
What does it matter whose body I walk in?

The air hurts my nostrils —
In my room, the air warm and dry as a slap.

Outside, the skin shrinks from frost.
Go away, then. I bury myself in the duvet.

The duvet smacks the floor with a flick of his wrist.
But tell, how much time do you have?

I can tell only once I am out of bed.

He snaps his fingers, the flourish of a maestro.
Let's go out for coffee then.

I am prompt as a dot. Off the bed.
He snatches my car-keys. Off the desk. *Hop in.*

II.
We climb slush on asphalt, and he hums
a familiar tune at 81 Ave.
Ever wondered why you get to sing?

I glance around to be sure he meant me.
I don't know that I can sing.

His eyes leave the dahlias in the sky
for the bloom on my face.
This serious shit is some joke to you?

I am no singer. I only write.

What singing is not words? What writing is not song?

White against the window, silence lengthens.

III.
On Whyte Ave, he points: burly bikers
bragging at a bar-front, laughing as though the city
were a trip they've taken many a time;

a man protests on the curb, his beard long and sturdy:
I'm citizen. Terrorist, not me. I only sit down a little.

The cop lets out a laugh, smooth as his bald head.
How do you know? That's for me to find out, mister.

One airport scene begins to bud in my head,
but the mock-parade of preschoolers
along the sidewalk dispels anger:

Summer, please come.
Winter, please go...

IV.
Right on time. We find ourselves in a cafe,
slouching across each other, between us stands a face
more Mexican than Filipino, her voice,
too much syrup on pancakes: *May I take your order?*

My father's double picks up the daily. *What's news?*
Pardon me? Chestnut eyes level on him.
London Fog. He smiles away her confusion.
My spine straightens. *Green Mango.*
He puts away the paper. *Oilers lost to Maple Leafs.*

Squelch — rivulets of snow on the road.
I hear him say:
What's new under the sun, Peter?
I frown to show disinterest in weather talk.

V.

He stares ahead of me, familiarly,
as would my father when he mumbled
about the war in future tense.
He tosses what's left of his latte
down his throat and says,

The women of Lesbos and their god.
The men of Lampedusa and their altar.
What does the island know of bones?
What does its people know
of bones beneath the flow?

A village adorns itself
with bones from the water's gut.
And whose bones are those?
Whose bones are those?

But may your voice sing.
May your voice sing, Peter.
May your voice sing,
Unafraid of chokehold.

The refrain enfolds me, its echo long and earnest.

I wake to light between the slats,
the tang of berries on my breath,
the stink of sweat on shirt,

and the mind that I just rode
with a man who's travelled here before

whose poems told of the war
my father mumbled about

only in our dialect.

About the Author:

Uchechukwu Peter Umezurike is an assistant professor of English at the University of Calgary. An alumnus of the International Writing Program (USA), Umezurike is a co-editor of Wreaths for Wayfarers, an anthology of poems. He is the author of Wish Maker (Masobe Books, 2021) and Double Wahala, Double Trouble (Griots Lounge Publishing, 2021). His poetry collection, there's more, is forthcoming from the University of Alberta Press in spring 2023

Three Poems

Kelli Russell Agodon

Before I Walk Out the Door,
I Grab My Switchblade

Because sadness wears a leather jacket, I carry
  a butterfly knife—
all weapons should have names so tender

—I know a woman who sliced the tops
of her thighs while telling her teenage daughter
how wonderful the world was

like loving the butterfly while pulling off your own wings
holding the hand of a toddler and dragging along the devil
        with the other
feeding dolphins while wrapped in fish netting

maybe this is why I keep a switchblade in my bra
you never know who needs freeing or who is drowning
  in what's been thrown away

when I see this woman in her cargo shorts setting a blanket
out
  on a blacktop beach I sit next to her and tie us together

with haloes of fireflies
with plastic bags and twist ties
with daisy chains
with the underside of a cloud

from the top of a mountain if you look down
if you turn yourself to another
  view
if you stare too long at the shadows of women
you can hardly tell us apart.

Men Write Us Love Poems

'Tis true; for you are over boots in love.'
The Two Gentlemen of Verona

Tonight, my muse wants to put her mouth
on my poem. As I write she bites the rhubarb
galette, says she wants a Kelli of her own.
As if. As if we could buy creation like a clock,
tick tock tick tock. What's the secret to being
a wildflower? A distinction from weeds.
In a superbloom, we're more likely to avoid
the pantofles of the careless, the lawnmower
men. Sometimes I hope my hallucinations
include sandwiches and slam dancing
at a Shakespeare festival because dear Bill
had only 144 speaking parts for women
in his plays. Let me be the one who holds

the dagger and safely return it to its sheath.
Let me place the poison high on the shelf.
Our voices echo over balconies—we do not
need to be compared to a summer's day, we're
already the sun; we are everything that blooms.

Ways to Fly

Back from the second ring of Saturn she points
to a clothesline covered in cobwebs she found inside
the second ring of the patriarchy. Today, a blowback of blue,
blue warblers of a nation. Who tied our wings together,
who stole our feathers? When she says, I love a woman who
loves
a little destruction, and I want to remodel my life, become her
green delight of grass, untamed, an uncommon patch
left untouched by wildfire. And when I fall into the burning
woods of her, she says, The universe is our sideshow—how
easy it is to be dazzled by the meteor landing in a neighbor's
yard.
We are praying to the sky but unlike those who believe
they have sinned, we pray like joyful saints and praise the
summer
of flower crowns and the girls who called themselves
sunshine,
who called themselves a verb—so wild, so many ways
to fly away above what's left of the forest that continues to
burn.

About the Author:

Kelli Russell Agodon is the cofounder of Two Sylvias Press and lives in a sleepy seaside town in Washington State on traditional lands of the Chimacum, Coast Salish, S'Klallam, and Suquamish people where she is an avid paddleboarder and hiker. She serves on the poetry faculty at the Rainier Writing Workshop, a low-residency MFA program at Pacific Lutheran University. Her fourth collection of poems, *Dialogues with Rising Tides* was published by Copper Canyon Press in 2021. You can write to her directly at kelli@agodon.com or visit her website: www.agodon.com.

Five Poems

Adeyele Adeniran

This God Called Woman

I have woman beaten onto my back
female sewn into my skin
weakness embroidered into the thing
that makes me me
I have strength for years that
make your tongue wag
when it comes to spilling my pride and pains
I survive through it all rising above
the things that call me soft

you call me rib but I am the mother of nations
the womb that give things air
you say men before me
like my womb didn't seed their bloom

I am woman
besides God
I make all.

self-adornment

for the days you feel strange in yourself, remember to hold yourself and love you well

hair is a halo
reaching up to heaven
bursting out
"Hallelujah"

skin is a testament
gold from God's kiss
when he blessed me
"this is my child"

body is a vase
holding a soul
of scents and colors
"for now you are at home"

some days you hug your
body
because it feels ancient
you squeeze your skin
begging it to once again
be warm, be kind, be mine.

Mother's song

on my mother's back
i first saw the world
on her back, i knew hills
and elated mountains-
i learnt the language of peace
and-
i knew what safety was
it was like ...
learning the name
of God on your tongue.

My Mother Bathes Her Pain in Prayers

We stare into the darkness ridden with brightness.
That comes from the heart of the generator outside the barbershop.
Nights like I wish the secrets going on in my mother's head will set me free
I long for her dreams and interpretations to help me breathe
Most times I lose focus I see her, it comforts me
She is here right in sight, face hard but soft eyes
It is the world that baked her brown but still she's tender inside.
She's looking into times that only her irises can define
Rising in age yet young whilst old in wisdom
Finding answers in her own world of patient breakthrough
Surviving like a peasant but still living as a queen
Learning our nos and yes'
Raising us in luxury even with kobo we are penniful, feeding us drunk in bountiful
Giving us lessons to teach our own daughters, pouring her stories to fuel our experience

This night I stare at my mother.
Tight lips, scrunched nose.
She is only perusing our future and praying grace falls upon us.
Staring into the darkness asking God
"let my daughters have light so bright it rules over darkness"
a pause
"let my daughters be bright that they are moon
the only big star in darkness, let them be sun
the energy of a whole world"

origin

this is to all my sisters
who bled before
it was their time

trauma is the signature of
your past
your weakest memory shows
a blue room
where the first man held your small
frame then tried to take you
he didn't care that you were six
you ran and you never told anyone
swallowed the key to that door
like it never happened
you live with it like you're getting
ready for the next ones

Ten years later, you're at a small supermarket
two male attendants walk up to you
they try to corner you then laugh
at your shaky hands and seized breath
"what's wrong with you?"
they don't know their small play
just caused a panic attack
you leave the supermarket
with your heart in your throat

sometimes when you're alone
you think about why it happened to you

what exactly did i do
you blame yourself
then hate your body for causing you grief
you want to abandon this skin
but the sins you burden yourself with
are not yours to bear

the realization of this
draws you closer to the truth

you suffered first through pain,
then grieved the child you weren't allowed to be
everything morphs into anger

you realize there are little girls out there
like you
who don't know it's a rapist disguised
as an uncle, father or brother
women who are made to feel like
things
their voices only to be heard when spoken to
body taken by force and beaten when unwilling

sisters who wear scars as tattoos of
oppression
some as far as a thousand miles away from you
or the next block from yours
you find a way to reach out to them
they don't all know the word

but the prospect of freedom
gives them hope,
it installs a light in their eyes
they call it unwarranted
but it's one voice
for billions of women
around the world.

-feminist because we are one.

About the Author:
Adeyele Adeniran is a Nigerian poet, creative writer, and feminist who resides in Lagos, Nigeria. Her poetry and storytelling are greatly inspired by her part as a spectator in a world filled with humanity and chaos. Besides writing, she loves to get lost in her imagination, enjoys music that make her feel like a rockstar, and loves to have a good time and a great laugh with people who make her happy. She studies History and Strategic Studies at the University of Lagos. Her works have been published in *Kalahari Review*, *The Young African Poets Anthology*, *African Writers*, *LitQuarterly*, *NoteWorthy*, and *Women's Peace Magazine*; and is forthcoming elsewhere. She hopes to be a voice and influence of change.

Four Poems

Joanna George

The Chant

'Be a few days late, but never abandon like last month or the one before'
I chant through my sweaty smiles.
A plate of juicy papaya, a few sliced pineapple pieces
and a packet of exotic seeds sit everywhere I turn.
I take an extra mile walk for this week, while my breasts are still tender
and then I meditate, pin on subliminal therapy
for the Red Goddess to appear.
"Shower on me. Bleed on me."
I keep reciting, every day every month,
yet she misses me, or I'm convinced my body misses her,
with these ovaries that are already ballooned with cysts,
decorated with tiny beads on the edges, like a string of fairy lights.
I sacrifice the little joys of coffee, ice cream and everything sweet,
While stress builds up, molesting my skin scattering its knives of acne
and extra hairs on my jaw, chest and everywhere it pleases,
leaving a trail of missed periods like footprints and bookmarks.
I try sleeping through this mayhem of hormone imbalance
But somehow end growing tighter in my new clothes.

I just have to keep my calm the doctor says
prescribing a handful of pills colored and shaped for geometry
lessons.
I pray to the moon, the grains and the banyan tree,
yet when I bite into the orange flesh of the papaya angrily,
staining the floors with the orange red juice of it,
it's already 80 days past the time, and I have not been stained,
with the asterisks of my period blood yet.
O How I wish for a miracle of red, a pain of joy and a rain of
blood.

The Chair

There is a chair that stands at the corner of our drawing room,
which is also our master bedroom.
Since, the chair is placed near the front door, duppattas fly on
its arms,
just in case someone needs to rush into the godly hours of the
smoldering sun.
Now, the chair is in front of the window as well,
fetching enough amount of wind as well as heat,
that's how the wet towels reach up the back of the chair, lying
shoulder wide.
The seat can't be left empty, can it?
Hence the clothes dry from the line, now blown up by
removal of water
Occupying the seat, waiting to be pressed to a line.
Somehow the cats like the height and being attracted to the
warmth,

leaving a shiver of ultrathin fur like vermicelli strands on the chair and all its way.
Bed sheets, blankets, hankies; every kind of cloth find an excuse to land up there,
like the chair itself was a Bermuda triangle attracting everything towards it.
At night, with the lights switched off, it brings out silhouettes of anything but a chair.
And I wonder, mother what shape you mould into at night,
as you crumple on your side to sleep,
is it yourself at least now?

Microwave Oven

That Friday when you voluntarily ordered a microwave oven,
I imagine sniffing the aroma of melting ghee,
The heat of dal wafting, clutching the scent of minced coriander,
The sweetened warmth of milk in tea and coffee,
Glasses clanking and laughter echoing.
But when the showroom people arrived,
in their shoes and caps for publicity,
you decide by yourself to keep it inside your cabin,
"For all." you gleam like a lottery was won.
And I think of the red-orange flames of pyre,
the blazes of witch hunt and the sunburn of your stare boring into our backs,
tracing the rounds of our bottoms and the curves of our sides.
Finally, you place that box spitting heat radiation

to the cornered junction of your room,
I can only think of mousetraps now,
how your hands would brush while helping,
how the tiniest squeak of mice is always unheard.
It asked for the cheese you would then say.
You being our guide can say a thousand words
an oracle from the flames and the men in your world would simply believe.
But what you don't understand is, how over centuries
the mice learnt well to smell traps like yours
and avoid them, while leaving you to eat the poisoned food you kept for her.

Periods in times of PCOD

A Pleiades of bright ruby sparkles, ripple on my underwear,
staining it in my red outcry of joy.
I feel the waves of warm slick of blood
between my thighs rush out in hurry,
as if the whole ghosting game for the past months has been tiring on her as well.
Since the last ultrasound illuminated
tiny grapes of follicles sequinning along the
boundaries of my swollen ovaries,
what I yearn for the most is the hopeful rustic smell of ache drilling my back and melting my knees.
Now that they all have arrived in grandeur after months of hibernation,
I feel new as an old version of me, before curbing to the possession of PCOD,

ready to teleport myself to the ancient times
where people celebrated their monthly surge of blood
and I would readily host a festival
for the arrival of my untimely and ever delayed splash of
menstrual blood.

About the Author

Joanna George (She/Her) is a research student at Pondicherry University. Her poems appear or are forthcoming in *Borderlands: Texas Poetry Review, West Trestle Review, Lumiere Review, Literary Shanghai, Mookychick* and others. She tweets at j_leaseofhope.

Balls of Mess

Muyera Sokoo

There once was fire in our bellies,
A spirit to fight injustice.
There once was a swag in our feet,
A need to accomplish.
There once was a song in our hearts,
A love so encompassing.

All that is gone,
The fire now only ashes,
We can only but drag our feet,
And live out days filled with wailing hearts.
We have no voice; we sold it on the dusty streets of Harare.

We cannot protest this violation,
For we are both oppressor and oppressed.
So we watch and we bleed.
What hope is there for us?
Torn in two: one part right,
One part who we are.

How can we fight when there is no fire in our belly?
How can we sing when we have forgotten the lyrics of our heart?
What is the point of dreaming when the sun never rises?
When the world is a dark and gloomy night.

What is the point of dreaming when we never awake?
When life itself has been drained from our bodies?
What is the point of dreaming now?

Why would we dream?
For dreaming reminds us of our barrenness.
Why would we dream?
For dreaming brings us face to face with helplessness.
What is the point of dreaming now?
When the sun never shines,
And our dreams are empty.

How can we dream when the fire in our bellies has been drenched?
Our helplessness turns our dreams into nightmares,
Haunting ghosts in a dark desolate place,
Filled with the stench of a fire which once burned so bright?

We can no longer dream but wait,
For what is life but one long wait,
A constant shift between hope and despair.
Confused and hurting.
And longing.

We tire.

Parts of us have forgotten that which we yearn for,
Scared in part to acknowledge it,
Scared to describe it,
Scared to put a name on it,

For doing so is coming face to face with our lack,
It is seeing our nakedness in full color.

So we wait for it to happen,
Our longing is a part of us,
An extension that goes on and on with no end,
Like a web,
Kneading our heart into doughs of anxiety.
Becoming,
Yet never reaching a conclusion.
Disjointed,
Broken pieces never coming together.
An incomplete puzzle.
A yearning for that which we cannot face
For facing it is to open a place long shut,
A place we refuse to honour.

Yet the longing remains still.
It pains. It hurts. It scares,
An uneasy date with demons we refuse to see,
Hearts at war,
Like a storm, destructive.
Like a force, indescribable.

We are scared, scarred,
Holding desperately to a little hope,
Taking pride in our suffering,
Resilience we assert nervously.
Wearing our scars like badges of honour,

We make believe,
That the scars we wear are a testimony of trials,
They tell a story which no words can ever say properly.

We tell ourselves that these scars on our hearts,
Are memories of love we felt deeply and of trust misplaced,
They are like rich, ancient text telling tales of sorrow and pain.
They adorn our hearts as expensive ornaments,
Worth their price in blood and sweat.

The scars on our minds were fashioned from broken dreams and missed opportunities.
We got them when we were foolish warriors shooting for the stars.
They are our crowns embedded with sparkling courage and hope.
We will tell of the scars on our feet, they are struggles of those who came before us,
They tell how they fought for the spaces which we now occupy.
They are the treasure to be passed to those who will come after us.

The scars on our hands are from the many responsibilities viciously dumped on us,
They tell sad stories of a system which takes and takes yet give so little in return.
They are palms begging for leniency, and a little balm maybe?

The scars in our eyes are from seeing too much injustice.

Too much violence, too much discrimination.
These scars are our spectacles helping us see the world more clearly.
These scars scattered on our bodies are reminders that we survived the horrors, and we live to fight again.

Yet we know,
That we are all balls of mess,
Chaos.
Explosions in waiting.

About the Author:
Muyera Sokoo is a Zimbabwean poet and storyteller. She is based in Marondera, Zimbabwe. She is passionate about all things women. She believes in making women's voices heard and in the power of words to bring on healing and change. Her work also appears in *Sesu* and *The Weight She Carries* magazines.

The One Good Eye of the Room

Susan Rich

When you left, I felt exhausted
and so was the room we fought in.
The front door stammered behind you
and in came silence—a recreational drug,
a fast forming habit that untied its shoelaces,
sank into the loveseat and prepared to stay
up with me all night.

Survival depends on the breath and its silences—
the in-between spaces and their rumors.
When I claimed silence during our fights, you'd
answer me with anger as if quietness
was a personal affront instead of a house of ruin
where gravity bore down on us—
a horned instrument—all the notes gone.

What if I told you silence worked as a sweetener—
Boston eclairs or an island vacation where
we could rely on a good time. When you left,
silence looked me in my one good eye, believed in me.
Let's play a game, silence said. *Let's see who
speaks first.* Then we washed and salted
the pasta, the delicately spiced sauce.

About the author:

Susan Rich is an award-winning poet and essayist based in Seattle, Washington. She is the author of five poetry collections: Gallery of Postcards and Maps: New and Selected Poems (Salmon Poetry) as well as Cloud Pharmacy, The Alchemist's Kitchen, Cures Include Travel and The Cartographer's Tongue /Poems of the World (White Pine Press). Her poems have received awards from Artists Trust, PEN USA, and the Times Literary Supplement (London). Individual work appears in New England Review, Oprah Quarterly Magazine and Poetry Ireland Review among other places. Rich's sixth collection of poems, Blue Atlas, is forthcoming from Red Hen Press. She is the co-founder and executive director of Poets on the Coast: A Writing Retreat for Women.

Six Poems

Sarah Rebecca Kersley

Tropical ache

Tropical ache
is worse

than April in the north.

It's worse
than the ache when you plunge your head
into a Scottish loch.

Worse
than when the tips of your fingers push out through the wool
of threadbare gloves, which even before being threadbare,
never fit.

Worse
than getting home
and there's no firewood, no matches
and no tea.

With tropical ache
everything glows.

With tropical ache
the sun shines on both sides of the street.

And with tropical ache
everyone
hides when it rains.

You edited me

I did the same to you.
I can't remember how things were before.
You selected, pasted, took away
what was in brackets; opened spaces
where there were none. Saved as,
configured margins, saved it all,
closed it, went back, changed some more.
Subject pronouns all got lost. You commented on the near
absence of pathetic fallacy,
you highlighted, underlined, gave the thing a body,
turned mud to crystal. Nothing
carnal. It was someone, it was you,
it was me. I can't remember how things were before.
Now, filed away, this version stays
right here, with nothing to be found
in the attachment.

Opening times

Near the registry
there was a viewing point,
a sign

to be read
just after things got dark.

It said in dialogues
of comic romances

there's always missing spaces
in the clouds.

Poem in which a foreign national carries out activities of a political nature

Doing nothing is an activity of a political nature.
Looking at antennas in a storm
is an activity of a political nature. Listening to Bowie
in deep water is an activity of a political nature. Repeating
what you read at school in dis-
united kingdoms is an activity of a political nature.
Stepping off the curb is an activity of a political nature.
Holding your hands over your ears is an activity of a political
nature.
Declaring yourself to be anti-marriage followed by
enthusiastic participation at your own wedding

is an activity of a political nature. Hoping
people from down the road will send you invitations is an
activity
of a political nature. Hoping people from outside the small
city borders
will send you invitations is an activity of a political nature.
Hoping people will send you invitations so that you can say no
is an activity of a political nature. Occupation is an activity
of a political nature. Interrupting into an unplugged
microphone
is an activity of a political nature. Standing up at the start
is an activity of a political nature. Sitting down at the end
is an activity of a political nature. Closing your eyes
whilst positioning your camera is an activity
of a political nature. Using the first person
is an activity of a political nature. Keeping to one side
is an activity of a political nature. Deciding what to bring
is an activity of a political nature.
Deciding what to leave.

Branch

The translator is
a machine says the myth
in bed too it says
legible solutions
are drafted
through the dreams
of sworn attested hearts.

Continental drift

Here, the irony
is different. But
the weight belt
still pulls you in
to the abyss.

For the *nth* time
I say yes,
it *is* the same sun
that heats up
what I suppose then
must be the same
Atlantic.
And no,
I'm not inclined
to beans,
but thanks again.

Here,
the velocity
of the mermaids
at the surface
is different. There,
the mermaids
are insured
for everything. For their
fishy tails,
which also seem from here
to be less green.

About the Author:

Sarah Rebecca Kersley is a poet, translator and editor born in the UK and based in Brazil for over a decade. She is the author of two books published in Brazil: *'Tipografia oceânica' ['Ocean typography']* (poetry, 2017) and *'Sábado' ['Saturday']* (memoir/biography/creative non-fiction, 2018). Her writing and translation has appeared in places such as *Manoa Journal, Modo de Usar & co., Washington Square Review, Denver Quarterly*, and elsewhere. She co-runs Livraria Boto-cor-de-rosa, an independent bookshop and small press focused on contemporary literature, in the city of Salvador, Bahia, where she is based.

* The poems "Tropical Ache", "You Edited Me", "Opening Times", "Branch", and "Continental Drift" are versions of poems originally written in Brazilian Portuguese and published in the book *Tipografia oceânica* (Brazil, Paralelo13S, 2017).

Three Poems

Chisom Okafor

In another life, I am twenty-two, gifted and curious

and dreaming of fleeing the world, while perched on the transom of
a stallion of the sea, breathing stale evening air off the
waterline, an entanglement of sodium chloride and ancient seawood.
The boy on the other side is waiting, arms outstretched, as though
to receive a prodigal advancing
to the interlocking welcome of an embrace.
Worn by the ways of the sea, I have mastered
the art of smearing my sternum with white and green watermarks,
and this is the year of my first diagnosis, and I'm pressing
a miniature paintbrush to my chest, tracing the shape of a heart,
feeble with cardiomegaly, and whispering
the words of the scriptures into it:
Tabitha cume. Tabitha cume. Feeble girl, rise up. Rise up.
And I'm thinking of what happens to the heart when its vessel — an
entire body — is immersed in water
and left to slouch against the rippling music of immersion.

I am thinking of the calculus of bodies, the time between
Point X and Point Y —
time between immersion and the bottom of the sea —
the exquisite mathematics of drowning.

Woodsmoke

Each one of us is born sensible
a heart incensed then falling.
— TJ Dema.

Falling, by which I mean a synchronized
art of dying. By which I also mean
something
burning in my chest
as I skid in full velocity off the middle
of a rail track.
I want to say to a century
of twinkling species overhead: I too
have been touched by wildfire
in a previous
life
I too, have memorized
the simple art
of free-
falling.

Echo-cardio-gram

Cut your heart open, you say. And I open:
Who says the dead are farther away from us

than the distance between my failing heart and yours, which I count
as nothing, even now, as we soak up the noonday sun. Who says there are no

murmurs grinding away beneath me, when a miracle of hands pressed on my chest
leave me gasping for a last violence of air in sunlight. Take air as vehicle, or fuel

for naked light, as it travels in a freefall through a vacuum, half expecting to be caught.
Do you know what it means to fall, and not be caught till a shattering arrives to offer some relief?

Like an agony of lights from a thousand distant stars: cellphone-holding species,
whose illuminations, shed a million years back, but without the malevolence

of being caught midway, are just reaching us tonight.

But there are no absolutes, you say, and time, like truth, is relative,
which is also to say nothing of the benevolent earth that stops all freefalls.

Earth, to which all travelers must return, when the day is spent

and the dance is over, and I see all the men I ever loved rise before me,
like the steam from chamomile tea. And I see all the cities I ever fled from, return to reclaim

from the barren fields, souls which were theirs before time began. These days,
I philosophize more on death than the last man caught in the volcanic rage of Pompeii,

with his daughter, a mass of solidified ash, freshly preserved in his arm, as though
he was saying to the fire: Let her body only be taken by the things she never saw.

For the things you possess the least knowledge of don't really kill you.
Hear me out: On my first trip to the cardiologist's,

a man had stared at me in the waiting room,
as though he was a teacher who had scribbled questions on a rough cardboard surface:

What caused your heart dysfunction, son?
Was it an excess of nicotine or the freedom of alcohol or lack of both?

But I know nothing of these things. Just as an owl dies
knowing nothing of the etiology
of its nocturnal fondness, why only in empty darkness is
where it finds home.

But we misinterpret emptiness as guilt,
which is why the owl is so strange to us. See how easy it is to
confuse

the act of falling with the act of failing. See?

See how we fall into the things that fail us,
like the reverberations of this cardiac machine, faithful in its
representation

of how much closer I am to the end of my heart dysfunction
than I think.

About the Author:
Chisom Okafor is a Nigerian poet and clinical nutritionist. His debut full-length manuscript, *Birthing*, was a finalist for the Sillerman First Book Prize for African Poets.

Nonfiction

Art by Seth Depiesse

Sense Of Touch

Nora Nneka

I've always had a strange relationship with the sense of touch.

My earliest memories are of gripping my mom in an attempt to shield her from my dad's hands. I can still feel the tension in her muscles and our shared sense of fear. It was a palpable static. I was three.

Next, the stinging bite of a belt on my skin; punishment for talking to boys at preschool. I was five.

My dad's touch was the most painful of them all. Like a snake in grass, he would slither into my bed at night, under the guise of tucking me in. While I longed for the embrace of my parents, I recoiled from his caresses, repulsed as he pressed his musky adult body against my small frame. I can still feel his scratchy body hair. I was nine.

As I grew into a woman, carrying the physical and emotional scars of my childhood, I peeked wearily into the realm of sensuality. Looking back I see that, because of my trauma, I normalized aggressive sensual interactions. I loved hard; not only with my sexual partners (enjoying chasing and conquering my prospects), but also with my friends, who I embraced each time as if it were for the last time. On the other hand, I rejected the touch of strangers. I remember being disgusted by the slightest brush of a classmate sitting near me in a lecture hall. It was as if cotton fibers were tiny pins on my skin.

I will never forget the morning I woke up and said "I want to have a baby," almost defiantly, to my husband as he wiped sleep from his eyes. Though a part of me secretly always wanted to be a mother, my feelings of inadequacy wore a public mask of indifference. The truth is, I didn't want to hurt my child the way I'd been hurt by my parents, and my medical mind feared my trauma and adverse coping skills would be woven into the DNA of my future beloved. That morning, to bear a child as soon as possible, bellowed from deep within my soul and echoed loudly in the walls of my brain. It was an undeniable and all-consuming force. As the months passed and my womb lay vacant, my soul withered in agony.

I rejoiced at the news of my pregnancy in March of 2017. As my child grew in my womb, my conceptualization of what "touch" meant changed. No one can articulate how fascinating it is to feel a fetus moving inside of you. While my traumatized brain recoiled at the idea of my body being invaded by another being, my heart rejoiced at the miracle of space and science happening within me. I bonded with my fetus-baby-person. By the thirty-sixth week though, I couldn't wait to deliver him. I was physically uncomfortable and emotionally more anxious by the day. On December 1 at 10:48 pm, Theory made his grand entry. I was relieved to have my little "intruder" out but I longed to touch and feel my baby. Things didn't go as planned after the delivery. As quickly as he was laid on my chest, ashen and quiet, he was rushed away to be intubated and taken to the Neonatal Intensive Care Unit. My heart sank as I feared the worst would happen and I would lose my baby boy. In the end, he was fine. No one could and ever did figure out why he was delayed in taking his first breath...but I wasn't the same after that. The trauma of his birth sent my mind into a primitive mode. I became a shell of myself; a wounded new mother clinging to her baby.

Postpartum care in my culture is called "omugwo". The matriarchs of the family and/or close female friends come to care for the tired mother and new baby. This care includes feeding the mother spicy pepper soup, tidying the home, tending to the baby while the new mother gets some much-needed rest, and massaging mother and baby to help them both recover from the delivery itself. My mom and sister were able to come the morning after Theory was born and I was grateful to have the women most important to me there for this pivotal moment in my life.

My relationship with my mom has been wrought with painful memories and words that can't be unspoken. After a year's silence, for my own mental health, I decided to resume communication with her when I found out I was pregnant. I wanted her to be in Theory's life because I didn't want him to feel disconnected from *any* of his roots. I've always longed to know more about my paternal family but have been distanced from them because of my dad's actions and his family's primarily monetarily-motivated interests. My knowledge of my maternal family is sparse beyond knowing the names of her siblings and my first cousins. While other people discussed family trees and hyperbolic stories of those past, I would sit and smile with a crushing sense of emptiness in my heart because I didn't have those connections. I didn't want that for my son.

Prior to arriving, my mom made her own salve of coconut oil, shea butter, and other (secret) ingredients. Immediately after we got home from the hospital, after the excited words and hugs, my mom took the baby and prepared him for his first bath and massage. I was nervous for these moments whenever I contemplated it during my pregnancy, but because of what we'd been through during our hospitalization, I was in shock. It was therapeutic watching my mom carefully and lovingly handle her grandson. I watched as she bathed Theory while my sister and brother cooed over his every gesture. The sense of family and belonging was euphoric. I was entranced by the sight of her gently but firmly pressing the oils onto his skin from his limbs to his core. My turn came a couple of days later after delays and excuses on my part. That massage was the longest time my mom had ever touched me in a positive way, and I wasn't emotionally prepared for it. It was awkward, to say the least. I sat in a lounge chair and breastfed the baby while she strategically lotioned and massaged me as she had done days prior to the baby. I avoided eye contact and made small talk about my swollen feet, healing uterus, and engorged breasts. While my muscles relaxed, my mind tensed more and more. If I'm honest with myself, I couldn't wait for it to be over. That's what I remember most about that massage: that I couldn't wait for it to be over… and that fact pains me to think about.

It got better from there. With every touch, caress, and breastfeeding session with Theory, we established our relationship and wove a tight bond. His interactions with me are pure. There isn't an ulterior motive; he simply loves and wants to be physically close to his mommy. I still occasionally flinch with unexpected pokes and grabs from him, but they are all welcomed.

As I sip from the honeyed tea of motherhood, my feelings toward my own mother have changed. "How could she say those things to a person who is *a piece of her*?" I wondered, while watching my darling laugh and play. "How could she sleep at night knowing the welts on my skin came from *her* hand?" Over time, the trepidatious yearning I had for a closer relationship with my mom has turned into a deeply seeded hatred for her; a woman who spitefully raised her first-born daughter only to chide pridefully later of her daughter's hard-earned material success.

I kept the container my mom brought with her during her visit, using it for my own concoction of oils and butters for Theory. It's sentimental in that it represents my family expanding, bonding, and a shared excitement for new beginnings. I keep it now, though, as a reminder to myself of the power of touch to heal and destroy. I open the lid every time with intention and a silent prayer that my son will never experience the physical pains I have… and that he will always cherish his mother's touch.

About the author:

Dr. Nora Ekeanya is a board-certified adult psychiatrist, storyteller, poet, wife, and mother. Born to Nigerian immigrant parents in Tallahassee, FL, she was raised in the United States and Nigeria, though calling Jacksonville, FL, her hometown. She is a practicing physician in Kansas, where she currently resides, and writes under the alias Nora Nneka.

Feeling Your Way Home

Uche Osondu

It was a Wednesday in December of 2018, that much I remember. The exact date slips through my mind's grasp just when I think I have it. I let the date go. After all, it was a period in my life where I was not too bothered about dates. I had just finished school, after seven years, and was preparing to leave Ibadan, this city that I had grown to call mine, to call home. It did not matter that I could not, and cannot, speak the language. All that mattered was it was the place I allowed myself to grow, make friends, and be myself just a little bit more; it was the city that I found love in. As the airplane rose into the sky and the landscape of this city—*running splash of rust // and gold-flung and scattered // among seven hills // like broken china in the sun* (J.P Clark)—lay before me, my heart could not keep still. I was finally heading home, but why did it feel like I was leaving home?

The plane touched down and started taxiing to a stop; the *fasten seat belts* light had not gone off but the cabin was filling with sounds of buckles being unfastened. While the rest of the passengers rushed to get their bags from the overhead compartments, I sat still. My legs were unable to move, crushed by the weight I was feeling in my chest. Memories of the corkscrew I received from a close friend with the note: "*and if our paths never cross again…";* memories of the shirt I had left behind with the most amazing woman I could ever love; memories of goodbyes to close friends filled with awkward long hugs and dry eyes, all flashed through my mind with searing clarity. I put on my phone, plugged in my earpiece, and listened to silence. What next? I had left shortly after my graduation from secondary school, eager to start life afresh. It was taking all of me to believe that I would find another place where I belonged other than the city I had just left behind.

I was a child. I was heading back to the house with my uniforms caked with dirt, my legs throbbing with the memory of bottles kicked on football pitches. I would sigh in relief as I saw the red gate that led into my compound, rush through the other three burglary gates, drop my bags in the kitchen, and scream into the empty sitting room: I am home. Home was a place of respite; structured learning would stop and I could now continue taking in the world at my own pace. It did not matter that in an hour my lesson teacher would arrive bringing structure and order to my well-curated chaos. For that hour, home was a place, an ideal of freedom. Then the cracks would start to appear—a bath, a plate of eba I did not want, all culminating in the visit of the lesson teacher, and then bedtime by 7 pm. For that hour, as Maya Angelou wrote, *home was that youthful region where a child is the only real living inhabitant*.

Home was silence. If the world around me was alight, then I needed a place where I could breathe without the smoke. I would hide away when family came over. I was not interested in their gifts, or their stories. And sometimes, when my mother scolded me for doing something I believed was me feeding my curiosity—in retrospect, most times to my detriment—I would retreat, or if I was enraged enough, would try to run away. I ran away more times than I would like to remember. My favorite clothes packed in a hurry, the current book I was reading at the time (thank you, Enid Blyton), and a voice (mother or grandmother) shouting at me to get back into the house while I tried to climb the second gate that led into the compound. I never once ventured past the huge red gate onto the street. Home was also an escape, but I like to believe I was smarter then. I would never have survived.

As time passed, I withdrew into myself and stopped trying to escape. It also helped that I had gotten admission into a boarding school that, while being far away from my house, was still in Abuja, the city I had always known as home. I don't recall feeling homesick, not once. The idea seemed odd to me. Home was escape and I was finally free—within reason, of course. As school progressed, I needed home to be more than an escape, to be more than silence. I found myself trying so hard to find a group of people I could call my *squad*; I would take whatever form I could to fit in with a group. I never thought the real me was enough. Home was still escape, but now I was escaping from myself into other people and their versions of me. I would not think anything of it until later, pining over lost friendships and hurting over friends who left. What if they left me because they could tell that I was not being authentic enough to myself? Or they had gotten tired of this version of me I had curated for their pleasure; or how eager to please I seemed? Warsan Shire would write years later: *you can't make homes out of human beings, someone should have already told you that.*

I would continue, still do sometimes, to navigate spaces like that as I searched for a place in the world. The search for home, a place to belong, was consuming me; I handled it the way I handled, and still handle, most of my problems—by denying it. In secondary school, I weaved in and out of organizations and sports. I tried rugby and cricket. Latin and Spanish. Reading and singing in the choir. I enjoyed the activities immensely, and remain grateful for them. But looking back, I find that how long I stayed interested or committed to those things was closely related to how I felt around the people with whom I shared those activities. It was always, still is, about the community for me. Then, it did not matter if I could be myself fully, just being able to feel I belonged while escaping myself was often enough. It was home.

When I first moved to Ibadan, I was distraught. Not because I was homesick, but because the new environment was too much to take in—into the compound, out on the street. I had never heard that many of my peers speak their native languages before, or feel confident about them. I was scared that I would be exposed here; how could I blend in, escape into people's versions of me if I could not communicate with them in the language they preferred? Growing up in Abuja meant that all my interactions with the world had only been done in English, the Enid Blyton English. I was proud that the pronunciations of 'ask' and 'gigantic' rolled off my tongue with ease, but the mere thought of which Igbo words to use, how to shape my mouth, left my tongue heavy and numb. I could understand some words, simple phrases, but these words were typically commands to do chores, food-related or animal insults I had picked up from the only Igbo textbook I had seen then. This meant, of course, that if one was not scolding me, offering me food or exchanging simple pleasantries, then I did not understand what they said. It also meant that I would most likely reply in English, which often lead to awkward silences and nervous laughter. My first acquaintances would be two young men who had joked about me behind my back, in Igbo, calling me an *ofe mmanu*—a term they told me meant I was

Yoruba. I would discard what they said, only pointing out that I understood a little of what they said, and I was in fact not Yoruba. The first few years would continue like this: me always on the periphery, flitting through Igbo student meetings and church fellowships, dodging classes or just going there to sleep. I was learning that maybe I didn't deserve a home if I wasn't going to be honest with who I was. I spent more time asleep than awake that year, I guess.

It would take time, but I would learn to at least be honest with who I was. I ignored the collective and chased my curiosities for once, content to find myself alone in any activity. And that would open the city up to me in a way that I could not have imagined. I found friends who saw me and thought I, the way I was, was enough. Even when my flaws reared, they addressed them and stayed. It didn't matter that some left, the ones that stayed meant the world to me. I found a community of people who showed me that it was okay to express myself through my words, in the stories I told, and for three years, my book club meetings—on the first and third Tuesdays of every month—were all I lived for. I found singing again, and I enjoyed it as I did before. It felt intimately similar to singing back in secondary school but wonderfully unique in its own way. I found jokes in last-minute rehearsals and a family in my part. My home had sprung forth from a city that I thought had nothing to offer me. And yes, there were many bad days and periods where I felt that to breathe my last would make it easier for everyone involved. But that's the thing about home: it can be an escape, support, or silence.

It's been over a year since I returned to Abuja, where I was that child fixated on the idea of home as a place of respite, of freedom, and still, my heart is often crushed by the weight of this feeling that I don't belong here anymore. School is over. I had gotten comfortable; I had just found love and now, I had been thrust into the real world. *The universe was conspiring against us*—we thought. I left the woman that I loved, my friends, and this home I had stumbled upon; I have never felt so alone. It doesn't help that the environment has changed vastly from what I remember, from what was. We no longer reside in a house with that many gates to pass through and scream *I am home*. Buildings have sprouted up where before there was nothing but bare ground. I am often still visited by the urge to run away when things get rough, but I am an adult now (unfortunately), and the difficulties of running away drag me back. So I am withdrawn, just like I was those years ago, begging myself to figure it all out so that I can make this place home. It seems like life comes in cycles, and I am in the process of redefining what home should be to me again.

Kurt Vonnegut—a long time before I was born—addressing a graduating class, said: *No matter what age any of us is now, we are going to be … lonely during what remains of our lives.* I have spent the past year battling with this loneliness and the way it washes over me unsuspecting. It does not help that Mr. Vonnegut points out that this is a battle that I will fight for the rest of my life. I am tired for now and the foreseeable future. The loneliness feeds me the nostalgia of the home I created for myself in a time that only my memories have access to. Memories of laughter shared with friends on the basketball court during a blackout or a Nollywood cinema viewing experience under the influence of good wine and good company. The memories taunt me, and fill me with dread: I might never find another place as good as what I have now lost. On other days, they flood my heart with hope: better days are coming.

There are days when I am certain that there is no place for me, no home at all. I have imagined the whole thing, my mind playing grade-one tricks on me, and I am better off not existing at all. In those moments, home becomes a journey, and alcohol its vehicle. I am chasing the ideal home, a place that resembles the place nestled in my memories and also one born of idealistic thinking. As the warmth of the alcohol spreads through my chest, my heart and mind travel to that place where I am content and it seems like nothing else matters. And once my heart gets there, and I am all giggles and smiles, home becomes the destination; *home is where the heart is*. I am learning now though, that maybe this is not the best way to find home. How many bottles will I go through searching for this fleeting definition of home? How many times must my liver cry out for mercy before I realize that this journey is not a road to be traveled so often? I am learning to hold on to the ideal in my heart without the warmth of the bottle, to bear the pain that comes with the nostalgia. I might not win every time, but I am trying. I am not drinking tonight.

The lights are off. I am beneath my navy blue blanket. My phone rings. It is one of my closest friends, this one I have named after Arnold Schwarzenegger—it is a joke that has been running since we first met about eight years ago, during my time in that city with the *running splash of rust*. We are laughing over something that does not make sense, talking about little things, big things, and all the things in-between. The call lifted me out from beneath my blankets and the loneliness that was threatening to crush me then. My friend has no idea. We are still laughing. At that moment, I am grateful for this piece of home that makes itself available to me when I am least expecting it. The call ends, and I am made to promise to go out more, to stop being afraid and join something, do something. It seems like my friend is echoing Mr. Vonnegut during his address: *So I recommend that everybody here joins all sorts of organizations, no matter how ridiculous, simply to get more people in his or her life. It does not matter much if all the other members are morons. Quantities of relatives of any sort are what we need.* Home is a promise made to a friend to do better, to be better.

I reckon that I might have to endure this for the rest of my life—the struggle to define home for me, watching as each definition evolves beyond itself, taking a life of its own in order to fit whatever phase of life that I find myself in. I reckon that maybe it will culminate in a great discovery, or maybe it will not. I reckon that maybe home is as dynamic as the mind that needs it, and that trying to define it is an endeavor that serves little to no purpose. Feeling your way to home is the surest way to prove its existence. In the end, I can only hope that I make it through this current phase alive, and with a home that I can call my own. Maya Angelou ends her essay "Home:" *We may act sophisticated and worldly but I believe we feel safest when we go inside ourselves and find home, a place where we belong and maybe the only place we really do.*

About the Author:

Uche Osondu is a Nigerian, tragically. He swears by two things: food and anime. He is currently working on writing and living, in equal measures. He writes from Abuja.

Serengeti Saga

Sylvia K Ilahuka

This is the true story of how I almost died a month before starting university. Okay, we didn't almost die…but we could've.

The month was July, the year was 2009, and the occasion was a cross-country road trip—the first vacation my family was taking since my mother passed. She had been with cancer for almost a decade, and in the latter half of her illness there had been no time for teenaged me to partake in sleepovers, let alone for my father to truly breathe. And so here we were, two years after her funeral, in our family's double-cabin 1995 Toyota Hilux, driving from Dar-es-Salaam to our ancestral village in the north-western corner of Tanzania.

It was a leisurely trip, with an initial overnight stopover in Arusha to visit a maternal uncle. The next stop was to be a night in the Serengeti, then a night in Mwanza town on the shores of Lake Victoria. We'd cross the lake by overnight ferry, then continue on to our final destination in Kagera region. The trip was a reprise of a 1997 tri-country road trip which had taken a longer route via Kenya and Uganda, partly for the reason that Tanzania's interior cross-country roads were still untarmacked and the rural stretches tended to be prowled by armed robbers at night. Even commercial buses took the Kenya-Uganda route, as I knew from ending up on one such trip at the age of twelve. One of my brothers was being sent to the village to visit our grandmother and ostensibly reflect on his teenage misdeeds, and I made the mistake of laughing at him at the dinner table. Next thing I knew, I was seated next to him on the bus. It's funny how with harrowing trips you remember the going but not really the return. All I recall was moments like the miraa-chewing Somali in the seat behind us eyeing me dubiously when the bus stopped in Nairobi at midnight and my brother got off to buy us food. When traveling in pairs, one person should remain on the bus to keep an eye on the bags and also alert the driver should they attempt to drive off before all the passengers have returned. That is actually what happened at one of the borders, I think it was Kenya-Uganda, when my brother disembarked to go get our passports stamped. I hadn't wanted to remain on the bus alone, but he insisted—and just as well he did, because the bus had started rolling by the time he jumped on. There are instances in which you realize how much you love a person, and that was one such.

But I digress.

In 2009 the interior main roads of Tanzania were finally tarmacked, and so this was a chance to see regions of the country that we might otherwise not have had reason to visit. And so we set off from Dar es Salaam very early in the morning, armed with a paper map—the very same one we'd used twelve years prior—and this time a technological upgrade in the form of my dad's Samsung cellphone with a stubby antenna and a screen that lit up blue. What could possibly go wrong?

A mere three days later I found myself standing shin-deep in Serengeti mud, alongside my brother, pushing the Hilux while our dad revved the engine in a frantic bid to unstick the vehicle. There was a large herd of wildebeest less than a kilometre from where we were, intermittently eyeing us as they grazed, one sudden move away from a stampede. And this was only the next day after we'd already almost died the first time.

Oh yes, that. That's what I'd come to tell you about.

There we were, driving around a national park with a paper map, no ranger, and no cellphone signal, as one does when one is local—after all, armed guides are for foreign tourists, aren't they? Our self-guided tour was going well, we'd seen a good number of animals, and it was Great Migration season so there were plenty more to look forward to.

Just before sunset, we stopped at the gate to inquire how to get to our planned lodging. The gatekeeper was friendly enough, probably counting down the minutes to the end of his shift as the park was about to be closed for the day.

"Ah, Serengeti Lodge?" He had been leaning with his ear cocked towards the driver's window, and now straightened his back and raised his head towards the distance ahead. "You driiiveee until you come to a fork in the road. On the right you will see a small bridge over a hippo pond; cross that bridge, and the hotel will be straight ahead."

Straightforward.

Or so it seemed.

We droooveee and then it got dark and began to rain, bestowing a very Jurassic Park feel upon the environs. There wasn't a soul in the vicinity, not even a Maasai herdsman to at least wave at in biped kinship. In that kind of darkness and stillness, shapes come to life. Trees resemble giraffes. Any rock resembles a large cat.

As sure as the gatekeeper's directions, we eventually came upon said fork in the road. And there was indeed a pond of hippos on the right. The only problem was that the bridge he had said would be there did not seem to exist. Dad edged the car closer to get a better look in the beam of the headlights; nope, no bridge. A sigh of bafflement. Did the gatekeeper perhaps mean the left fork? You know some people can get their left and right confused, the same way others get their "l" and "r" mixed up. Let's try and see. We put the car in reverse and so began a macabre game of Which Door Should I Pick, only this time the prize was survival.

Back at the fork, we took the left this time. No sooner had we driven down it than I heard a gasp from my dad, the car swerved, and a nervous laugh emerged from my brother in the front passenger seat.

"What happened?" I asked, craning my neck to look out of the rear window.

"Don't look back," Dad replied, "we nearly hit a large animal."

The "large animal" was a hippo, whose cute rotund depiction in cartoons belies a deadly temper when provoked or threatened—and we had shaved by it with barely an inch to spare.

A male lion that had been lounging in the middle of the road leaped up, startled by the car, and glared at us from within his mane. A small elephant grazed by the side of the road. While we seemed to be hitting all the sights that would be the envy of any game drive, this was not ideal. Even less ideal was the swamp in front of us: the left fork had in fact been a dead end.

Time to reverse again.

Did I mention that the fuel gauge was broken, so we actually had no idea how much fuel was left in the car? And with all that driving around in circles, we could very well have been close to running out. What had started as one wrong turn had evolved into a safari drive crossed with Russian Roulette.

Back at the fork, Dad proposed: how about we switch off the car, leave the parking lights on, and sleep here until morning?

Say what now?

My first thought was how I needed to relieve myself, and the logistics of that would probably be more in favor of the gents than I. Not to mention the other very real issue of the car potentially getting attacked by wild animals overnight but, you know, that concern takes second place in the face of a full bladder. Priorities.

My brother and I vetoed the idea and suggested we follow the sign that we had seen earlier, one that read "KILIMANJARO LODGE: 20 KM" and pointed towards a third road opposite the fork.

Dad agreed, put the car in gear, and we held our collective breaths as we followed this winding road through grass that engulfed the entire car. Nothing was stirring in the nighttime stillness, nothing at all; not a sound aside from the roar of the Hilux engine as we chased an uncertain destination. At some point we noticed lights twinkling on the brow of a hill in the distance—yet every time we rounded a bend the lights would disappear. Was it a mirage? Would we even make it on this gamble of a gas tank?

Eventually, after what felt like an eternity, we came upon a campsite—the type that probably charges a pretty penny for the "authentic" experience of sleeping amidst African wildlife. At the sound of our arrival, some of the occupants came out in curiosity; I say, I have never been so relieved to see another Homo sapiens. The guides welcomed us warmly, gave us dinner, and a tent to ourselves. The tents were equipped with raised beds, Western-style toilets, and even a hot shower. This was not roughing it, this was glamping. With stern warnings not to venture outside during the night, we went to sleep with the sounds of hyenas breathing noisily, separated from us by only a thin canvas.

We awoke the following morning to the glorious roar of lions at sunrise, and it was then that I understood why people left their home countries, boarded twenty-four-hour long flights and endured bumpy bus rides to get to this experience. Whenever possible and as money allows, we should all tour in our homelands. Truly. Kwetu pazuri.

Our hosts offered us breakfast and we in return left them with a monetary token of gratitude for all their hospitality. The tour guide taking a group of tourists into the park invited us to follow in our car so he could point out where we should've turned the night before to get to the hotel, and then direct us to where there was a petrol station within the national park.

Standing by the Hilux while waiting for the tourists to get ready, we laughed for the first time—Dad with his hands on his waist and head hanging in utter relief. He laughed so hard he was almost doubled over, then stood up and let out a deep breath with one hand over his mouth in disbelief. On the drive out of the camp, he told us how he'd really felt during the ordeal. He said the whole time he was wondering what sort of parent he was, to have taken two of his children into a national park full of wild animals with no ranger. On my part, whatever fear I had felt was offset by his presence; I was nineteen years old, but the ordeal had triggered in me the childish perception of parents as invincible superheroes. That innocent no matter how complicated it is, my parent will sort it out trust—or perhaps it was more of a jaded teenage you got us into this mess and you're the parent here so it's on you to get us out of it placing of responsibility? I have since learnt that adults are also just figuring it out as they go. I have my own child now and were we to find ourselves in such a situation, best believe I would still be looking around for a grownup.

Trailing the tourists, we retraced the route we'd taken the night before. We got to the fork, eager to see where we went wrong; lo and behold, though we could've sworn it hadn't been there the night before, there was the bridge. There could be a number of explanations—such as that this bridge was so low as to be nearly flush with the water, so perhaps we just hadn't seen it in the darkness, or that the water levels had been slightly higher the night before and obscured it entirely. Personally, I maintain that the Serengeti clearly holds many secrets which it perhaps just hadn't wanted to share at that particular time. We were nevertheless privileged to have seen the park in its most private hours.

We found the petrol station, refueled, and the day began promisingly—the sun was shining, the sky was blue, and a giraffe even stopped to pose for our camera right in the middle of the road. The drive was uneventful until it wasn't, rudely interrupted by a patch of mud thick enough to ensnare even our four-wheel drive. There we were, cruising along with renewed hope for a smooth journey, admiring a large herd of wildebeest to our right, only to hear the dreaded sound of spinning wheels. Yes, those were the wildebeest I mentioned earlier. The slightest startle and we risked finding ourselves in a modern-day enactment of that scene from *The Lion King*. The goal had now become to unstick the car with as minimal fuss as possible but also be ready to run to…somewhere. Anywhere. Every (wo)man for themself. Several expert-level manual gear maneuvers by Dad were insufficient. There were only the three of us, of whom the only one licensed to drive was also the only with the most muscle strength of our lot. The calculus boiled down to my brother and I getting out to push while Dad steered. Many grunts later it was looking like a lost cause, until we were saved by a lorry coming from the opposite direction—carrying, as fate would have it, young men who had the necessary rope and vigor to free us. As we drove off, I looked down at my ruined jeans and resigned myself to whatever the rest of the trip would bring. I wondered what would next befall us; whether we'd make it to the village in one piece and whether I'd even get to see America with my adult eyes—because, remember, we still had to drive back…

We made it to the village in one piece. And made it back to Dar as well, taking a less scenic route this time in the name of efficiency. As I recall the near-misses today, I suspect my memory of the fear is shielded or perhaps tempered by the aforementioned padding of youth in the presence of a parent. Or perhaps I was just so exhausted by the time we rolled back into our home driveway, and the aftershocks never quite got to me since I had to start packing for college almost immediately thereafter. They say traveling with companions reveals a lot about one another; it tests relationships. If a long layover in a cramped airport is test enough, imagine getting lost in the Serengeti. Our family was already riddled with tensions of various origins, many of which were exacerbated to traumatic degrees by the nature of long-distance road travel. So while the experience did bring us closer, the way rollercoaster rides and shared spicy food do, it also left scars. Knowing what I know now as an adult, about grieving and about parenting (and, heck, about how tiring driving can be), I occasionally revisit the unpleasant moments to see if perhaps I would have responded differently to the stressors. However, some things are best left in the rear view mirror—until you turn a corner and they show up again. A decade later I found myself experiencing nightmarish déjà-vu as my then-boyfriend and I skidded along the muddy main road of Uganda's Murchison Falls National Park, in a rickety Rav4, him driving and me silently panicking, having been let in after dark by a gatekeeper who made us swear not to mention his name if anything happened. But that is itself a tale for another day.

About the Author:

Sylvia K. Ilahuka is a Tanzanian writer based in Kampala. She has essays and poetry published in literary journals *Lolwe*, *Doek!*, and *Iskanchi*, and has written about music for Bandcamp Daily.

Personal History Of Cantaloupes

Theo (Dot) Armstrong

Cantaloupe sprouts smell like fully-formed cantaloupes when I water them. The air in the greenhouse is already heavy with moisture; the thermometer says 90 degrees by 9 a.m. Water hits the rounded leaves and I smell it, soft and mellow, the scent of ripe melon. An orange dreamsicle, twin rockets melting to white on my hand. Cubed cantaloupe at breakfast, served in shallow yellow bowls beside plates of toast or bowls of cereal. My mother prepared the melon before we got up in the morning, cutting the wet fruit into uneven pieces, squaring the circle. On special occasions and some Sundays before church, she left the melon in fat wedges with the thin, bumpy rind still on and the tan seeds scooped out. A seed or two stuck like barnacles on boat hulls. We braced our hands on the sticky prows of the little gondolas and dug in. Spoons dripped with sweet juice. I loved paring away the creamy meat from the mottled shell. Even the strange rind tasted delicate: soft orange faded to crunchy green in one scoop. Vivid empty cantaloupe coracles joined the seeds in the compost pail after we finished our excavations.

The catalogs came in the mail. Pages of glossy color photos showed prime specimens with names like race horses. Ambrosia, Bush Star, Emerald Gem. Hale's Best Jumbo. Healy's Pride. Hearts of Gold. Petit Gris De Rennes, Pride of Wisconsin, Minnesota Midget.

The name *Cantaloupe* refers to a papal estate in Rome. Cantaloupo, allegedly a place where wolves gathered to sing, was the site of the melon's arrival from Armenia, around 1739. These lupine fruits are, in fact, muskmelons masquerading: cantaloupe, Australian rockmelon, South African spanspek, and sweet melon are all variations on the *Cucumis melo* theme. Two major differences exist in appearance. European cantaloupes (var. *cantalupensis*), have gray, ribbed hides while North American cantaloupes, (var. *reticulatis*), bear the familiar doily-decked look, all tan and pebbly. Regardless of texture, *C. melo* varieties fall into the family *Cucurbitaceae*. They are in good company with cucumbers, squash, pumpkins, zucchini, calabashes, bitter melons, and watermelons.

Choosing a good melon is essential. Too ripe, and the flesh is squishy and half-rotten; too firm, and it's bland and dry. At the produce section of the local grocery store, Mom explained the technique. Hoist a likely candidate to check size and weight, then press your ear to its roundness and—knock. Yes, knock on it with your fist, as if it's a door. A ripe melon echoes roundly, with firmness and depth. When I was little, I liked to hold the melon in my skinny arms and pretend it was a baby, or a pregnant belly. Feeling the weight. Once, when my sister was caught in the swift updraft of a panic attack, she sat at the dining room table and put a cantaloupe on her lap. The heaviness grounded her, she said. Later, someone bought her a weighted blanket.

Advice from the Farmer's Almanac regarding cantaloupes.

"Dry weather produces the sweetest melon."

"Don't be discouraged when the first blooms do not produce fruit."

Something about adversity and perseverance. I will be in the greenhouse all day, all month, observing incremental alchemy so small and fervent I must use all of my senses. Water, heat, cloud. Chlorophyll, nitrogen. These sprouts hum with mute energy. I am their servant and progenitor. I protect them from heat and drought and neglect. I watch and wonder as they unfold. My charges, becoming more of themselves every moment, grow up. Sturdy stems stand in the humid air, producing soft orange smells I remember from my own childhood. Soon, the fragrant plants will produce tendrils and start climbing. Then, flowers; then, doors to be knocked on, weights to be carried, delicacies to taste.

Advice from the Witch's Almanac regarding cantaloupes and their curative properties.

"Place six seeds, dried in the noon sun, underneath your pillow to ward off bad dreams."

"Rub cantaloupe rind on afflicted skin under a full moon to rid yourself of warts and blemishes."

"When anxious, grasp the melon with both hands. Count thrice and lift. Caress the surface as if stroking the face of a lover, or your own face in the mirror. Feel the nubbly texture; sense the hollow middle, the heavy moisture inside. Sit down, preferably on a chair that your grandmother sat in. Place the melon atop your thighs and wait. Breathe deeply, expanding your whole belly. Sit thus until the world slows down."

When the fruit comes, it comes on fast. Melon season lasts many weeks: the warehouse overflows from mid-July until late August. The harvesters bring in bin after bin and I learn to recognize the varieties by their grooved hides—deeper furrows and a slight football shape means the sweeter, more flavorful kind. All my children. By the time we planted them, I had forgotten their names. I fantasize as I wash them and place them in boxes. This one looks like a Sweet Granite, or a Schoon's Hard Shell. A crossbreed rumor; a genetic anomaly, fragile and full-flavored.

On a summer's day in 1620, the Bishop of Rennes spotted a grey hue on his crop of cantaloupes. Curious, he knelt and peeked under the leaves. Three days later, the melons were ripe. He served the fruit at his birthday banquet and saved the seeds in an envelope labeled "Petit Gris De Rennes." In 1886, W. Atlee Burpee opened a package from William Voorhees. Inside were twenty seeds and a letter, which extolled the virtues of a melon variety with a rich green rind that Voorhees had grown the summer prior—he called it the Emerald Gem, claiming it was "altogether unapproached in delicious flavor and luscious beyond description." Legend has it that Neil Young christened the Hearts of Gold variety while on tour in Michigan. After a set at Northwestern University, he played on a farm near Benton Harbor owned by Crazy Horse's cousin's stepdaughter. The farmer could only pay him in melons.

Morning and afternoon, at break time, I slice open orange miracles. I carve the seeds off the flesh with the tip of my knife, making the little boats clean like my mother did once. I pass my coworkers the half-moons running with juice. We sit on our haunches in the weeds, dripping. We sweat and grin and devour, exhausted and sunblind. We toss the rinds behind us, dust to dust, compost on site. By September, I will no longer crave the taste. By November, the scent will be a memory.

CSA pack is on Tuesdays. With one hand, I shove the waxed cardboard along the conveyor belt; the other scoops brown paper bags of russet potatoes, heirloom tomatoes, and hot peppers from harvest totes. I need both hands for the cantaloupe. The sticker listing the contents of a stranger's box calls for one melon: I rummage for the largest and nestle it between the red leaf lettuce and the eggplant. As I fold the box closed— left, right, tuck, tuck— and sign my initials on the side, I think of my sister pulling her chair up to the table.

About the author:
Theo (Dot) Armstrong is a queer, nonbinary freelance writer and movement artist based in Brooklyn. I received a BA in English Literature and a BFA in Dance Performance from the University of Iowa. My work has appeared in *The Dance Enthusiast*, *The Daily Iowan*, and *Culturebot*. This past summer, I worked as a farmhand at Featherstone Farm in Rushford, MN.

Adjuncts In The Age Of Coronavirus

Frances Cannon

I am about to turn thirty years old, and I have finally found an answer to the age-old-question, "Why do you write?" Do I write for fun, or for fame and glory? No, no. Do I write because my literary family encouraged me to pursue this career? Well, sort of, but I'm sure that my engineer father would have preferred if I had chosen a more stable and lucrative career. I write to cope; I write in the face of natural disaster, racial disparity, social collapse, financial ruin, rampant homophobia, ignorance of politicians. I write when I don't know what else to do, how else to make myself useful, what else to do with the maelstrom that is my internal landscape of anxieties and thoughts. I write when I'm on the verge of a panic attack—and this is the current state of my mind as I set out to write this essay.

This essay is about the relationship between adjuncts, higher education, and the coronavirus. I am an adjunct professor, and for those who don't know the ins and outs of this job, it is neither noble, nor fulfilling, at least not in the way the teaching profession is romanticized in movies and books. The relationships that I form with a handful of students each semester saves me from the doldrums of these jobs. I teach at three different schools: one high school and two colleges, which is more than a full-time teaching load with a fraction of the pay of a full-time professor. I have no health care benefits from either of the colleges, no office, no overtime pay, no paid time-off or any other salary benefits, no job security; my courses are often cancelled last-minute due to low enrollment or other inexplicable changes in the department. I am paid per course, and even when I am at full adjunct capacity at these colleges, I still make less money than I would if I were to work as a full-time barista. I used to work primarily in the food industry, so I know how grueling those jobs are, but at least they are transparent and straightforward: you get paid per hour plus tips. As an adjunct, I found myself halfway through the summer designing and implementing a handful of new syllabi for a mysterious "flex-hybrid" model for the fall. This is the new face of education in the times of the coronavirus. And no, I was not paid for this extra work. Adjuncts are not paid for course design or preparation, or to attend meetings.

I recently attended a Zoom meeting with a representative of the "Center for Learning and Teaching" at Champlain College, which made me question my career even more than I do on a daily basis. What am I doing with my life? I considered texting my partner something urgent and vague like, "I can't do it anymore, I want to quit!" but I could see in my mind's eye that this would only cause me to feel more shame than comfort. I want my partner to see me as strong and intelligent; he is a research professor at the University of Vermont—a school with better reputation, higher budget, and more resources for part-time teachers. In many ways his position is the ideal that I'm striving towards, even though his job is technically part-time and equally precarious. I considered writing a list of grievances to the director of the Writing and Publishing Department. In other words, I nearly sent my boss an angry email. I stopped just before hitting send—what good would it do? My boss often remarks in faculty meetings that his "hands are tied" or that certain decisions are out of his "ballpark"—meaning, he's not the one who makes decisions regarding salaries, hiring and firing, or benefits. Champlain College does have an adjunct union, and while we are lucky for the tireless work the union organizers do to argue on our behalf, I still feel that we are at a standstill—last fall, we convincingly bargained for higher wages, more benefits, and extra protections, but the concessions from the college were disappointing. Our new contract includes a 17% increase in wages. To put things into perspective, adjuncts at Champlain College, no matter which department, make about $4,000 per course. So, the new contract offers a whopping increase to: $4,120. Meanwhile, full professors with the same credentials as adjuncts, who teach the same number of courses, same subject material, to the same students, "make an average of $60,000 plus benefits" (VT Digger). Adjuncts at the University of Vermont, which sits half a mile away from our campus, make about $7,000 per course. Students pay full tuition of $42,662. Where is all of that money going, if not to pay the teachers who provide the content and guidance for students? Into the salaries of the higher administration. According to the Burlington Free Press, "Former Champlain College President David Finney was paid over $1.1 million in his last year at the college. Much of the money came from a one-time $700,000 payout, on top of his salary and benefits, federal-tax filings show." The president of Champlain College who stepped down in 2017, Donald J. Laackman, earned a salary and benefits package worth $551,511, (Seven Days). I am also paid about the same amount per course at the MFA program at the Vermont College of Fine Arts, where I teach in the Writing and Publishing department. My combined annual "salary" from both schools amounts to about $24,000, if I am lucky to be given at least one or two courses per school. This is before taxes. At each school, adjuncts are only permitted to teach three courses, so even if I wanted to take on a heavier load, I would not be allowed to. I am stuck in my lane, in a rut. These reasons prompted me to seek additional employment, which is why I accepted a new job teaching visual art and English at the Vermont Commons School—a private middle school and high school, 6th grade through 12th. This position is also part-time, but so far this small school has made steps to take care of my well-being, including offering partial health care coverage. Hallelujah, finally!

Yet this begs the question—why am I putting myself through this maelstrom? Why must I juggle three jobs and seven classes in one semester? This fall, I am teaching a total of 108 students. As you can imagine, I barely manage to stay on top of my to-do list. I have four email accounts, one for each school and my personal email. I am part of four separate academic departments, and have to attend all of the requisite faculty meetings. Why am I stuck in this *particular* rut? How did I get here? I have an MFA in creative nonfiction from Iowa, which is considered a "terminal degree" for creative writing instructors. In other words, in our field, a PhD is no guarantee for getting hired, and many hiring committees for teaching positions in creative writing would consider an MFA a more appropriate degree. I have four books published; the most recent of the titles was published by MIT Press. Is this not reputable enough for me to get hired as a full professor, or an associate professor, or even an assistant professor? To clarify this confusing ladder of job titles for those unaware: adjuncts are on the very bottom rung of the ladder of higher education: in order of salary and benefits, the scale is adjunct, lecturer, assistant, associate, full. In any case, one would think that an MFA from one of the nation's top creative writing programs and four books under my belt, not to mention a CV packed with jobs, internships, conferences, writer's retreats, residencies, and awards would qualify me for a step up the ladder. Before I got the job teaching art and writing at the Vermont Commons School, I applied to every full-time teaching job that came across my desk, no matter the location or teaching load. I have applied for teaching jobs in the subjects of nonfiction, poetry, rhetoric, composition, from California to Florida. I made it through the first to the second round of interviews on a handful of occasions, and yes, my hopes were high, but the rejections streamed in. I have been teaching for six years, and I consistently receive positive, often glowing evaluations from my students and colleagues. I wouldn't normally write about my accolades in such an unapologetically frank manner, but I do so out of rage and frustration, not pride or vanity. I am qualified, and I deserve better. Adjuncts everywhere deserve to be adequately compensated and rewarded for our hard work.

I have been teaching as an adjunct for over half a decade, so why am I only now crumpling under the weight? Covid-19! All teachers had to dramatically alter their approach to education in the spring, and now schools everywhere are trying to solidify a safe plan for reopening in the fall. I am not alone in thinking that this is a terrible idea. If we have not yet "flattened the curve" of this deadly virus, why invite thousands of students to travel across state lines from all manner of cities to stay on campus and sit in a classroom together? Why not continue to teach online? The answer, as usual, is money. Colleges are businesses, students are the customers, and if the customer is not satisfied, they will not buy the product. If students and their families do not see the appeal in getting a degree online instead of partying in the dorms as a rite of passage, why would they proceed? So, to avoid a massive drop in enrollment, many colleges in Vermont and beyond have devised a monster of a plan; a cyborg version of higher education. Champlain College chose a "flex-hybrid" model for this academic year, which basically means that whoever is brave or stupid enough to come to class in person will have to wear a mask, sanitize every inch of their body multiple times a day, and get tested weekly. This includes the faculty. We are expected to put ourselves at risk, daily, and I will say that teaching with a mask on is frustrating, to say the least. I can barely speak without fogging up my glasses, and my words are muffled through any style of mask. Not only are we expected to teach in person in this compromised state, we are also expected to create simultaneous digital content for those students who do not wish to come to campus. In other words, I have had to design a dual-mode, a two-for-the-price-of-one, double-headed beast of a class. Twice the work, for the same pay. Soon, after Thanksgiving break, all classes will shift online—so, in a way, the class is a three-headed hydra. I elected to teach many of my classes entirely online, to save myself the complexity of these two modes.

I'm operating on low morale here, and it's hard for me to attend all of these Zoom meetings and put on a "good sport" smile. To add to this confusion, my program director offhandedly announced during one of our online faculty meetings that "we" (the department) have hired a new full professor of creative writing. What does this mean? It means that unbeknownst to me or the other adjuncts in our tiny writing department, a secret teaching position for a full-salary-with-full-benefits was filled by a candidate with nearly identical credentials to my own, from several states away. Why? How? At this point, I was almost too tired to ask, but the answer came back just as unsatisfying or illuminating as always, with phrases from my superiors like "I wish it had been handled differently" and "I was kept out of the loop." Who is responsible? Who is accountable?

I am at my wit's end, but I can't quit, not yet. I don't have a back-up plan. Many of my friends who lost their jobs when the state of Vermont closed businesses to slow the spread of covid-19—artists, waiters, cooks, hairdressers—filed for unemployment, and struggled throughout the summer to find new jobs. Yes–it is tempting to quit, but what then? All of my skills, passion, experience, training, and education have shaped me to be a teacher. I love teaching. I love my students. I love the subjects. I practically live inside of a stack of books. I can't even begin to imagine what else I would or could do for work.

So, dear reader, what would you do? Should I quit, file for unemployment, and start my career over from scratch? Or should I keep limping along, perpetuating the broken system that is higher education—the business that sucks money out of the pockets of students, creating future debt and lifelong worry—The business that rewards only the upper crust of its administration—adding dollars to the six-figure salaries of its presidents while the staff and faculty scrape by—the business that runs on the underpaid labor of adjuncts? If you're shaking your head, know that I am too. This is where my writing finally comes in handy for me—as a coping mechanism. If I can't write myself into a stable job, at least I can temporarily quell my fury by typing this piece.

Addendum:

Nearly two years have passed since I wrote the preceding essay. I have since entered my thirties, without fanfare; I quit my teaching job at Champlain College, without any acknowledgment of my services from the administration or even from the director of my program; the residential MFA in Writing and Publishing program at the Vermont College of Fine Arts was shut down without explanation from the administration, thus ending all of the jobs in our program, including mine; and we are still experiencing a pandemic. After the Champlain and VCFA jobs ended, I continued to plod along at the Vermont Commons School, teaching middle school and high school classes. I was the only part-time instructor at the school, which signaled to me that the administration did not value the arts as highly as any other subject. Although my contract was technically part-time, at 75%, I felt as though I were teaching more than a full course load: they had me teaching six courses per semester, which is nearly twice as many courses as a full course load at many undergraduate institutions.

Up until my time at VCS, I had been teaching at the college level, where a full teaching load is anywhere between two and four courses per semester. For example, at the University of Iowa, according to the current faculty handbook, the "full teaching load is two three-semester-hour courses per year or equivalent."

At Champlain College, the full time load is a bit higher; according to the Catalog of Faculty Rights, Responsibilities, and Expectations, "The normal teaching load is typically four (4) undergraduate courses per semester." At the Vermont Commons School, my course load felt quite high for a part-time instructor, particularly considering the low salary of around $30,000 annually, before taxes. For example, in the spring semester of 2022, I was teaching the following courses simultaneously: high school visual art portfolio, high school elective: comics, 6th and 7th grade art, 8th grade art, 6th grade English, and PE. This does not include the extra courses that I helped to plan and lead that were part of the experiential education "E-Weeks' which occurred four times each year, including a photography and creative writing E-Week, an interdisciplinary dance and visual art E-Week, and a film-making E-Week.

I was also part of two different departments: English and art, and I attended at least one department meeting for each of these departments every week. That's twice as much meeting time as any of the full time faculty. I also advised several seniors for their senior projects each year, which is a hefty commitment—weekly meetings, editorial assistance, advice, and assessment. I also coordinated the production of the yearbook, with no extra compensation. I helped the music teacher to organize the Open Mic and Arts Night events each semester. I served on the Social Justice committee. This is all, of course, in addition to meeting with students in-between classes and after school, and emailing and meeting with students who needed extra help. I know that all teachers put in extra time and commit to these extra tasks at every institution, but I felt in my bones that the amount of work that I put into the job was not reflected in the salary, and perhaps that's the bottom line—I simply could not pay my bills and mortgage and afford to live on this salary alone, and I therefore felt pressured to take on another very demanding job as the managing director of a poetry nonprofit, called The

Sundog Poetry Center. For the sake of simplicity, I will stick to describing the problems with academia, and I'll save the details of leading an arts nonprofit for another essay.

I felt burned out at the start of the pandemic, and the wick simply continued to burn, long after the end of all of my energetic wax. The model was simply unsustainable. I finally scheduled a meeting with the headmaster to request change. During every one-on-one conversation that occurred with the headmaster or the assistant headmaster at this school, I made it very clear that juggling multiple jobs to make ends meet was unsustainable and frustrating, and that being a part-time instructor was extremely confusing and exhausting, but I hadn't yet threatened to quit as a bargaining point until this spring semester, two years into the job. When I finally made it known that if nothing changed, I would leave the position, the headmaster shook his head and said that there was nothing he could do, "we simply don't have the funds." He noted the low enrollment due to the pandemic, and the small size of the school. We were sitting in his office during this meeting, and as he offered excuses for why he could not increase my salary or change my position to full time, I glanced around his office—a large room with floor-to-ceiling windows, three or four leather armchairs, and artifacts from his global travels, in comparison to the office that I shared with two other instructors in the older building. This building, housing this spacious room, was a brand-new acquisition. I thought about the plot of land in Charlotte that the school had purchased for recreation. I thought about the new alumni outreach coordinator that the school had hired. I thought about all of the catered parties that the administration threw for alumni and students and faculty throughout the year. Take note that this is a private school, for which parents pay $28,950 per child to attend. That's nearly the equivalent of my salary. I teach about 16 students in each art class, so the school is making about $463,200 from their tuition. True, I'm not taking into account all of the expenses of running a school, but in the end, what is the school selling? Education. Who provides this service? Teachers. Who gets paid? Administrators. No funds to pay the art teacher, eh? I left the meeting feeling defeated and resigned to quitting, although I asked him for some time to think things over. He replied, "Yes, certainly, but we may need to begin posting your position soon, just in case." Thank you, sir, for the support.

The next day, the assistant headmaster pulled me aside in-between classes and asked me in a strangely cheerful and aloof tone, "I hear you might be leaving the school." My breath caught—had the headmaster already spoken with the other administration about my departure? I hadn't yet given him my decision! I held my tongue, lest vocalization released the flood of tears; I had to return to the classroom in five minutes and wouldn't want my students to see me fully break down. She took my silence as a prompt to keep interrogating me, "Is your heart not in it? Do you not feel at home at this school?" What I wish I could have said in reply: "Are you f***ing kidding me? That question is entirely irrelevant. My heart is here. My students love me. I'm damn good at my job. I work tirelessly every day for this school, and I feel undercompensated, stressed out, and at my wit's end. I have made this discrepancy very clear, and yet the only option that the administration has is to let me exit the side door, quietly." Instead of saying any of this, I choked out a meager, "Yes, but it's hard…" and I backed out of her office with the excuse that I didn't want to be late for my class. She never followed up with me on this conversation.

Not too long after these meetings, perhaps a mere week or two had passed, this assistant headmaster made an announcement to the entire school in the middle of our 'morning meeting', during which every student, staff, and faculty member gathered in a feel-good circle in the volleyball field. She shouted out to the circle, "We have a candidate for the art department visiting today, if anyone would like to meet her and ask her any questions, she will be in the art room from eleven to noon." Panicked, I glanced across the circle to the music teacher, the only other art faculty in our tiny department. He raised his eyebrows and shrugged. After the meeting concluded, my students rushed to pester me with questions, "Are they adding a teacher, or are you leaving? What's going on? Don't leave us!" I had to rush to the classroom, with my students clinging to me like barnacles on a very wobbly rowboat. I had no answers for them. I hadn't been warned about the candidate's visit, nor had I been notified that my art room—the only art room—would be occupied for this interview. This scenario occurred several more times the same week with new candidates, and then another whopper of an announcement occurred the following week in an email to all staff, faculty, and parents: the school had hired a new, full-time music teacher! Neither the headmaster or assistant headmaster pulled me aside with any explanation or condolence. After the fourth candidate, I decided to take my free period to knock on the headmaster's door and ask for clarification. He welcomed me cheerfully into his office and closed the door, as though nothing untoward had occurred. The next hour dragged along through a dense, putrid fog, which calls to mind T.S. Eliot's *Love Song of J. Alred Prufrock,*

> And indeed there will be time
> For the yellow smoke that slides along the street,
> Rubbing its back upon the window-panes;
> There will be time, there will be time
> To prepare a face to meet the faces that you meet;
> There will be time to murder and create,
> And time for all the works and days of hands
> That lift and drop a question on your plate;
> Time for you and time for me,
> And time yet for a hundred indecisions,
> And for a hundred visions and revisions…

Perhaps there will be "time to murder and I create," and I hope that soon I'll find the energy, once I rest and heal from the trauma that is working as an underpaid, part-time teacher at a private high school. Here are a few choice tidbits from my meeting with the headmaster. I was not taking notes, and in retrospect it would have been wise to record the meeting on my phone, but keep in mind that although these are paraphrased, these quotes convey very much the mood, tone, and meaning of the headmaster's words.

When I told him, once again, that I was struggling to make ends meet, and that teaching full time at the school would at least offer me more stability and a slightly higher salary, he reminded me that it simply wasn't possible this year, but that each year my pay would increase according to the salary scale. To this, I mentioned that the salary was rather low to begin with, he replied,

> "I have great empathy for your position. I was once in a similar position, although further along in my career, with a few more publications and a higher degree, but I was still making under 40,000 a year, with a baby on the way. So, I left teaching and became an administrator. You may have seen my salary somewhere on the internet, and yes, I make more than teachers do here, but I can assure you that this directly correlates to the extra hours that I put into my job. Annually, I work more hours than teachers do. It's just logical."

There are a few aspects of our conversation that are a bit too complex to explain here, but I should mention that one pivotal disagreement centered on the aforementioned 'salary scale,' which had only recently been made public to the faculty, towards an effort for transparency, as demanded by the faculty. The school, being private, is not unionized. The scale combines two factors: time (how many years has the instructor been teaching) and experience (does the instructor have a higher degree or not). I do have a higher degree, and I have been teaching for about eight years, or up to a decade if you include student teaching experience. Somehow, the headmaster had calculated my total teaching experience as four years. When I asked him about this, he explained that prior to teaching at this school, I had taught at colleges and universities, which does not directly translate to a secondary education course-load. He did not explain how this would reduce my years of teaching by half, but he would not budge.

I asked him about his decision to hire a new full-time music teacher without offering me full-time employment. I had, after all, been teaching at the school for two years, and my students trust and appreciate my teaching, according to their course evaluations each semester, and their frequent verbal affirmations and thank-you notes throughout the year. He explained that this teacher had been hired to replace the current music teacher, who was moving on to a different job. His expression then soured, out of the blue, and he asked in an accusatory tone, "Are you suggesting that we reduce the musical offerings at our school, in order to increase your position?" I felt caught off guard by this, but I managed to respond, "No, I never suggested that. Why can't both subjects co-exist, in full capacity?" He shook his head, and said, "As I have explained, we cannot afford to expand the art department this year. We simply cannot afford it."

I should mention that throughout our conversation, I cried uncontrollably. This seems important, albeit a bit embarrassing; I have a very hard time turning the faucet off once the tears begin. I used nearly an entire box of tissues during our meeting. It was physically uncomfortable to continue my conversation, with a throbbing headache and my nose stopped up with emotional snot, but I felt the need to push through to the end. The end arrived: he offered me nothing. He also advised me to be careful about how I shared the news with my students. He said, "You could tell them that you're turning your focus to your other job." Completely exhausted, I nodded and shrugged, and made my way to the bathroom to cool my red-hot face down and stop the flow of tears before my next event: my star students' senior presentation in the auditorium.

That night, I wrote a long and rambling email to my colleagues, none of whom had any clue that I would be departing the school, aside from the music teacher. The next morning, my co-worker and office-mate, the other English teacher, greeted me with a bouquet of flowers and a hug. As soon as she handed me the mason jar filled with blooming peonies, she began wailing and crying. I couldn't handle carrying my grief as well as hers, so I accepted the flowers and rushed outside to catch a breath of fresh air, where I was immediately accosted by a cluster of my favorite students—the beloved, queer, atypical wallflowers and geeks and nerds from my 8th grade art class. They surrounded me and showered me with overlapping exclamations, "Why are you leaving?" "What happened?" "The new art candidates suck! They're all boring!" "Don't leave us, we'll miss you!"

This all occurred one week prior to graduation. Those seven days were a righteous slog. I volunteered to be a chaperone for prom on a cruise boat, and I brought my film camera to take portraits of my students in their snazzy outfits, but just before the ship left the dock, I fled back to solid ground—I knew that if I stayed on the ship I might have to lock myself in the bathroom to sob. I haven't cried this hard since my stepdad left our family when I was a young twenty-something, or when Trump was elected. I've never felt sad before about quitting a job. In this case, I knew I was leaving behind something bigger—not only a job, but possibly academia altogether, and my vocation as a teacher. I don't think I have the energy or resilience to return.

Maybe this was a blessing in disguise? Maybe I dodged a bullet? Maybe now I can turn towards my own creative projects, or get a job as a barista (again) and write poems on napkins while I wait for the next customer? In the meantime, I'm going to try to enjoy having only one job—the part-time poetry nonprofit—and enjoy the remaining hours of the day as a human, with a body, with needs, hobbies, passions, projects, pets, a garden, responsibilities, bills, and yes—I will take time, every day, to heal from my decade in academia.

About the author:
Frances Cannon is a queer writer, professor, artist, and dog & cat-mom currently living in Vermont. She is the managing director of the Sundog Poetry Center. She has an MFA in creative writing from Iowa and a BA from the University of Vermont. She is the author and illustrator of several books: *Walter Benjamin: Reimagined*, MIT Press, *The Highs and Lows of Shapeshift Ma and Big-Little Frank*, Gold Wake Press, *Tropicalia*, Vagabond Press, *Uranian Fruit*, Honeybee Press, and *Predator/ Play*, Ethel Zine.

On The Feminine & The Oracular

Itiola Jones

As the story has been told to me, I come from three generations of pastors and prophets, and in this way, the prophetic has always been in my blood. I was raised in the Celestial Church of Christ, a denomination of Christianity founded in Benin, where my mother's family is from. In every house I've lived in, we've devoted a room or a corner for an altar to prayer. Only my father and brothers were allowed to touch the altar, where we placed candles and offers for God on Sunday, while my mother, my sister and I were not allowed past the halfway point. All Celestians ('Cele' for short) wear what are called 'sutanas' (also called 'white garments' in Nigeria), but only the women have to cover their heads. We cannot wear shoes while we wear our sutanas. Men and women sit on opposite ends of the church and there are no pews. I did not sit in one until I was well into my twenties, when I went to an American church for the first time. Though I wasn't allowed to learn Yoruba (my first language before English) as my parents believed it would slow down my developmental process, we almost exclusively prayed in and sang in Yoruba. I memorized songs, believing my people's language to be the language of angels.

As a child, I did not question what was often accepted to be the rules, that although God loved me, He saw my body as a site of contempt. When my body began to open, to awaken its machinery of creation, my father was angry because now I was no longer a girl-child. Yet, I was happy because I wanted to be a woman, so I presented to my father this new development of my body. A promise, red as shame. Now, every month, my body would shed and release its labor. When my chest began its slow, yet rude blooming, my father stopped hugging me, unable to reconcile with nature's betrayal. When boys in my grade grabbed me and gestured towards my shaping body, when grown men would holler profanities out of their car, when my mother threatened if I got pregnant, don't bother coming home, when the world named me and my body before I had language to name myself, I began to understand 'desire' and 'shame' were the cornerstones of womanhood as I could make sense of.

When I sought understanding of the world's workings, back then I turned to the Bible. I was raised to understand that with all the world's problems, God gave humans answers in the Great Book. In the Western canonical Bible, Eve is the first woman named, yet in the Hebrew Bible, Adam had a wife before her, Lilith. Depending on which translation you trust, her name means "female demon" or "night banshee". Lilith was the first woman punished for denying a man pleasures of the flesh. It was then that I began to question: "What does pleasure look like outside of the male gaze/God's approval?" The Bible told me it does not exist. Eve sought pleasure for herself and paradise was set on fire. She was gifted and punished with childbearing. She was punished twofold by losing both her children, one to death and the other to banishment. Mary's sole function in the Bible seemed to be birthing a boy-god, only to watch him crucified trying to save his people from damnation. Lot's wife was not only denied a name, but was disavowed by God for looking back, for being a woman who could bear witness to His most blatant savagery. While it was true that Jezebel ruled Israel with a brutal hand, her name is often associated with a woman who is evil or scheming. Paul acknowledges Junia as a member of the apostles and Mary Magdalene was one of earliest followers of Jesus, one of the few, alongside Mary, to witness the crucifixion of Jesus, yet neither of them are that widely recognized as followers of Christ.

Men in the Bible are given the grace to inflict outright cruelty, to kill God's worshippers, to offer up their daughters in exchange for clemency, to be complicated figures, but a woman tells God 'no', a woman refuses to lay beneath her husband, a woman looks back, and she is either erased or relegated to secondary roles. For years, I struggled to reconcile my relationship to God with a book of His teachings where I could not see my face. Now, I'm not sure if I am still religious, but I know the Bible was my first book of poems and I know poetry is the medium by which I make tangible sense of my living.

When I moved to New York, my sister and I lived together for the first time as adults. Before she arrived, there was already tension—years of unresolved frustration and anger crammed together in a two-bedroom apartment. It was never a serious strife between us. Neither of us endangered the life of the other, but we were both capable of enacting impressive cruelty against one another, incapable of forgiveness. She accused me of gaslighting her by shuffling her objects around the living room, would throw violent fits when I wouldn't listen to her. I accuse the patriarchal forces of the Bible for wielding unlawful power, but at every turn reminded my sister I was the eldest and she could not oppose me. We screamed and cursed each other, and it went on like this. In *The Wild Iris*, Louise Glück evokes the voice of nature to connect with God and to use language to strike back at forces that reigned above her:

And all this time
I indulged your limitations, thinking

you would cast it aside yourselves sooner or later,
thinking matter could not absorb your gaze forever—

We were kids and she told me, repeatedly, to kill myself. She said it in childish rage, initially, but then as we were older, she said it again with more precision—the kind that cleaves flesh from bone. It seems dramatic to write this all out—two sisters needlessly quarreling—in a two-bedroom apartment somewhere in Queens, yet in the middle of this heat, it felt Biblical that one of us would strike the other down with the fury of Kingdom Come. It was the closest I had ever felt to her and the farthest. Blinded by rage, I turned to other women in literature who could possibly understand. Louise Glück and Brigit Pegeen Kelly felt like a proper introduction to the Divine from a feminine perspective, a voice I was so hungry for, especially then, at a time when I was consumed with rage towards my sister, I was afraid of what I had become. Glück finds a way to meet God's eye without ever saying His name. Here, she crafts a voice, which returns us to the natural world. Who better than God's most noble creatures to confront him:

I've watched you long enough
I can speak to you any way I like—

I've submitted to your preferences, observing patiently
the things you love, speaking

through vehicles only, in
details of earth, as you prefer,

And then as the poem progresses, there is risk and veracity. Glück never flinches from exactness:

I cannot go on
restricting myself to images

because you think it is your right
to dispute my meaning:

I am prepared now to force
clarity upon you.

A voice of the oracular, from a feminine perspective allowed me the gift of sharpness, to negotiate the complexities and nuance of desire that was lawfully denied of women in the Bible. What does the Divine sound like coming from a body that menstruates? How does the Divine transform inside a body that must negotiate obligations often thrust upon its form? How does shame and Divine function in a singular body with all of these complexities?

To understand my rage towards my sister, I looked towards the oldest sibling rivalry in the Bible. I wrote the first poem titled "Cain", guided by the works of Glück and Kelly. Having only read *To The Place of Trumpets, The Orchard* opened, for me, a new door:

Bright shapes in the dark garden, the gardenless stretch
Of old yard, sweetened now by the half-light
As if by burning flowers. Overture. First gesture.
But not even that, the pause before the gesture,
The window frame composing the space, so it
Seems as if time has stopped, as if this half-dark,
This winter grass, plated with frost, these unseen
Silent birds might stay forever. It seems as if
This might be what forever is, the presence of time
Overriding the body of time, the fullness of time
Not a moment but a being, watchful and unguarded,
Unguarded and gravely watched this garden—
The black fir with its long aristocratic broken branches,
The cluster of three tiny tipped arborvitae
Damp as sea sponges, the ghostly sycamore shedding
Its skin, and the sweet row of yews along the walk
Into which people throw their glittering trash....
And who, when the light rises, will come up the walk?
We can say no one will come—the day will be empty
Because you are no longer in it

The greatest strength of this poem is Kelly's remarkable ability to combine the tangible ("silent birds") with the intangible that transforms the body ("the presence of time") giving me nuance to speak of the oracular. We begin in the natural world, in a world governed by ever-shifting time, and arrive back in the human world, burdened by "glittering trash". Kelly teaches me to observe, to mythologize and reshape the world as I see fit. The following poems in this anthology are poems guided by women and non-binary poets engaging in the Divine through a multitude of lenses. Many engaging in both established and borrowed mythologies, such as Leila Chatti sitting next to Mary in a gynecologist's office. New writers Carly Joy Miller, author of *Ceremonial* and Analicia Sotelo, author of *Virgin,* while both their works are different, there are poems which come together as sister poems, both evoking and mythologizing desire from a feminine gaze. In "Ceremonial For The Beast I Desired", Miller confesses:

Tragic, how ceremonies
bitter: my body a door

always closing.
Beast, when done,

blurs my chest still:
missed shadow, phantom

gift. Still I kiss
his jaw wild with yellow

jackets. I shepherd
too long in his furs.

"In his furs" segues us to Soleto's "The Minotaur Invents The Circumstances Of His Birth":

I am born: her birthing dress is a mast in my mouth,

a moth wrecked in specks of sarcophagus black,

a parasol in the twelve-armed wheel of a phaeton,

a crinoline smoking in a fragrant fire—

I crawled through her human body

to meet her spectators head on

& in the high forceps of the evening

I wanted more complicated women in the Bible and, to that end, consider this anthology a glimpse into what that Bible could look like. The women and non-binary persons in this anthology both question God and question desire that morphs the body. They implicate the Divine, in their own language, drawing threads that bind one another together while allowing their human nature to be a driving force. The poems here do their best to be ordered in a thematic structure, a structure that I trust any reader could follow and witness how these poems, emerging from different voices, amalgamate to become a singular one. It is an immense honor to complete this anthology with a poem of my own as I see my work in conversation with every single one of these luminaries. I invite you to walk through the door and read.

About the author:

I.S. Jones is an American/Nigerian poet and music journalist. She is a Graduate Fellow with The Watering Hole and holds fellowships from Callaloo, BOAAT Writer's Retreat, and

Brooklyn Poets. She is a Book Editor with Indolent Books, Editor at *20.35 Africa: An Anthology of Contemporary Poetry*, freelances for Vinyl Me Please, *Complex*, *Earmilk*, *NBC News Think* and elsewhere. Her works have appeared or are forthcoming in *Guernica, Washington Square Review, Hayden's Ferry Review, The Rumpus, The Offing, Shade Literary Arts* and elsewhere. Her work was chosen as a finalist by Khadijah Queen for the 2020 Sublingua Prize for Poetry. She is an MFA candidate in Poetry at UW-Madison.

This Is Not My Hand On Your Back

Tyler Orion

It is snowing heavily outside as the gloaming deepens. I am watching an old Barry Jenkins movie filmed not quite in black-and-white, but almost. A few colors bleed through palely, like the main characters' shirts in faded red and yellow, and the effect is an old photograph that has been manually hand tinted. There was a one-night stand and now I'm watching a scene from the following day where the two people are exploring the streets of San Francisco together. At one point they walk through a park caught between buildings where there is a waterfall flowing over a concrete ledge. The couple walk behind the water and stop to view the engravings carved on the wall. Although this is all besides the point.

The man, who is carefully but persistently pursuing the woman, reaches out a hand and places it on her lower back. He guides her in front of him with this touch and she follows, allowing his hand to rest there, lightly pressed, in a gesture that says, *I want to touch you, I want to pull your body into mine, but instead I will show you through this touch how I respect that we hardly know each other.*

And there lies the point. They hardly know each other. Yet he feels it is appropriate to touch the woman's back. And she lets him, and follows his hand, lets him guide her, and she pauses just long enough to let his hand linger showing that she doesn't mind.

This gesture embodies everything about masculinity that I still don't understand.

I almost pause the film on the shot where I can view his hand against her back. The light touch. The delicate but intimate pressure. The desire held back with restraint. The man gesturing in a way that only men gesture.

I let the film roll on, but I am stuck there on his hand reaching out and touching.

I would never know how to do this. I wouldn't even think of doing this. As a trans guy who is just learning how to interpret and maneuver though masculine terrain, and as someone who was socialized as female and is all too aware of how men's hands wander into places they shouldn't, I am exceedingly cautious about keeping my hands to myself. I have never gestured in this way, even with intimate partners. I can't imagine wanting or needing to control another person's movement in this way.

But yet men make this gesture constantly, and women seem to accept and even sometimes enjoy this touch (I have almost exclusively observed this specific touch between heterosexual couples, but I do wonder why it doesn't translate to queer couples. Is it too old-fashioned? Too associated with heteros to bleed into queer relationships? Which leads me to wonder what the intention is behind this touch and to surmise that most likely it is built on men's control over women: cis men believe they have the right, and even expectation, to move women about as they please).

The placement of the hand on the lower back is intentionally intimate. A touch to the shoulder or the upper back does not have the same effect. Although men do this regularly also, particularly to women they don't know well but still feel it is appropriate to touch.

But this isn't about appropriate gestures and isn't about men's inherent confidence to put their hands where they please. It is, in the end, about my inability to touch a person (of any gender) with public intimacy which stems directly from the shame I carry as a trans person.

Oh. Right. This is about shame.

I don't know how to write about shame because it is so woven into my being. I am too close to it. It is the skin I wear. It is every bone. It is in every smile. It flows out with every exhale.

In watching this brief shot in the film, I see in that man's hand, as if he is cupping the depths of my soul, all of the shame that I carry deeply within me which has become as natural to me as breathing. I accept it, allow it, even embrace it as freely as I do each inhale that is so inherent to the rhythm of my body.

All roads lead to shame the way every vein leads to the heart.

About the author:
Tyler Orion is a queer, trans writer and photographer living in rural northern Vermont. Orion works at a small, independent bookstore, is a reader for the *Maine Review* and has work forthcoming or published recently in *Orion*, *Brevity*, *Allegory Ridge*, *Mount Island*, and in an anthology from Damaged Goods Press.

Cracks In Glass Identities

Oluchi S. Agboola

As mosquitoes dined and wined on all ten of my toes one Tuesday night in the middle of a Lagos hair salon this August, I looked into the mirror in front of me and came to a shocking realization: the hairdresser that my mother and I have been patronizing since I was at least four, well over a decade and a half now, was twisting red wool into my hair when I realized I did not know her name.

At first, I thought it was the heavy generator smoke clouding my memory and killing the last two brain cells the summer semester mercifully spared me, but I truly did not know and was too embarrassed to ask.

This woman has known me throughout my primary and secondary school education. She knows every member of my extended family on my mother's side. Her firstborn, my age mate and namesake, is about finishing university. I know what school she's in, what she's studying, what issues she had with getting a room in her first year. I know this woman's entire nuclear family and even her sister, who lives in the East. I know where she's from, a village near ours. I know where she lives, where she worships, and what denomination she belongs to, but I could not tell her actual first name, which seriously shocked me.

As much as I referred to her, I've only heard her be called Mummy So-and-so, her own name never having come up in conversation with myself or others. That night, I just felt too ashamed to ask. It made me question why the thought of her individuality never occurred to me.

People say I'm a rude child because I call my mother by her first name. People say I'm a rude child for less, especially for that. How can you call your mother by her name? Don't you have any respect?

I say I'm a rude child regardless, but that has nothing to do with it. If my grandparents did not intend for her to be called that name, they wouldn't have given it to her. Barely anyone calls her by her name (no pun intended, but shout out to Lil Nas X).

She's Mommy "S" to most, and perhaps it was my angst and hormones at work, but between the pubescent angst and hormones, I decided she deserved to be called what her parents named her, and it stuck.

Becoming Mrs. Somebody and Mummy Someone is like pushing a shiny glass under a rapid river. A once sharp image reflected to you—a clear, glass identity—soon becomes a hazy, distorted reflection of an identity that no longer belongs to you. Even when the cracks begin to form in the glass, when its sheen begins to dull, it is kept underwater because the owner is not around to claim it, and there it stays, drowning.

One of my favorite, and arguably, one of the best Disney villains, Cruella De Vil (portrayed by Glenn Close), once said, "More good women have been lost to marriage than war, famine, disease and disaster." This line resonated with me right from the first time I heard it as a child.

Growing up, I wondered what it was about marriage that

melted the hardest of women into a pool of water that never solidifies again. Observing people around me, I could never get it. I still don't.

Each family comes with its unique flavor of dysfunction. It all falls back on what you decide you can tolerate. There was never a flavor that followed that I quite understood. Looking at a no-nonsense woman I knew growing up, desperate to marry a man who threatened to beat her in her own father's house while visiting. He almost did, if not for the people at home with her. And I wondered what molded a love so cruel that you would swallow a dysfunction coated in thorns. Something that would scar you from the inside out. It was then I realized what marriage could be, a heavy wind to knock down even the sturdiest of trees, pulling away at your roots.

I saw friendships lost due to a habitual cheater who would never leave his wife's friends alone, moving with the verified knowledge that she would choose him each time. I wondered if the woman had no fear when it came to swallowing their dysfunction. People half her age coming to her as a woman, her own friends lost to this man, and still, she stayed. I wondered if she would never break. I wondered if she had broken a long time ago and the ease with which she took the dysfunction in stride was the reluctant surrender of a battle long lost.

I saw a man lose out on having a relationship with his children because they refused to be pawns in his game of mental manipulation. I saw him try to pin it on his old wife with shaky hands, as though she has the cunning to turn their children against him, as though she was not against him also. And yet, she stayed, through arguing, mental subjugation, manipulation, and many nights where the tension was thick enough to smother her, she stayed.

Despite all these, these women would shine their teeth and ask young girls, "When will you marry?" It all appeared as a major ruse, a grand charade to convince society, who is not well on its own, that all is well with you despite the odds. Marriage is a mask worn at a masquerade ball that everyone is trying to convince you is their real face, even when you know that there is a lousiness, something so lackluster, hiding behind the monumental farce.

I wondered, for all a woman is taught to endure and submit to, would a husband ever reciprocate? Would people cry for him to stay with a notorious abuser, would they advise him to pray more to keep his cheating wife, would they ask him to sing a song of endurance because he was now Mr. Somebody? Would they beg him to drown in a tempestuous family because at least he had a family? Let's not even go too extreme: would he let go of his name? Perhaps, but not often.

Above all else with most cishet marriages, even those without the abuse, without the infidelity, or any other moral dilemmas, there is a heavy reliance on the stripping away of the individual to form the unit that bothers me. We spend so much of our lives as other people: our parents' children, the sibling of our siblings, somebody's spouse. Who are any of us without the ties, without the noise? If we silenced the voices of everyone in our bubble, what do we have to say in isolation? Many people spend an existence living as the "them" in their parent's minds, in their family's expectations. I often wonder who any of us would be without it? If we shed away people's expectations of us and just decided to be, freely? I think many people head into marriage without trying to figure any of that out. What does it matter anyhow, your individuality muddles into your new family regardless?

Even the Bible says, "For this reason a man shall leave his father and his mother, and be joined to his wife; and they shall become one flesh" (Genesis 2:24). One flesh, except he keeps his last name. One flesh, except he is not the one tasked with the role of returning home from a job, the same as his spouse, and being expected to slave away in the kitchen. One flesh, except he is not the child constantly reminded of how his mates are married in the North and how he should be learning to cater to his future family that doesn't exist yet. One flesh, but he is not the one berated with questions of "Is this how you will be behaving in your wife's house?" One flesh, but it is rarely called the "wife's house." And it makes me wonder, how tightly can the molecules in flesh combine to become one anyhow?

There is no beauty in loss of self. There is beauty in the change of self, regaining of self, but never in losing self. We expect women to lose themselves to marriage and admonish them if otherwise.

We expect them to claim to be "a wife and mother first." Not whoever they were in the two seconds before they took on those roles.

We expect them, even before becoming wives or mothers, to spend ages praying to be wives and mothers. Going to retreats, revivals and restoration services to pray for their husbands and offspring. While married, we expect them to keep being this altar, this pillar of spiritual powers, as though the Head of House went missing.

We ask them ridiculous questions like "Does your husband know you do that?" and justify complaints with, "Well, her husband likes it like that," as though she means nothing, is nothing, but an extension of her husband. As though she is not enough to like something for herself.

We strip them of their names. Their maiden names are nowhere to be found, their states of origin might as well have never come to be, and the children that they built in their body cannot even claim them. We refer to them by their first names, barely. We forget who they were before they became a Mrs. or a Mummy. And I cannot help but wonder how hard it might be, to let go of the concrete identity you have had all your life, to trade it in for a glass identity that can smash at any time.

Living under a patriarchal society demands this for the cishet structure to survive. Women who challenge this norm, especially in traditional, conservative communities, face backlash and pressure to conform. The man gains ownership rights; the man gains a Head of House title like it's Big Brother on steroids; the man gains a cook, cleaner and babymaker to dominate. And the woman? She is left with a name that is not her own, which brings her added responsibility, the expectation to be a caretaker, and the unquestionable idea that she will place her family's needs above her own each time.

When I was a child, a woman from my church had the most beautiful voice. She had two kids but no husband. When the time came for Mother's Day, she was not allowed to sing with the mothers on stage because the Women's department executives had issues with her being unmarried. I watched each tear roll down her cheeks, her back hunched, as she recounted this to my furious mother. I watched my mother call the Women's Department head and pastor's wife to tell them she didn't know the meaning of their nonsense, but she wouldn't be attending the Mother's Day event. I watched them beg and fawn, like headless chickens who had no parts in the decisions leading up to that moment. I wondered how the lack of a husband negated her identity as a woman and a mother, especially since Mother's Day has nothing to do with husbands. It was a big issue where the pastor's wife had to apologize to her and my mother, but it made me realize just how much society stresses the package deal. Your womanhood does not depend on you growing to be a well-rounded woman. Society defines womanhood by marriage (happy or not) and kids, full stop.

I do not know where the willingness for this sacrifice comes from and I do not know if I will ever be ready to swap out my identity for one so demanding of me. I do not know if defining my life around children and my husband, rarely me, is something I am ready for.

Hopefully, there will always be people to remind you that there was a *you* before you became somebody else's. Before my mother was "Mommy S," she was what I call her. It is easy to lose sight of you in trying to be someone else's. It is easy to let the concept of self suffer loss. It is easy to follow the new customs marriage and childbirth bring. Marriages take work, but women should not have to relinquish their identities to it.

My hairdresser's name is Joyce.

Here is to one less crack in her identity.

About the Author:

Oluchi S. Agboola is a student whose soul has been sold to medicine, but the arts still possess a great chunk of her heart.

Since streaming services are yet to make her life a reality show, she writes creative nonfiction pieces and personal essays, mostly for her blog found at mattersofdedrea.wordpress.com. In love with the art of storytelling, language and bending reality, she also writes poetry and literary fiction. When she is not writing, one can find her crying into her chemistry notes, drawing or pretending to do one of three.

An Odd Sort Of Thursday

Ria Dhingra

I drink black tea and cups upon cups of coffee at small cafes, editing essays and twisting words. The setting makes me seem rather intelligent and pretentious. I am neither of those things. In fact, I feel rather stupid. But all great writers craft stories in cafes; and if I aspire to be a writer, I too must sit in these outdoor, Parisian seats.

The tea is now cold and the coffee was always bitter; I cannot seem to grow accustomed to the taste. But I finish each cup for it is Thursday. I dislike Thursdays. The kind of weary days where the week is close to being done, but not close enough to feel giddy about. The kind of days where activities and events seem to blur and burden you altogether. I order another drink.

Laid out before me are pages upon pages of literature, people's drafts and stories and moments all captured in text. I wish to write the next great American novel. I am neither great nor American.

To be American is to be hungry and ambitious and selfish. I'm starving—but I cannot bring myself to eat. There are too many choices. Instead, I pacify my ambition with the sweet taste of succession. After all, what a writer wants most besides harnessing art is garnering reputation—relying on legacy. What an artist craves most is memory. What compels an artist to move, to create, to craft, is neither inspiration nor aesthetics—but fear.

There is fear in endings, but an even greater fear in losing the story itself. Artists cannot seem to stand the thought of it. So, they sing songs, sell stories, and produce poetry. Anything to emboss greatness onto the hunk of metal known as aesthetic history. There is desperate urgency as they work to capture life in order to be remembered after death. I am done with fearing death. I stared him down once before and I am ready to embrace him yet again, so I will never be a great artist. Instead, I wish to be a teacher. Or, at least, that's what I tell myself.

In high school, my English teacher once told me that if you cannot create greatness, you should teach it. That way, you can be credited for producing it, and maybe—one day—some writer can inscribe your name as his dedication. You can be someone's muse. Teaching, that's succession.

I had once adored the way this teacher had chosen his words. The way he always inspired me to find my own. The way he crafted stories and commented upon others. Not once did he ever call me an artist.

Soon, I began to see the overlap in his stories. The lies he wove into the truth for emotional emphasis. The interchangeable themes and names and tragedies. I found this to be very compelling—these lies. In fact, my teacher got so good at telling them that he won an essay contest and soon traveled the world to share these stories. I guess the classroom got too small for him. I am not an artist, so I hope to be a good person. *I do not lie.*

I take a break from editing the stack of stories before me. The texts hungry writers from around the state mailed editors, not expecting their work to be weighed by a burned-out Literature student. I look across the table at my boyfriend, hard at work finishing a term paper for his class.

I concentrate on his hands as they type. He does not seem to wrestle with his words. In fact, he is articulate and American and hungry. I am sure he will one day grow up to be great. It takes effort to contain my jealousy.

He fell in love with me for I am neither American nor destined for greatness. In fact, he believes that I embody most things he is not—I'm "different." From him. From other girls. It seems the difference is alluring, attractive—refreshing.

Here's a secret: Women are not snowflakes. Not unique fleeting entities ever meant to "refresh." Most of us are the same, which is not the tragedy narratives would like you to believe. The true calamity resides in the fact that we have all internalized this expectation, and none of us can ever live up to it.

Most girls are the same. They represent nature, until they lose themselves to the role of nurture. They are dreamers, until their dreams are forced to die. They are beautiful and naive, until they are old and ignorant. They are young and "free" until they attract someone older and sterner. Someone who will be sure to remind them of how "different" they are. A woman's life is defined by a switching. From one thing to another. Girl to woman. Writer to teacher. It's not a slow transition or a metamorphosis; it's a sudden snap.

Blink. My boyfriend once lamented on how time moves too fast. Blink, and you're in college. Blink, and you're working for someone. Blink, and you have people working for you. Time blinks away, and you hardly ever get to enjoy it all.

I don't believe time truly works like that. At least it never has for me. For time to move too fast, you have to be aware of owning your own time. You have to know what you want to do with it. Time, like most things, is a sudden snap. You never have agency over it, and once you realize you want it, know what you want to do with it, the time is already gone. No spare moments for greatness.

Upon sharing these thoughts, my boyfriend had remarked again how this different way of thinking fascinates him. Now, I say nothing.

I fell in love with him because he once told me that my hair looked like "crashing waves." It was comments like these that first made me swoon and then made me envious. Poetry flows out of him. The kind of soulful phrases and aphorisms that come with being told repeatedly that you have the potential to be somebody. He gets told that often. And if not for his patented pragmatism, I think he would allow himself to be a poet.

He seems like the sort of man my mother would want me to marry. The kind whose pragmatism leads to the sort of houses she admires. My mother is a big stickler for pragmatism. My father would find him dreary and boring—which he is. My father likes to say that I do not need a man to complete me.

Regardless of what each parent may think, there is unanimity in the fact that we must start considering what is deemed marriage material. My mother was married by the time she turned twenty-three, had me at twenty-seven, and worked on and off ever since. I'm twenty, I beg for more time. Time to study, work, and edit stories in cafes, hoping for the creativity to craft my own. Art takes time. Takes inspiration. Takes experience. Art cannot be penciled into a timeline with marriage. So, it is men like the lover across from me that force women like me to want to become teachers. What's more infuriating is that it is never their deliberate fault.

I long to be capable—to be loved. To be told my hair looks like waves while being allowed the opportunity to author opuses about the ocean. For a woman, it seems the two must be mutually exclusive. This was a grounding revelation. One I wish I could unlearn. But last night, I spent the evening baking banana bread. A treat to get me through today.

I adore baking. It allows me time to clear my head while creating something tactile with my hands. I get to produce for the sole purpose of my own enjoyment. My mother always told me that my future husband would love this about me. She would say, "Most men deal with bitter remarks when their woman gets angry, yet yours would receive sweet baked goods." I never said I was angry, but I bake for myself.

Yet, as the smell of bread wafted through the kitchen last night, I could not help but imagine grubby children running around the room. I felt the sudden urge to hold these imaginary children close and love them. The amount of love I felt was terrifying. The desire to drive them to and from school, to kiss each bruise, and carry them off to bed overwhelmed me. My panacea of baking suddenly became a means to appease a family, to care for others. An act of love.

Artists cannot afford to spend that kind of love. I would have to be thrifty to save my affection. Each spare penny, hidden in a jar under the bed like an emergency fund. I would be diligent in my spending. Split the bill evenly for each student at work and not impulse buy for the children I keep at home. I would have to hold my jar tight to not let the pennies spill out if I heard them cry. My love must be worth more than a rainy day.

I could collect the coins until I had enough love, enough soul, enough energy to stay up one night and spend it all on a page. I would write till my funds ran out and sell the story in order to buy more. That was how I would sustain myself. Teach and love and care, and hopefully—maybe—create on the side until it proved worthy enough to take up more time. Maybe, I too could win an essay contest and go around the world selling stories.

I pull out the box of banana bread from my backpack and remove its plastic lid. Two thick slices, each iced with cream cheese and decorated with walnuts. I watch my boyfriend's hands slowly stop typing. I watch him first eye the bread and then me, waiting for me to push the box over and offer him the first slice like I always do. He loves my bread.

Today, I scarf down both slices. I make an effort to pick out each crumb from the box, to lick clean each finger. Today, I refuse to share. *I'm hungry.* I know that later, I'll feel sick and regret the sweet taste of bread, but for now I savor each bite. This is my bread, my labor, my love—today; I choose to feed it to myself.

I zone into work and edit at an astonishing pace. I'm motivated and diligent and provide insightful comments. I open a new tab on my computer to start compiling these critiques, my bright ideas—saving them for myself rather than handing them to the hungry.

My boyfriend, having wrapped up his term paper, reaches over to grasp my hand. I swat his touch away. I'm focused. I'm writing. I see a future in the scripts before me. A pile of stories, a choose your own adventure. I wish to take the best paragraphs and merge them all together into one. *An artist, a teacher, a mother, a lover, a free thinker, a loner, a critic, and a composer*—I want it all. But, of course, that's not how this works. And when I think long and hard about it, I have learned to be okay with that.

For now, I revel in time. My time. Full on my bread, I write. Chasing glory before it all runs out.

My boyfriend packs up his laptop, and says he'll head back to his place early. He kisses my cheek and says he will meet me later once I've finished. Today, he is feeling rather uninspired. He remarks on how odd the day makes him feel.

Yes. What an odd sort of Thursday indeed.

About the Author:

Ria Dhingra is a Sophomore at the University of Wisconsin-Madison and is pursuing a degree in English Literature. Her work has been recognized by her university as she was the recipient of the Mackaman Undergraduate Writer's Award in 2021. Her work appears in or is forthcoming in *Bridge Literary Journal*. Ria is a lover of stories, car rides, post-it notes, and trying to find beauty in the ordinary.

Notable Mentions: Short Stories

Glowworm

Tayler Bunge

Death creeps through like a glowworm. It steadies itself and readies itself on a campsite of your memory. "When we used to." "The last thing she told me."

Eventually it's late summer and she's been gone four months and the house is cleaned out and the only finality is the truth that time is abandonment in motion, and the only life that death spins is the one that catches all your wispy, sticky, ghostlike forgetfulness.

Jamie keeps bringing glowworm larvae into the house. I'll wake up to a matchbox of glowworms he's made beds for with beef jerky shreds. He's been doing it for weeks and I don't mention it.

Out here in Sardis the blue-green dusk stretches itself long. It's the constant faintness of almost-evening. I'm outside picking at this scab left by some bug, some bloodsucking little thing. I'm eating Double Stufs on a pair of pillowcases because Gobi peed on all the blankets.

Jamie walks up with Gobi at his side. "I lost his collar." He sits down and gives Gobi half a cookie.

"That's chocolate, he can't have that." I fish it out of the dog's mouth. "Where's his leash?"

"I lost it."

He looks like his mom, but only in the way that my eyes can deceive me, in the way that they can remember the eight-year-old sister I once knew with my four-year-old eyes. All blonde, all curls, all grown out to his shoulders, just like Brandy. He whips his head every five seconds to get it out of his face and every few weekends I'll ask if he wants me to cut it. He's tiny. Were kids always this tiny? In the past ten years, how many children have I seen?

"That cloud looks like a Transformer." He points.

"Oh, yeah." I don't see it.

"Are we going to the mailbox today?" Jamie asks.

"Do you have something to mail?"

"No."

"Can you take the dog inside?"

"His name is Gobi. Not *the dog*."

"Okay. Sorry."

Gobi is eleven years old, has a limp, and is covered in fatty cysts.

We're staying at Dad's house, the house that for a few years was ours as a family though I can barely find even faint memories of how two adults and two daughters lived here together.

It's white, symmetrical, compact, bears a porch with a porch swing and a roof with a chimney and a rolling Southern yard with a willow tree in the front and pecan tree in the back.

I started the cleanout last fall, a full year after Dad's funeral when I could finally make it down. The bare cabinets and half-filled moving boxes sit in silence to remind me as they were being packed, my sister Brandy was only blocks away, living and breathing. I was here and she was breathing. Her father was here, his twelve-gauge was here. We were all here and the *could haves* start to drown my stomach in acid. Each box reminds me of the biggest failure, my biggest shame, that the only person I could save was myself.

"We need more juice and pickles," Jamie tells me, standing on a chair.

"Can you get off the chair?" I ask.

At first Jamie didn't want to stay. Not in this house, not with me. His home was taped off so we couldn't go back in for his things. Most of Jamie's clothes, mostly underwear and pants, were taken as evidence.

It doesn't seem fair. Your mom is dead and now you have to live with someone you've never met, doesn't look like you, calls herself an adult. Keeps trying to cut your hair and throw away your worms.

When Jamie and I moved into Dad's house, we opened every window and door and let the mosquitos fly in and bite us as we lay on the linoleum kitchen floor, hating it together. Jamie hated the permanent mildew smell that is in every memory I have of being young. He hated that he had to wear a Dollar Store swimsuit as pants for a full week, hated that he had to wear some of my shirts.

After a few days he started breathing again. I think he saw how I knew the space, how he could hide in the weird cupboard in the living room that only fits an eight-year-old, how the place started molding around him and he around it. One night I saw him turn off a light switch from behind his back without looking, the house and its corners creeping into the memory of his muscles.

I've been on the pullout couch that's been pulled out for four months and now is just "TV Bed," Jamie calls it. He has the bedroom but most nights he ends up on TV Bed with me.

"Can we get Muddy Buddies?" he asks.

"We need a vegetable. What do you want for dinner?"

Jamie and I both do a thing where we just stop talking if the answer is *no*. I don't remember if he did that before or after we moved in together.

We head to the store in Brandy's '96 Accord. Stuck in the tape player is Side One of the *Jericho* cassette by The Band. I can't pull it out and now Jamie and I have memorized "Atlantic City". People have started waving to me out of their cars or on the street when we pass. I'm not sure if I'm *the girl with the kid whose family died* or *the girl who bagged our groceries ten years ago*. Or, for the new-in-towns, *Is that an Asian?*

We pass the small brick bungalow that used to be Dad's place, the only Chinese restaurant in a fifty-mile radius. People came to it like church in droves and flocks on Christmas and Easter to worship at the altar of the immigrant with the six table scoop 'n' serve dishing four dollar portions of chow mein with his two employees "Kevin" and "Marie"—who were given nametags that the locals could pronounce. Tuesday through Sunday, Dad would come home soaked in grease and smelling like sesame oil and fish sauce. I smell hot oil and I can hear my father coming in the front door.

Every year he barely made it, though he did make it. Most days, he had six customers, max, but those major blessings from the rare Southern Protestant saved him—helped him spread it year-round, or at least make it to the next round of debt financing.

A year after Mom left, he let it go under, his stamina burned out, his capacity for defiance obliterated by shame. His body was a shrine of what she could no longer love and even more, what she grew to hate—grease-soaked hands she grew to hate, the smell of egg drop soup she grew to hate, the monolids and bridgeless nose that I'd inherited she also grew to hate.

The restaurant went down, and he went down with the ship, falling to the creeping suspicion that she was right, that he and I were meant to tighten ourselves down to compact units of muted, invisible nothing.

Our cart is full of SpaghettiOs, chicken nuggets, frozen fish sticks, tubes of ground chuck, tomato sauce, ramen (not the cup of noodles, the rectangles), Mountain Dew, and fresh brown mushrooms. Jamie's decided he wants to collect onion skins, so we'll get a plastic produce bag and gather old skins that have fallen to the bottom of the bins, go through the same dance with the same cashier who pretends it costs one million dollars.

On one of Jamie's and my first Walmart trips, back when we didn't know how to talk to one another, I picked up a tiny Smart TV even though it felt blasphemous to stream premium television within Dad's walls. I could hear his scratchy voice: *Think of the energy bills, V.*

I know we should be watching something educational, but I've somehow gotten Jamie into *Grey's Anatomy*. It's me, Jamie, a bowl of baked fish sticks, eating on TV Bed while watching *Grey's*.

Tonight, as he eats, I'm poking through yesterday's mail from the PO Box. Energy bill. Junk. Junk. Coupons. Reminder to go to the dentist. Junk. Nothingness is the truest sign of life.

After Jamie is asleep, I wander the house and sit on the porch, listening to the cicadas and crickets, the soft wind—damp from dinner rainfall. The hammock Jamie loves, stretching from a hook Dad drilled in the roof out toward the giant willow, is in a slight sway. A ghost in repose.

Nighttime feels like a second new dimension of the same

day. In the day I shrink myself tightly the way Dad and I would tuck ourselves into the corners of this town, holding ourselves still, never knowing how to act or what to say when we were being watched. Just trying to let time pass us by. At night I unravel.

On nights like this after Mom left, Dad and I would lay on the roof. He would tell me the stars were glowworm webs, the willow branches were constellations, and that astronomers look at the world wrong—upside down and inside out. We'd both lay there, both yearning to not know what we already knew, that Mom would never return.

One day I'll take Jamie up there but he's not ready. He'll think he's been putting tiny planets into matchboxes, little larvae from the sky, and I don't think his heart could take it.

Back inside I lay down beside Jamie and he wraps his legs around mine. I hold him tighter. A stretch of moonlight streaks his face, the soft eyelids, the drooling mouth. He took the best of Brandy in the way she took the best of Mom—the way Mom couldn't replicate with me.

His tiny head and lion's mane have more secrets buried in memories than I'll ever know, more than a detective or a social worker might be able to find. The fact that he carries around with him the horrors that we, taller and bigger and older, are struggling to comprehend, the horrors that are weakening our stomachs, is unbearable to think of for too long.

I am stricken in this moment by the hope that possibly, maybe, grief can pass him by. How do you build a soul at sea? He doesn't even know how to spell *grief*. Maybe I can hold onto his sorrow for him, maybe I can let it ooze into the house and let it go for the both of us. Maybe we can just lay for now, Jamie and I, the two mourners, the little orphans holding each other in a matchbox.

One morning I drop Jamie off at his friend Marko's. Marko lives around the corner from my dad's, within walking distance, but I drive him.

Jamie brings with him a Ziploc bag of Oreos and a stick that he's chewing on.

"How long am I here today?" he asks.

"How long do you want to be?"

"Not very long."

"Okay. An hour."

"Okay."

I'm turning him into an agoraphobe. An agoraphobe who makes onion beds and watches soap operas.

I'm heading to town where I have a meeting with the Detective and the Social Worker, the start of a good joke. Before I get there, I veer off and drive by the house, Brandy's house, where her dad's broken trailer in the backyard has been hauled away but left a rectangle patch of brown death beneath it.

Once the estate is settled, they'll fix it up and try to sell it, or raze it entirely because those stains are deep, but until then the house lives as a mausoleum of *empty* and *gone*. The longer it sits the longer the stains will blur and the brown grass will grow over, the air will breeze itself anew, the ghosts living in concentration where love once was and death now reigns will saturate themselves deep into the earth. Until then it sits much like Jamie and me, not sure what we're waiting for anymore, the sneaking suspicion creeping on us that if *transition period* lasts long enough it just becomes *living*.

In the dark of my closed eyelids, I suddenly see Brandy on the front porch, Brandy as I last remember knowing her. It's us at five and nine, making a funeral procession of our stuffed animals. I see her at sixteen, leaving town. I see her at eighteen, coming back with a black eye and a belly scar. I see her at twenty-three, moving back in with her father and her new infant son.

I see a dark secret sitting in the silence of all that love—all that love and all those secrets, the performance of a love that might've meant nothing in a house that curled around its own puppet show. I see the silhouettes dancing on the walls against the glow of a television, the one that was still on when his grandfather let off nine rounds in April.

And there, suddenly, is my mother who left this town like Brandy tried to, pulled back by children and men. If Mom had taken Brandy, we wouldn't be here. If I had taken Brandy, we wouldn't be here. All the chances.

Finally, I drift back, parking in the alley that the bar shares with the grocery store. Today I'm with Jeremy the Detective and Kaley the Social Worker.

The detective and I went to middle school together, the social worker is from Kentucky. Proximity and routine haven't brought us closer, but I might consider them friends. Consider them something. I'd invite them to my funeral.

The three of us gather at the bar, the one next to the post office. We ditched the police station a few weeks back because they're trying to make it feel less like what it is—just disappointing emptiness, telling me they need me to stay for another two weeks. The town doesn't have a foster care system and outside of Sardis, anything could happen to the forty-two-pound freckled kid with a long, blonde lion's mane.

A few moments of niceties, we sit down with our beers, and I watch Jeremy and Kaley trying to make sense of my face, trying to find answers.

"So we've made some progress," Jeremy tells me.

"Oh?"

"We found your mom," Kaley finally says.

It drops into the air like an iceberg—a shatter, but not all at once, so vast in size that from the naked eye it moves in slow motion.

"When?" I ask, the way you ask the wrong question after hearing a gathering of four words you'd never thought you'd hear.

"She's in California. She has a partner—she changed her name. They're married."

It drops into the room like a cobweb—a slight flutter, a barely-there glow, so stringy and sticky. It sways and grabs the air but with a grip so light it can't catch on.

"Oh."

"She's being called in as a witness once the trial starts. But she has expressed interest in taking over as Jamie's guardian."

Suddenly I'm swimming in rage. The way she can pick and choose the life she wants, the life she doesn't. The way some things want you and the way some things don't.

"Oh."

"I don't know how much longer you wanted to stay," he says. "Obviously, we can assume you'll be called in as a witness, too. You could file a petition to try for custody under the grounds of the routine he's built with you—"

"No, I have to get back."

"Nothing's definite," Kaley offers.

"Does she want him?" I ask. What I mean is, *Like she didn't want me?*

"She has a home and a farm in northern California—good schools, and financially she seems like a strong support system."

For the next bit there's the silence of three people who don't know one another well enough to do much more than give sad looks. They were bracing for this.

As they move on, onto the search for Jamie's father that won't yield anything, I briefly catch the scent of fried rice on the old, burnt wok. I hear a sizzle and my name over boiling broth. I realize I will, someday, lose Jamie. I've been adjusting for so long to having him around that it never occurred to me I might lose him.

It'll just be us again, Dad—the last ones standing, the ones she left behind. Empty buildings, empty hands. One more thing she gets to take with her, one more time she gets to leave us in this town as I stand holding boxes of the dead, unattached and in stillness and pretending the world is upside down.

On the way back home the tape rewinds itself and starts playing again. I park in front of Marko's and watch Jamie from the car as he lets Marko kill ants with a hammer. I was told when it happened Jamie laid by his mother for thirteen hours until Brandy's coworker showed up looking for her. He laid there silently—I was told he laid there until morning with two bodies spilling out onto the carpet—that he didn't scream when the police arrived.

He's just a shadow now, he creeps in and out of rooms and stays travel-sized, sinking his toes into the weeds and bringing the outside inside to build himself a fortress that he can smell, touch, and trust, long abandoned by the naïve and foolish notion that love is steadfast and invisible. Maybe it is easier to lose that notion early.

I watch him now as I hold a new secret. *Someone is coming for you*. *Someone wants you*. This liminal space of lost and alone, you have an escape—you can make it out. Is that exciting? Is that good?

Later that night we go to the bakery which is really just a laundromat that's also a convenience store that sells pastries. Jamie and I get two chocolate donuts and I get a coffee that tastes reheated from the day before and we sit at the booth in the window, both scraping frosting with our plastic butter knives to suck on like a popsicle.

The sun sets and I watch his tiny fingers poke holes in the dough, chocolate staining his lips. He is wanted by her; he doesn't know it yet. It's a holy space to bear witness to. I sat at this booth every day after school, sometimes with Brandy, sometimes alone, pretending I also lived in that space.

But back then I didn't realize I was pretending; I didn't realize the yearning was hope or the hope was nostalgia, or the nostalgia was resentment. I didn't realize anything but the scene that replayed in my tiny head—the scene when they find her and she admits she's been searching for me all along, she's spent so long searching for me, and that I was wanted every moment in between.

I crept in and out of that moment, laying by it silently—not screaming. Life spilling out. After tragedy, she wants him. She's found him. Maybe Dad and I weren't tragic enough. Maybe I wasn't tragic enough. Maybe I hadn't lost enough because the only thing I'd lost was her.

I want to tell him he's lucky, I know that he's not. He's

somehow lost everything yet now holds the only thing I ever wanted. It's a pity to my sense of humor that my grief sleeps at night with my envy.

I let the stale coffee burn my tongue as I swallow down the shameful thought.

I am holding onto this moment. I am saving it for now. I will probably forget it someday, the way we probably forget most things we want to hold onto, and our phantom bodies hold onto so many of the things we don't need.

For now, though, it is Jamie and me and we are traveling together in the car, we are traveling and listening to the tape that's been stuck longer than my sister has been dead. If it stays put, we can hold time where it's at, which is there and with her in some still, spinning universe.

The sun is setting and blinding my eyes—we have to go to Walmart because I want to buy him a tent. I have no money but I'm going to buy him a tent. There'll be tents where he's going but not a tent that we've been in together.

It was just last April that I was called by the detective to come down to the coroner, because I'm next of kin or closest living relative, to identify Brandy, and collect the kid I've never met. The next day I'm on a plane and the next week Jamie and I are at my dad's house, both of us not recognizing ourselves there. Both of us reckoning with loss on different magnitudes but somehow a loss of the same, an abandonment and betrayal of same. His loss is soaked in trauma and his shadow itself is quieter than most shadows I've met.

We met at the police station where he was wearing clothes donated by some of the locals. Word had traveled fast. I crouched down but he didn't make eye contact.

"Jamie, this is Victoria. She's your mother's sister," Kaley told him.

"Hi," I said.

"I'll come back and check in on him tomorrow morning?" Jeremy the Detective asked.

"That works," I said, horrified. *You are leaving this living creature with me.*

I decided to do for Jamie what my father did for me—stay, and not reckon with the largeness of his tragedy. It felt like a second chance to love my sister, to know this child—a second chance to atone for abandoning this town.

Kaley calls me to tell me she's coming by the house. She's never done that before. I don't even know that she knows where we live. Jamie is at Marko's and I'm clipping my toenails, on hold with the water company as I rehearse my story about not receiving last month's bill.

She pulls up and I let her in. Kaley stands today in the middle of the kitchen, and I feel a pang in my neck like I might get in trouble for not telling my dad a guest is coming. For the first time I notice her eyes are green.

"This is your dad's place?"

"Yeah."

"Are these matches?" Kaley asks, pointing at the seven boxes lined up in a row like dominos on the counter.

"We've been cleaning out the drawers."

We go outside into the backyard where Jamie has been building a canopy of willow tree strands, tying them together and hanging them from the branches of the pecan tree. In their spindly, dangly flow they look like hanging webs. They look like hanging nooses. Gobi follows me, hobbling along and panting.

"Oh, you got trouble," she points at the silky glowworm nests that coat the trunk and branches.

"Glowworms. We've always had them."

"Those are webworms," Kaley says, crouching down.

"The larvae?"

"They're webworms. Those huge webs start coming out this time of year." She pokes at one with a stick. "They usually go after dead trees. See them, they clump up like this."

"Oh."

Webworms. I thought they were dying stars.

We are both doing a yogi squat at the base of the tree. Gobi breathes hot air into our faces. Kaley's not here to talk about pecan trees. I see the piece of paper she has in her hand. She's holding it the way you hold bad news.

"Do you want a beer?" I ask, standing up.

"Do you have to pick him up?"

"Not for a while."

In the kitchen we both stand across from one another, leaning up against separate parts of the counter, each nursing one of the two Miller Lites I had in the fridge.

"Your mom will be in town next month," she says, finally.

I do that thing where I don't answer. I don't answer and I want it to end.

"She's started the process to be Jamie's formal guardian. She'll obviously have to meet with him, but I have to warn you they give precedence to the grandparents," is what's said. I don't know who says it, Kaley, or the puppeteer of this cruel irony.

"That makes sense."

We both take shallow breaths with what's left of the air between us.

"Between you and me—" she starts.

"Don't." I stop her. *It's better for her.* "It's better for him."

"He'll have a good home. And you can visit. That's easy to set up."

"It makes more sense."

Neither of us believes any of this, but the truth has nothing to hold onto anymore, not in here, not in the remains of this empty tomb.

This town makes caskets of us all. We're just wisps in here, wispy empties trying to form around the corners, letting all that we can't bear any longer sweep itself out the door and get caught up in the limbs of the trees and stars.

Let it go, I'm telling myself, and I look at Kaley and know she heard it. A translation of my mind to hers sparks itself and she pulls me close in the kindest embrace I've had in this house, trying to quiet the moment as Gobi drools on our feet.

It's Monday night and Jamie has decided he wants a rotisserie chicken, so I indulge him. When everything is ending you save every moment, it is a privilege to be conscious of the last looks you have with someone. It is a privilege to know when it ends. It is something he never got with Brandy. It is something I never got with my mother. With Jamie I am now trying to watch it all. I want to see his feet, his sneezes, his whiplash head jerk to get the hair from his eyes. Our days are numbered.

I try to explain it to him. I try to explain it to him the way no one did for me. I squeeze my eyes shut as we sit on the porch, eating white meat with our greasy fingertips.

"I'll visit you a lot," I say.

"Every Christmas?"

"Is that when you want me to visit?"

"Can you live with us?"

"No. I have to go back home."

"To New York?"

"Yeah. But you'll like California. It's sunny all the time. Your grandma lives on an almond farm."

"Does she know me?" he asks.

They've never met. I stare at his face and I see Brandy—she pours out of his eyes and tiny mouth, the sister I knew to mourn stuffed dogs and cry out at night for her mother.

Brandy was a mother, I realize suddenly. This is her child. This is a child and she is a mother and here I am, sailing souls from mothers to mothers, affirming a kind of *want* that left me but that he might get to keep. Let him keep it.

I watch him dig a hole in the dirt with a chicken bone.

"She loves you," I say to the both of us.

I want him to have everything. She is part of that. I will never lose like he has lost. She is part of that.

It's Friday night, a week after Kaley's visit, and Jamie and I are laying on the grass, itchy, staring up through the gaps in the willow tree. He was afraid to get on the roof. Our bodies are sticking halfway out of the tent, halfway sprawled on the picnic blanket. Gobi is at Jamie's feet. I wonder if Mom won't want the dog or if she has a better tent.

We're eating Muddy Buddies and drinking Mountain Dew. The air is chilly but with the windless early evening, it doesn't feel cold, just clean. The symphony of birds and bugs is a curtain of sound above and around us, pocketing us in the safety that every moment might be self-sustaining. Sound, air, ground, stars. Everything at once—it is everything because it is nothing at all. It is the existence and the moments and the emptiness of life ongoing.

I hear him start to hum.

Maybe everything that dies someday comes back.

I start to laugh at the eight-year-old beside me as I remember how much I loved my sister. I remember how she loved our mother and how much she loved her father and how much she loved the sounds the crickets made and hated this tired, tiny town. I laugh at the boy beside me who I likely will never see again, and I laugh at the home we made together out of these withering things around us.

He and I hold ourselves together in a bundle a few seconds longer, tightening our grip on all that we can hear and touch, knowing we'll eventually spill out in time, knowing we'll break open and our hearts will burst. It threatens to at every moment. But not yet.

About the Author:

Tayler Hanxi Bunge is a queer, adopted Chinese-American writer with work that's appeared or is forthcoming in *McSweeney's, Tenderness Lit, CNMN Mag, Ghost City Review, Vagabond City Lit*, and others. She lives in Los Angeles and Philly.

What It Means to Be Free

Bono Sigudu

I was awakened by the gravity of tension and flickering notes on the red table that had my grandmother's face engraved on it, where my mother hosted her gambling sessions. There was always a toddler oozing with mucus and a hanging diaper, latched on to a mother's waist, another one crawling to get to the cards and disrupt the game, while a woman's grocery money, that her husband had sent her from the mines, ping-ponged on the table while her sanity hung by a loose thread. Tension was followed by laughter until a fight broke out because Mutshekwa from the next village kept on stashing coins into the bundle of plastic she'd hid underneath her tshiluvhelo when everyone was watching baby Naki dance to Brenda Fassie's "Weekend Special."

Mma was a turbulent host. She would bring her guests—who she called money-making machines—traditional beer made purely from sorghum, and depending on her mood and the person she was serving, she'd add some special ingredient. Sometimes the secret ingredient was sugar, choosing a more alcoholic calabash, saliva, or phlegm—especially if the participant was Rachel, who she secretly hated for snatching her first love during the reed dance period of her youth; or, if it was a new village woman that came to her yard wearing fabric too delicate to be hers.

I walked to the corner where my mates were skipping rope in their uniforms.

"Pretty, if you make me lose this game, you will understand why my name means *fear her*!" Muofhe shouted from across the table to her teammate Pretty, who was sweating under the headwrap she'd tied on her head. Muofhe had invested One Rand, with hopes of getting Five Rands so she could buy herself a matching munwenda set and Christmas clothes for her children.

Muofhe was building a nine. Nine was a number easy to overlook in Casino. Most people were fascinated by ten, the ultimate power player, but she was not. She was convinced that with her two nine cards–a heart and a club–she would win, calculating that one nine card was already on the deck that my mother won after taking out the ten she had built. One nine was left, which was not in her hands, but her prayer was that it was in Pretty's hands.

My mother was building a ten again, this time with full assurance that she was the only one who had the last ten, the powerful diamond ten–worth two points, but worth nothing if not used properly. Muofhe's heart rejoiced at what she thought would soon be my mother's downfall.

It was my mother's turn; her eyebrows tensed, signalling a potential failure. She had two cards left: a ten that she was building towards and an anonymous one, most likely an Ace. My mother looked at her teammate, mouthed a faint "I'm sorry," then vomited her dirty laughter of victory. She had a nine of spades—almost a clean sweep. No one had expected her to have it seeing that she was very nonchalant about the manufacturing behind it. She won. Muofhe tossed her cards to the ground in anger and stormed out, blowing the red loamy soil to the direction of my mother with her feet.

"Hulisani," Mma called me. "Come see how losers behave." She laughed, clapping her hands, and increased the volume on her radio. I was already there, watching everything but she had not noticed me in my school uniform.

That mechanism of being a blurred filter on her background described our relationship. She thought of me only after the wins and losses; never the in-betweens, never a *How are you, you look sad, tell me what happened*? Our relationship was that of a single middle-aged woman and a teenager who happened to end up staying together in one house. The only thing that convinced me that indeed she was my mother and I was not adopted was the bridge of my nose that resembled hers. That was the only thing that aligned us, along with our love for the steaming pot of yellow porridge, the brewed ginger drink, and the corn being burnt over the fire. I was a background in her imagination, a dim dwindling light of no significance, like the extras in a soapie–no one notices them nor remembers how their faces look–they are just there.

I announced my departure to school to the crowd of glistening faces. Mma nodded. Going to school was the one activity we were forced to do to keep us from roaming the streets like wild dogs. The Security Forces scouted around our classrooms and dysfunctional soccer fields, regularly, eyeing any possible future freedom fighters that might be propagated from the group of Bantu schoolchildren. For people that sought to maintain a system of separation from us, they were always within our space–not the other way round. They were obsessed with us in a scary way. To them, we were weapons that had to be guarded and destroyed.

The previous week, they'd dragged Joshua in his tattered

white shirt and khaki shorts, saying the poster he drew for a project defied the laws of South Africa. Mrs. Goodness had asked us to make a dream poster of where we saw ourselves in five years; she was now in hot water with the risk of losing her teaching license.

"This–*k-word*–drew a provoking poster and he has to be punished for it. Who taught him to write "WE WILL SET OURSELVES FREE?" Which curriculum is this?"

The class listened to the barking voice, and an AK-47 hitting the table for emphasis, all the way from the staffroom. Principal Mudi spitting apologies in a breaking voice. He knew what could happen to educators that taught about anything beyond how to draw caterpillars and fruits, sing hymns, and plough vegetables in the backyard. That was how the government wanted it–we had to, at our maximum capacity and talent, end up being teachers, mid-wives, or policemen. It was strange, we thought that since Venda was now an independent state, we would see less of the faces of those who were always ready to kill us. We'd all heard whispers about the schoolchildren that were killed in Soweto in 1978. We knew we were next.

My classmates were organising a protest for the 12th of September at Thohoyandou Stadium. There was going to be a celebration for the anniversary of Venda being an independent state, hosted by *Honourable* Gota, the President of the Republic of Venda, and the white people that oversaw him. All decisions passed through the white people in Louis Trichardt. The President and his cabinet were puppets being made to feel as though they were in power, but they were simply the faces indirectly campaigning for Apartheid.

My dream poster was a compilation of books I fiercely

loved, words I'd wished I'd written, a Black girl's picture I found in *Drum* magazine. She had a blooming afro, smiling while wearing a mustard-yellow dress that was probably made just for her. She was the version I wished I was–happily being, without pummelling into the challenges of being Black and a woman; she was eyeing an invisible horizon, which meant freedom to me. Freedom from the world, freedom from self-loathing. On the upper left corner was a quote from Audre Lorde's poem, *The Litany of* Survival: "So it is better to speak, knowing we were never meant to survive." I did not submit it to Mrs. Goodness.

My mother built everything she has from the ground up. Her house, her thriving business hosting a popular card spot, and all the glass kitchenware. The plate with purple flower petals was her favourite. She said it reminded her of the widening distance between where she came from and where she was now. No one was allowed to eat from it, let alone touch it. My father left for Jo'burg when she was pregnant to seek a job in the mines or railways,any place where they were using Black cheap labour. That was seventeen years ago. I have yet to see the person representing the other half of the chromosomes that formed me.

Gossipers said that he got there and fell in love with a Jozi woman who he probably ended up marrying. When fights broke out during my mother's Casino sessions, some women hurled insults at my mother, saying things like, "Don't talk to me like that, Mavis. My husband didn't leave me for a Jozi woman," and, "At least my husband still sends me money that he makes in the mines." My mother fell into attack mode after the insults, reminding them that they did not know what was happening beyond the Venda borders, that their husbands were probably basking in a woman's warmth.

The protest posters were secretly exchanged as covers for *vetkoeks* and boiled corn in the streets. The police were too occupied by the big things to notice the small ones: that the number of schoolchildren in the classes was thinning, that some pupils were made to remain in class in order to deviate their attention, that some of the teachers who were in the classrooms were not the licensed ones but merely a façade for the ones who were actively assisting in organising the protest.

Everyone who chooses to go to a protest sheds off their skin before they leave—they know that being alive is a privilege they may not come back home with. Even the ones not protesting, the ones randomly roaming the streets or going about their lives, know that they may catch a bullet, that their eyes could be blinded by teargas, that their wombs may bleed when they see their children's blood reddening the streets. Card games stopped, only the thickness of grief engulfed the air. That is the way of the police—they don't care who they shoot, whether it's a nine-month-old infant bruising its kneecaps while crawling, or a fifty-year-old woman carrying firewood on top of her head–it didn't matter, as long as the bullets penetrate someone whose skin is dark enough to be tar, or whose hair coiled at the ends.

I did not consider myself a freedom fighter per se, but knew that in order to get the life I wanted, I had to do something, and not just sit around the yard watching women break off each other's braids over coins and clothes. The backyard was where

I allowed people to host meetings. We would sit in a circle and pretend to be playing ndode, throwing stones in the air while discussing our plan. My mother did not know, and could not know.

"As soon as the cabinet stands on the stage, we enter holding our placards and start chanting. The Police will be ready to shoot, so the best way to protect ourselves from the intensity of the bullets is to put on two hardened cow skins inside our uniform. Mma Tshedza is handing them out for free. Hopefully, the bullets will not penetrate them,"Madzanga, the student leader whispered. He didn't know the speed of the bullet, and neither did we, but we trusted that if it was aimed at the heart we would survive. None of us spoke about the likelihood of the bullet tearing our legs, piercing the scalp, the possibility of haemorrhaging to death.

"The protest is tomorrow. We know the procedure. Comrades, be ready for anything." He paused. "Including death. We might not all come back alive, but such is the sacrifice for being Black. Our blood waters the dusty streets."

I wasn't sure if I was ready to sacrifice myself for something that would never be solved.

That evening, the steaming pot of porridge rumbled between my mother and I in the cooking hut.

She added maize to three-legged pot and continued in her stirring and swirling motion. Making porridge was an art of patience and concentration. There was something about the silence and the fire that forced a communication between us, with no questions asked, my mother started peeling the folds of her crusty heart off.

"You know, I never loved your father. He was just there

the one time when I thought I needed a man's touch. Even the marriage was a farce. I was groomed by a blanket and swerved through the dusty roads to come to this village. I am happy that he never came back. That was always my prayer. These women that you see me love and loathe are what make me happy."

I listened attentively, waiting to hear the source of her sudden vulnerability. Did she suddenly want to kindle a relationship with her only daughter, could she feel that I was on the death row, waiting to die like the students of Soweto? She passed me her favourite plate, told me I was allowed to use it that one time only, then filled it with porridge and kale.

"I wanted more for myself too, like you. When I was a child playing in the mud, we would hear aeroplanes roaring in the air. That was when I decided I wanted to fly one. I went to school till standard two. My parents could not afford to pay for me to be taught how to draw butterflies. That is when I started following my mother like a shadow when she went to play card games with the women in her village. I did not understand what my fate would be then, or what she derived from the long hours exchanging gossip there, but it was better than sulking about her husband who had been sucked away by the gold mines. No one knows what happens to the men when they get to the city of gold, no one can tell us. Some of them just disappeared, most times not to Jozi women but to the white man. My father was one of them. We thought he would come back, at least during holidays and funerals of close family members, but he never came. One day, a cousin brought us the news that he was one of the dead in the Sharpeville Massacre. We didn't know where he was buried, what the color of his coffin was, or even how he looked in his final years. My mother cried herself to death."

We lined up in four rows, our backs facing each other, forming a square, unable to see each other's faces and the anticipation of danger that was engraved in our pupils. We were at the centre of the stadium, the area closest to the eye of a cyclone—where calamity happens. It has been said that seconds before one dies, their life flashes before them. The stadium went silent, a brief calm before the storm. The tissue of my heart ready to break loose at any given moment. It seemed easier to prepare for death than a life full of wounds.

I was ready to say goodbye to the relationship my mother and I had never had, the legacy of playing cards that I was supposed to pass on to my children, the fabric and texture of joy like the woman in my dream poster. President Gota stood with his mouth agape, reading the posters we held up high. One read *King Makhado is turning in his grave!*, another *We want to be free!* My poster read: *I want to be me*.

About the Author:

Bono Sigudu is a South African writer, fourth-year medical student at the University of Pretoria, and spoken word poet. She is twenty-years-old and writes to set her mind free. *Isele* is her debut publication.

GMO

Desmond Peeples

Juno's talent for rage-naps had always been impressive. Like her mother, she disciplined those who crossed her by showing the ultimate control: opting out.

This nap was particularly bitter. Bored of playing Monopoly yet again, Juno had asked her mother politely if she could run upstairs to grab Life. By then Delilah had made it clear more than several times, as if the air-raid sirens and the bullhorn drivebys weren't enough, that there would be no going upstairs until the city said—so she had repeated the fact. Maybe a bit snappishly. Juno had replied by punching two holes into a stack of Monopoly money, stringing an old shoelace through them, and wearing the thing as a nightmask. And Delilah wasn't about to blame her. They'd been officially "hunkered down" in the basement since the first air raid—a week? Almost two? Maybe she'd ask Juno to measure her leg hairs.

From her spot by the washing machine, Delilah glanced between her sleeping daughter and the pages of *Architectural Digest*. Aware that her overhead light might fail again that night, she had to use this alone time to her advantage.

"I heard all that, you know."

But she never really had alone time. The voice, tinny and hollow, pursued Delilah from a rusted pipe in the wall beside her head.

"If she wants a game," said the voice, *"try Fuck, Marry, Kill. Ever played that?"*

Delilah pursed her lips. But elsewhere her muscles relaxed; secretly, she was relieved to hear her neighbor again. She leaned toward the pipe. "Not till she gets braces," said Delilah. "Nice try, though."

"Now, now—just try it. I'll start you off: the mailman, the chief of police, or the mayor."

"They're probably already dead."

"Suit yourself… Well, are you still reading last month's Architectural Digest*? I'm in the middle of 'After the White House: A Tour of the New Presidential Mansions'. Check page twenty-six when you get a chance—the President of California has a nice lamp. The one in some ballroom, next to a stuffy baby grand. I bet it'd look perfect next to your washing machine."*

Delilah's house was connected to her neighbor's thanks to some crummy old pipes running between their basements. Together they were the neighborhood's only black households, but Delilah's neighbor didn't admit to caring about that the way Delilah did. In the ten years since moving in, Delilah had never once seen her neighbor outside the house. She knew her as a silhouette behind kitchen curtains, and the occasional blare of game shows, the news, HBO through an open window. But they talked through the basement pipes regularly.

Delilah's neighbor lived alone. Her husband was in a cigar box on her mantle, and her children never called. More often than not, Delilah could count on hearing her whenever she was in the basement. She liked to send ghostly moans crackling through the pipes until Delilah replied with an "I hope you're feeling well today," or a sudden "Boo!" When Delilah had time, her neighbor liked to cluck over headlines and celebrity gossip, but her favorite subject was Delilah's life. She loved chewing on Delilah's stories and spitting out unruly advice. And Delilah loved hearing it, whether or not it was wise. Sometimes, when Juno was with her white family for the week, Delilah would spend hours in the basement, smoking cigarettes and chattering with her neighbor late into the night.

Delilah considered herself lucky, at least when it came to home. The whitest state in the Union, and she had landed right next to another black woman. One she could talk to, no less. When she left New York years ago, her mother had warned of despair and stir-craziness, told Delilah any black folks she'd meet in Vermont would be lawn jockeys. She wasn't wrong by much, but she was wrong, and so were all the smiling white folks here who loved saying as much to Delilah's face, laughing it off like crows. As if "some" were no better than "none." As if "nobody" felt as warm as "somebody," "anybody."

Another interruption came between Delilah and her magazine. It wheedled vaguely at her from across the room, an exoskeleton of a voice—the radio. Streaming from Delilah's phone in the dirt by Juno's head. Juno was still stretched out on her blankets, Monopoly money over her eyes.

"...from UVM's bioengineering program, talking with us about today's emergency GMO bill and the potential benefits, as well as some concerning risks it brings."

"Remember when the scariest GMOs were just carrots and peas, Jane?"

"I do, Tom, and I still won't touch the stuff."

"And how about people, then, Jane? You never know who's a GMO these days unless they—well, snap."

"Of course you can't avoid them, Tom, and you shouldn't—

millions of GMOs lead perfectly happy, productive, stable lives. It's true we're not as exposed to them in Vermont as folks in New York or Texas, but we can't let the horror stories turn us into bad neighbors."

"Well said, Jane—you know, a close friend of mine is actually a GMO, and you'd never know it if he didn't tell you. Folks who are nervous about this coming GMO wave should remember there are already GMO Vermonters all across the state, and they're contributing to our communities just like anyone else. In fact, we'd love to hear what GMO Vermonters have to say about this emergency bill, or just about the GMO experience here. If you have something to share with Vermont National Radio give us a call at 1-800-639-2211, that's 1-800-639-2211."

"Good thinking—don't be shy out there folks, we welcome your perspectives. You know, Tom, Dr. Carol mentioned that some lawmakers want to follow up today's bill with one to implement an ID system like there is in Texas. Now that's a sore subject for—"

An otherworldly wailing drowned out the radio. Air raid sirens. A cottony thunder of bombs buffeted the house from somewhere across the city, and Delilah watched Juno's lips for a slip-up, a grimace—nada. Juno had stopped letting the ruckus disturb her a few days ago, after her dad skipped town without her.

Delilah's skull roared with the spotless attitude of her ex-husband's Silverado. He had called to check in while packing it with his wife, toddler and home essentials, advising Delilah to let him know when she and Juno were somewhere safe. She could have chewed him out, just for Juno's sake, but she knew it was for the best. And she liked to think Juno knew it, too. Pale as she'd come out, Juno had always had more of her mother in her.

In time the sirens petered out, breaking back down into radio jabber.

"...the Executive Council, no civilians will be allowed to enter Burlington until further notice. And folks, don't forget to come by the Montpelier Farmers Market if you're hungry, or if you just need some company."

"That's right, Jane, it's potluck breakfast and lunch every Wednesday and Saturday, and free care bundles are—"

Bubbly xylophone tones cut off the radio.

"Mama!" Juno was up, bounding across floor with the phone in hand. "It's Aunt Diana."

Delilah's eyes drifted up from her magazine, and she suppressed a sigh as she reached out for the phone. "Hello?"

"Delilah—is this Delilah?"

"Yes, Diana."

"Oh, I— ...sometimes Juno sounds just like you. Have you left Burlington yet?"

"The buses still haven't come to my neighborhood."

The phone filled with Diana's breathy, oxygenated silence, and Delilah felt a growing thickness in her lungs, new layers of chemical residue from nights spent burning magazines and underwear.

"I know that's not true, Del. They've been showing drone footage on the news every night. Hell, I saw your house just yesterday, people lining up on your street to get into a bus. What do I need to do to help you? The bombs aren't gonna stop."

There it was again. Diana had a cross to bear. She was a copycat of course, riding their mother's coattails as always, but Diana bore all that certainty with too much ease, as if she were born with it instead of pure flesh and blood. That was what their curse mother liked to say—they were born with it. The truth that lives underneath us, the fly in America's soup. But Delilah didn't even like soup.

"Have you tried having sex with the president?"

"Very funny, Delilah. You need to get out of that house."

"No, no—we've got guests coming."

"What? Stop that—be real with me for half a second."

Delilah hesitated as her ears began to ring. The sound crackled faintly, like papers being shuffled—she began to make out her neighbor's whisper eking from the pipes.

"Hang up. Hang up, Delilah, that sister of yours is too uppity. What does she think, you gonna run back to Queens and raise your girl in her broom closet? We're at war. Does she think you're about to shack up with your white friends in Stowe? So they can pat themselves on the back, call CPS on you for not straightening Juno's hair? Hang up. We'll figure this one out for ourselves. And shut off that radio too. It'll make Juno as soft as her father."

Delilah hung up on her sister, and, before the radio could fade back in, she turned off the phone and laid it in the dirt beside her.

"So guests, huh?" her neighbor whispered. *"Gonna throw a party for the neighborhood? Good idea. Now there's no excuse not to whip that basement of yours into shape."*

"Shh," said Delilah.

She looked to Juno. Back in her corner, she was hunched over a mess of Monopoly money, her eyes hard and nitpicky as she tore and folded a blue bill into an origami person. Delilah doubted Juno would ever be as soft as her dad. But half of her was always hidden from Delilah, just as the other half hid from her dad. Delilah had never been sure how to make sense of that.

"Come over here, Negroni," she teased. "Let's pick some new colors for the walls. Nothing wrong with sprucing things up."

Summer in Vermont could make up for any shortcoming. When Delilah first visited with her family as a teenager, she knew she would need the place. Her parents spent the trip hating it, worrying at the windows of their rental cabin over bears and buck-toothed home invaders. Her sister dismissed the whole state before they even booked their stay, warning the family they'd be put in a zoo if they went out in public. And they did attract stares on the village green, and they did see Confederate flags billowing from passing pickup trucks, and they did not see another black family in the village or at the lake. But Delilah had seen worse in far uglier surroundings. What she had never experienced before, and what she would chase forevermore, was calm. A moment away from somebody's plans and opinions. Roads that climbed away from town into nowheresville, the otherworldly destination that kids back home avoided like homework. Well it was good enough for Delilah. There was music in the mountains, and the lyrics never sucked. When you heard a gun going off, you didn't assume it was ruining someone's day. You could drive miles and miles, all damn night, without seeing a cop. And if you really just *had* to do something, there was, Delilah discovered, the city of Burlington. No bigger than a breadbox, if you asked Delilah's mother, but Delilah often daydreamed of cutting down on bread.

After that first taste of Vermont, Delilah spent most summers working at a summer camp on Lake Champlain, where every night she watched the sky burn until it, the lake, and all the mountains melted together —poof, gone.

When she enrolled at UVM she was hardly the only Black student there, and the city opened up to her with every color and attitude she could imagine. She could dance herself sick with someone different every night and at dawn meet tomorrow's victim on the beach. One night outside a Church Street bar, she watched a drifter stroll up to some kid staring at his phone and stab him in the neck. A mighty iron bolt ran through her spirit, pinned it to the earth.

In time Delilah's father died, and the money he left her to spite his wife went toward a two-bedroom bungalow downtown with the medical student she'd met and kept. A blue-eyed, blond white man, handsome, and relatively nice. He seemed easy to please at first, but by the time Juno could talk Delilah must have worn out her welcome. All of the sudden her jokes weren't funny, she watched too much TV, she didn't scramble eggs right. So he moved across town, and they began trading Juno back and forth while her father tried again with a summery yoga instructor and herbalist. Delilah's mother said it was because with Juno he could still be with a piece of Delilah, except the piece got to look white.

"Ugh—blue? We don't play tennis, Juno." Delilah's index finger trailed down a crack in the wall like it would a distant lover's spine. "I was thinking a nice red."

"I don't really like red."

"Oh, sweetie, don't say that... Red is one of the most beautiful colors out there."

"It reminds me of blood, though."

"Blood isn't so bad. It's salty. You like salt. And you wouldn't have been born if I couldn't bleed."

An image gurgled up in Delilah's mind: syrupy blood dripping from the ceiling to curtain the walls, and her body alone, engorged on the floor. She shut her eyes and turned away from the wall, and when she shook them open Juno was gone.

She had wandered over to the pile of crumbled cinderblocks and bricks by her corner.

"What could we put over here, Mama?"

"Where?" Delilah kept her eyes on the wall, pretending she hadn't noticed.

"Right here. The pile—maybe we can clean it up. And put a pretty table there, or some big plants."

"Oh, plants—yeah... We'd have our own little mountain."

Delilah turned to scan the basement; she landed on last year's snow tires, leaned up in a row against the opposite wall. She advanced on them, and while Juno looked on she rolled them one by one toward the stone pile. She stacked three on top of each other just beside the pile, and the fourth she balanced upright on top.

"There." She smiled wide at Juno. "A tree. Just until we can get the real things."

"What we need is a Persian rug. A super ugly one."

Delilah and Juno faced each other crisscross-applesauce on the bare floor. Between them was a burning heap of *Home Living* and *Bon Appétit*.

"Daddy has a Persian rug."

"Do you think he left it here?"

"...Has he texted you?"

"I don't think so. He might have lost his phone. He does that all the time, doesn't he? I bet war only makes worse."

They were interrupted by a chiming from Delilah's pocket. She sighed as she slid her phone out—she had forgotten to turn it off after listening to the radio earlier.

"Hi Diana."

"I'm about ready to call the police up there and tell them to get you, Del. I don't know how, but I will."

"They're very busy. How's Mom?"

"She's fine, she's fine, I— ...Do you even have food there?"

"Plenty."

"And what'll you do when it runs out?"

"I said 'plenty.'" She hung up, rested the phone in her lap, and switched it to silent mode. "Aunt Diana says hi."

Delilah stared down at the phone, forgetting to throw Juno a smile. She began tapping out a text message:

– Don't ever call us again. I won't pick up. Love you.

While Juno slept that night, Delilah told her neighbor what she had done.

"The police? So they can shoot you dead in self-defense? What will they see when they barge into that basement? A little white girl—Jewish, at best—cowering behind a mad, dirty Black woman. That's all anyone ever sees, isn't it? Your damn sister included. Well, I say good riddance. You certainly don't want her talking to Juno anymore, it's not good for a girl like that."

"...What do you mean?" Delilah whispered. "A girl like that."

"Oh, please, you know what—she's a GMO. They need to hear consistent messaging. Or they'll snap."

"...Juno's not a GMO."

"Oh really? She may have come right from you and that cracker,

but she's just like the lab ones. She ain't natural. Now I suppose there's nothing wrong with that—but you've got to be careful around her. I hate to break it to you… Your sister may be a princess, but she's right about one thing—half-devil doesn't cut it in heaven."

"…I'm going to sleep. Goodnight."

Delilah gnashed in the dark. A GMO. Unbelievable—even her sister wouldn't say something so dumb. Her mother might have—-she'd have said it just to toy with Delilah, then call her back in the middle of the night to say she couldn't shake the thought, that something told her she was right. And what if she was? Delilah couldn't be sure she'd ever met a GMO, but they couldn't be much worse than regular people. Maybe being a GMO felt nice sometimes. Every one of them was created with a purpose. To be tireless, or brilliant, or ravishing, or survive their parents' diseases. Whatever wrong in the world their creator saw fit to right. Must be nice. The only purpose Delilah ever heard for her creation was the same her mother would spit out for a stranger: "To praise the Lord and resist the White Devil." And in her mother's esteem, Delilah had already failed at both—Juno was the proof.

Delilah couldn't tell you why she created Juno. But Juno had never asked. Most likely her dad already told her something unoriginal, and she figured the truth didn't matter. Or maybe Juno already knew what Delilah took decades just to suspect. The truth does not exist. Even if the whole world wants you born, you still come out a screaming, gory, useless animal, your mother wounded and in mortal danger. If Juno were really a GMO, Delilah would have had the power to imbue her life with purpose. She would have chosen the purpose she used to believe was her own: to be loved.

Before the war, but not a moment too soon, Delilah brought Juno to New York for the first time, right to her mother's door. At the bridge over Lake Champlain into Upstate New York they hit a road block and waited bumper to bumper for hours while staties enforced the new Governor's cap on refugees. Delilah's driver's license passed inspection, and she answered the trooper's questions politely enough to cross the border. Along the highways as they drove south, they passed signs of the nation's unrest as reported in the news—travel centers along the highway gutted and boarded up, stretches of billboards tagged with swastikas, hate speech, messages of hope—but when they reached the city it was no different than Delilah remembered it. As her neighbor liked to predict, the sea level can't rise higher than New York's horse.

When Delilah and Juno arrived at the address her sister had relinquished, her mother answered the door and nearly scoffed, said, "Sorry ladies… I already did last call." But they went inside anyway. The next hour of their lives didn't matter too much. That's how Delilah resolved to explain it to Juno until the day she, herself, had the reason pinned. Her mother had been cordial, lowering the volume of the TV to host them in the living room. Even a little kind, offering Juno, who had never tasted fast food before—banned in Vermont, Delilah explained—a bucket of chicken scraps, still warm. While Juno squirreled through the ragged wing bones and drumsticks, Delilah and her mother took it to the kitchen, where Delilah dropped the real bomb: She had come to beg. Not for forgiveness, or understanding, or anything her mother would have relished giving—for her home. The collectors wouldn't stop calling for the mortgage, no matter how many times she told them to ask her ex-husband for it. To this Delilah's mother sneered, "Oh, you can take my money, baby. So long as you don't *ever* come back again."

Afterward, Delilah took Juno to the zoo and lost track of her while staring at the elephants. Five minutes, maybe, it couldn't have been more—but long enough for a small crowd to gather around a disturbance in the distance, down by the zebras. As Delilah ran she heard a steel shearing in the air—a child's wail—and as she neared the crowd she recognized a small, bright mass emerging, bursting forth like a solar flare—Juno. They were brandishing her, offering her to passersby who shook their heads, refused her. Delilah galloped into the fray spitting, "That's my daughter! Excuse me, that's my daughter!" And as Juno reached out to her she reached back—but the white woman holding her recoiled. The crowd constricted. Delilah heard them asking softly, "Is that the truth? Is that your mama?" And she watched Juno blubber, cheeks glistening, complete gibberish.

Delilah woke in the morning to a bug in her ear. A high-pitched nag, just barely whining through her morning grogginess.

"Psst. Delilah—Delilah, wake up. It's that daughter of yours, look what—"

"Shh."

Delilah opened her eyes, and she saw Juno in her corner with the phone to her ear. Her lips were moving.

In two bounds, Delilah unfurled from her pile of blankets and sweaters with her open palm cocked up like her mother's, and she appeared across the room and swung it down against Juno's cheek—an ember popped between them, and the phone clattered on the floor.

Delilah's skin beat and crawled with heat. Eyes wide, she stared down at Juno with her muscles wound tight as the minute, just last summer, when she'd had to pull Juno from a carriage's path in Central Park.

"What the hell do you think you're doing?" she blurted.

Juno cowered against the wall. "I was— …I was listening to the radio."

"She's a little liar, Delilah."

"Oh, I know," said Delilah.

Juno began to tremble against the wall, and tears boiled up in her eyes. She closed them. "I don't— …" She choked on gurgling stones in her throat. "I—I want to leave, Mama, I don't wanna be here anymore…"

The words raked Delilah. She crumbled to her knees and wrapped her arms around Juno, and she stared over her shoulder into the concrete wall.

The world she needed began to unfold from her skull: a fresh hardwood floor clapped into place over the concrete, and a crimson Persian rug alighted over it to match the slowly reddening walls. The dryer and washing machine became a clanky old turntable, maybe a jukebox glowing gently, too. Delilah's pile of blankets took on the legs of an antique daybed, and the nearby sediments of rubble grew green until they were rubber plants and young Venus flytraps. The barricade and the beach buckets of piss and shit at the stairs could be a darkwood bar, well-stocked with top-shelf liquors, glass vases plump and bright with citrus, and a built-in ice cooler. A few stools would be tucked under its counter, and around the room would be small, round tables for intimate arrangements of four or so. And Juno really was right about the little stone pile in the corner—a few potted Norfolk Island pines, some Boston ferns and… and peace lilies, and it was better than Mount Mansfield.

"I told you that 'Negroni' was—"

"Lay off," said Delilah.

Juno stiffened.

Delilah uncoiled her arms from around Juno and swiped up the phone as she stood. "Are you hungry, miss thing?" she asked.

Now curled up and sniveling in her blankets, Juno wiped her eyes. "We only have three rice cakes left. And some peanut butter."

"I heard that. Are you sure she's not being a primadonna?"

"No, no, that's— …I'll just, uh… We'll order some delivery."

"Alright, hold on—you've got to think carefully now. Who do you trust? Besides little ol' me."

As a rule, Delilah avoided trick questions, but this one landed. Nearly knocked her breath out. As she trudged across the basement back to her corner, her mind tripped over thoughts of the few people possibly left in her life. The mailman, likely no more. Her few friends had all fled the city at the first evacuation order or earlier, and none cared to please her enough to let her have her way.

"What about that man you like to string along? The white boy— you and these crackers… Noah the contractor. He's got big balls and no spine, doesn't he?"

She held the phone up to her nose to smash out a text message.

– Hi. Where are you?

The reply came in seconds.

– Down at my parents house. They're jarring preserves lol. Where are u?

– Safe with Juno. Can you bring us food?

– Where? Do u know when the supply trucks get there?

– We're in my basement

– Huh? Why?

– Cuz my house is still sexy

– Don't make me beat it up. How do I get past the checkpoints?

– Just have sex with the soldiers

– K. I'll leave in the morning

New York's presidential mansion was also featured in last month's *Architectural Digest*. It was the same brick fogey that used to house the governor, but the new president had installed a bowling alley in the basement and an observatory in the south tower, and he had revived the old backyard zoo from the 1920's. Delilah's eyes traced the page captions over and over, but her mind was busy with the image of helmeted bears, ostriches, giraffes, and penguins marching the perimeter of the mansion while the president fucked her sister on a bowling lane.

Last night Delilah had dreamt of Juno thrashing and screaming on the floor. At the base of her neck, oozing at the spine, was a clumsy incision. Delilah straddled her back and held her down with one hand—in the other she gripped a blood-smeared shard of glass. She dropped the shard, and she plunged her fingers into the wound to dig and dig for whatever was buried there. A glinting chip, a wire to snap, some claw-footed chemical micro-pump. Through Juno's screams and the grinding of teeth, she heard herself cooing an unintelligible nursery rhyme. She woke without finding whatever was in that wound, and guilt drove her to allow Juno two hours of radio time.

"...so no reinforcements from our friends the New England Federation, is what we're hearing."

"I don't doubt it, Jane, though I would hope for better from our neighbors. You know it's not an uncommon opinion that going it alone is what doomed us."

"There is that old saying, 'You can't keep trouble from coming, but you don't have to give it a chair—"

"Do you hear that, Delilah? That garbage you're letting her listen to? I swear, if I—"

"Shut up, please," Delilah murmured.

"Fine. But don't think I don't see you using up that magazine. Why don't you go polish the cutlery for once?"

Delilah let her hands drift up from *Architectural Digest*, and she stared into her palms. They didn't really seem all that dirty to her. But maybe they were. Everything else down here was filthy. She spat into each hand, and she began to rub the fluid deep into her arcane lines, up and down and between each finger, into her nails with the repetition of small circles.

"Mama! Mama there's a text from Noah—he says he's at the door! Can I go get him?"

Delilah lowered her clasped hands from her eyes, and there was Juno, standing by the greasy black remains of last night's fire.

"I'll get him. You just sit back down and listen to your radio."

She laid her magazine on the floor, and cold rushed back into her lap. As she rose, the chill spread over her body and tightened, but she dragged on toward the stairwell's dark.

The walls upstairs blared whiter than she remembered. She forced her eyes through the adjustment with recollections of the pride that followed every afternoon spent hunched at the walls to scrub away this or that offending mark. And the kitchen was as open house-ready as she always kept it, the living room and mud room, too. Delilah sailed through her wealth of proper placements and clever lines of sight, and she nearly forgot why she had come upstairs.

Feet away the front door rattled. Her blood thinned to a trickle—but it surged back, frothing, when she recalled Noah and food, promises, sex. She harried the locks and snatched at the doorknob, and a tall, dark figure swallowed up the doorway—she seized Noah into the house.

They embraced and did not kiss. Delilah's eyes darted to his hands—just a paper bag, a small bag—and back to his eyes, which were sad marbles. He smiled to himself, like he was on the subway.

"...You really look like shit, Del."

"My diet isn't working?"

Noah held her remark with wasteful silence, and Delilah felt an unusual burning in her cheeks.

"Come on," she said, "Somebody's hungry."

She snatched up Noah's empty hand and led him toward the basement. In the kitchen he pulled back, and Delilah bore her fidgets so he could awe.

"Man... Looks like you haven't been eating the mice, at least."

"Mice? No way—where?"

"Um... Everywhere? Well, that's where their shit is. Maybe they're out grocery shopping."

Delilah let her hand throttle the knob of the basement door as she eyed Noah and ground her teeth. “Nice try,” she said.

Noah’s boots paddled the concrete as he advanced toward Juno.

“Isn’t it quiet? What happened to the radio? Juno’s too good for it all the sudden? I can just imagine what she might have done while you left her down here, who she could have called… Do you really trust her? You don’t have to, you know.”

Delilah watched from her spot by the washing machine as Noah crouched in front of Juno. They exchanged inaudible whispers as he removed a wrapped sandwich from the bag, long and white in wax paper. When he stood up he bent himself into a bow, and he turned to thud back to Delilah. “So… I got you the usual.”

He sat down in front of Delilah with another wrapped sandwich in one hand—his other was crumpling the bag into a ball. When he slid the food into her lap, she went pale and grimaced. “Thank you,” she said. “Should I help you get all the food you left in your car?”

“This is all I brought, Del.”

She dug her shoulder blades into the washing machine. “…If I only eat one bite a day will it last till we win the war?”

“You’re supposed to eat the whole thing now. Or in the car. There’ll be plenty of food later. I’m taking you and Juno to my parents’ house.”

“Oh, they finally signed over the deed to me?”

“I’m serious. I’m not leaving here without you two.”

“…I’m sorry, Delilah. I wasn’t quite expecting that either. He’s been pretty good lately, after all. I guess we can give him more benefit of the doubt, if you like. But that’s how they get you, you know.”

"We're not going anywhere. I'm serious. Dude."

"Fuck, Del—why are you doing this? Do you think you'll be safe when they bomb the shit outta your house? Half the city's burning—dead."

Over Noah's shoulder, Delilah saw her daughter glance up from the sandwich in her hands. She watched her tired chewing until all she could see were the hollows in her cheeks. "Quiet down, please."

"No! I'm not letting you do this to yourself!" Noah spread his arms wide enough to bearhug. "What about Juno? You're gonna let her go through this lunatic shit when she could've been safe and clean and healthy somewhere weeks ago? You guys look like coal miners. It's freezing as fuck in here, and it smells like a septic tank, it fucking reeks. And I don't know what you were trying to pull in the kitchen, but you know the whole place is full of mouse holes and covered in their shit!" His open hands shrank into shuddering fists, but he reigned his arms back in. He tried to nuzzle Delilah's shins with his knuckles. "I'm not bringing any more food, I can't… I'm getting you out of here. I'm sorry, but that's final. *Final.*"

"Oh, it's final, I see now… Did you hear that, Delilah? That man is dropping F-bombs on your daughter. Is that how they talk around children where he's trying to take you?"

Juno tried to become as small as possible as she watched her mother breathe over the stone pile. She had seen Delilah count long breaths through crises in the past, but these now were dagger short and jabbed inward over and over, the kind of breathing Juno had only seen from frantic women losing control of their wombs on TV hospital beds. She hoped it would pass if she kept still and silent—but she heard Noah's careless boots thudding across the room.

"Time to get out of here, Juno," Noah whispered. "Go upstairs and get what you need. I'll meet you up there with your mom."

Juno had only just passed the black well of the fire pit when she heard a grunt. The room rattled, she turned. On the floor, facedown, Noah gurgled into a dark puddle. Delilah knelt beside him, a cinderblock cocked over her head.

She swung it downward and Juno looked away, she closed her eyes—she heard a terrible sound. Dull and stupid and wet.

Then quiet ballooned in her ears. The darkness in her eyes wriggled and jumped, alive with rashes of faint color. In time, through the haze, her mother's voice returned, muttering.

"Look at this red… Look at this. It's all wrong. It's—oh, come on… Red walls. Guess we'll just be red then, sure… Juno? Come lend Mama a hand."

About the author:

Desmond Saunders Peeples' writing has appeared or is forthcoming in *Big Bridge, Past-Ten, Goreyesque*, and elsewhere, and they write regularly for the Vermont Arts Council. They are the founding editor of *Mount Island*, a literary magazine for rural LGBTQ+ and POC voices. They hold degrees from Goddard College and Vermont College of Fine Arts. Desmond was born and lives still in Vermont. Learn more at desmondpeeples.com.

The Trial

Boluwatife Oyediran

"These are puritanical times. Private life is public business. Prurience is respectable, prurience and sentiment."
—J. M. Coetzee, *Disgrace*

It's a Monday morning, a busy day at the university. From the Division of Students' Affairs where I have submitted a proposal towards starting a literary club on the university campus, I receive this note: Student LIT/2017/229 to face panel inquiry at the DSA on Tuesday, April 2, 1:00 p.m. Failure to show attracts heavy penalty. No reason is stated as to why I have been called up, nothing about the proposal, nothing about the literary club. Just an inquiry. My mind raves but comes up with nothing. A quick shudder of fear tugs at me.

I arrive at the Division of Students' Affairs on Tuesday afternoon. After a brief wait, I am conducted to Room 203, the 'Panel Room', where I pass between two uniformed guards and the door closes behind me.

The Panel Room is a spacious yet cramped office, brightly lit, with tiled floors and walls painted white. Running around its perimeters, standing tall against the shuttered windows, are row after row of heavy metal cabinets marked Cases of Misbehaviours. In the center of the room are four chairs and a long table, finished in shiny black leather. Behind the table sits a fat, neckless man in a red tie and horn-rimmed glasses. He is clean-shaven, bald, and huge, like an animal from another world. From the ceiling a florescent lamp glows over him, leaving a dot of white shining in the middle of his head. He is soaked to midriff despite the air-conditioning, hunched over some papers, scribbling fast and pulling at his tie. His chest tag reads: PST (DR.) F. A. FOLAWE.

It is clear that he has been waiting for me. Without raising his head, he waves me over.

"Come on in, my friend," Dr. Folawe says, waving his short tubby arm above his head. "Come. Sit. Tell me your name and your course of study. I don't have all the time in the world. We have a long way to go."

"Yes, sir," I reply, sitting. "I am Samson Folorunsho, sir. BA Literature-in-English. 200 level. Yesterday I received a note, sir, to face a panel inquiry today."

"Yes, Samson Folorunsho, BA Literature-in-English. Your interrogator is coming. He's a Linguistics expert from your department. I'm only here to witness the interrogation and forward my report for adequate prosecution—which is very applicable in your case—to the director of students' affairs."

I am on the edge of my seat. "Sir?"

"Usually, three or more members of staff present themselves to tackle a case. But your case is different. Very different. It is straightforward."

I know too well I should not ask, should not say a word, but I ask anyway: "What is my case, sir? I don't understand what is going on."

Through the space above his glasses the man regards me briefly, dubiously, then lowers his head and continues to scribble. His pen dances over the papers, filling the room with a swift, scratching sound. He signs the bottoms of the papers with a flourish and packs them into a pile.

"You don't have any idea what's going on? You don't know what you've done?"

Silence.

There is a swift knock at the door. A tall, wiry man in a dark suit, with grey hair and rough stubble, shuffles in with an attaché case and hurries to take a seat beside the fat man.

"Sorry jare," the man says. "My car developed fault on the way."

"Ah," responds the fat man, "when does it not develop fault?"

There is a chuckling from both men, a chattery, luxurious laughter that shakes the tall man vigorously, almost tipping him off the chair. They regard each other with a knowing look as their laughter dies.

"Okay, er, since the boy is here let's get down to business," the wiry man says, reaching into his case for a sheaf of papers. "By God's grace, I am Johnson," he announces. "Pastor Professor Johnson Atanda, student advisor and associate professor of Stylistics, Department of English. You do know me, right?"

"Yes, sir," I say. "You always come to class with a pair of scissors."

"Good. It's good you know I'm a disciplinarian. I take a pair of scissors along to my classes in order to prune down extravagant hairstyles. And that's part of what we'll do here this morning, boy. Prune. Prune down!" He spits his words, emphasising the plosives, glances at the papers, shifting forward.

"We have summoned you regarding your proposal to establish a literary club and the sample short stories that came with it. You are a gifted writer, I must say. God has blessed you with an important gift, to be a voice of this generation."

"Thank you, sir."

"But," Johnson continues in a deep voice, a voice that demands silence, "but you have sent us stories that are way too—what do we call them now?"

"Disturbing. Immoral. Carnal," the fat man offers.

"Exactly! Carnal! Thank you." Putting on his glasses, the professor peruses the papers, whistling softly and shaking his head. "Too bad," he tuts at last, shifting forward again. "How old are you, boy?"

"Nineteen, sir."

"Nineteen. The Age of Reason. Do you know that the steps you take at your young age will determine how you'll end your life? You see, if you tell us the truth about yourself and your stories, we will be considerate, particularly because you are the son of one of our pastors. We want to help you. We want to lead you on the path of godly living. That is the core reason this private Christian university was established. To raise godly destinies. That is why all the lecturers we have here are children of God. That is why pastors' children like you are required to attend school here. May God bless Papa, our chancellor, unto whom was given the vision to start this university and the ministry that runs it. Er..." His fingers drum the table nervously. Then in a quick, smart gesture he extracts a single leaf from the sheaf, advances it across the table and stabs a gnarled finger on a paragraph.

"Okay, read this to us, boy. Where it says *will as well publish.* Read what you wrote. Listen to yourself."

I draw the paper closer, a photocopy of my proposal, the proposal to start a literary club on campus. Now I know for certain I am in trouble. They have made photocopies. Has my dad received a copy as well? Could he be facing an inquiry as well? A lump fills my throat like a morsel of fufu. I swallow and swallow, but when I open my mouth to talk, nothing comes out.

"Look, we don't have time," the fat man growls, leaning forward. Through his nostrils, which are thick with hair, comes the soft rattle of trapped mucus. Before him is a sheet of paper, his thick hand rests on it.

I read: "'The University'—that's what we chose to name our literary club. It's an adaptation of the 1580s sect of dramatists who championed the Elizabethan theatre."

The professor gives an impatient snort. "Yes, we know all that. We know how you came about the name The University Wits. Just read what's on the paper."

"Yes, sir. 'The University Wits will as well publish excerpts from books. There will be no thematic discrimination, nor will there be space for nepotism.'"

"Good. Stop there, boy. That's the bone of contention: No thematic discrimination. What is that supposed to mean? Elaborate, please."

I breathe in deeply. "It simply means what it states, sir. That any well-written story will be published without questioning whatever theme it contains."

"Any story?" the fat man interrupts.

"Yes, sir. Because, storytelling, to my best knowledge, and in our publishing, should be diversified. We want to listen to all sides and help these diverse voices reach the public. Excluding the ones directed at us as a literary community, we shall not be on the receiving end of any blame, criticism, or misconception launched against any of the pieces we publish on our blog. That's what we mean by no thematic discrimination, sir."

The old men glance at each other. Murmured words pass between them.

My palms are clammy with sweat; I rub them together, then straighten my trousers.

"You said *we*, boy. How many are you?" the professor demands.

"I don't yet know, sir. But I'm certain that students will want to join as soon as we start publishing. At the moment, I am backed by my guys, Mayowa, Adedayor, and Jesus Pet."

The professor nods his head heavily, resting back in his chair.

"So, my boy, to put words in your mouth, so to speak, are you trying to aver that your club will not publish stories that glorify God's name alone, as is the law of the university?"

My eyes wander, for the first time, to the poster of Christ on the wall, a white Christ of course, hung on the cross at Golgotha, battered with suffering, next to the university year calendar. The bright aureole around His head, the crown of thorns, His deep sunken eyes, mouth contorted in anguish, with streams of clotted blood running down His scarred body to His thin, tight hips. Hipbones of Christ, I think, as Michael Ondaatje puts it.

"I don't know what you mean by stories that glorify God's name alone, sir," I respond. "But I do know the story of Judas. Does the story of Judas glorify God's name alone? I don't know. All I know is it is a deeply emotional tale of betrayal, how he kissed Christ to His death. And that's all that matters, that's the essence."

A long silence falls. For a moment I cease to hear the soft purring of the air conditioner, the rustle of papers, the swish of a pen. I think I am deaf, stunned by the heat of the African summer noon. Have I been struck deaf in the middle of the interrogation? Did Galileo go deaf before the Catholic fanatics, Joan of Arc before the pro-English court, Christ before Pilate?

"You know what?" the fat man begins, leisurely twirling his pen in his fingers. "There is a problem with you young people today. So far as you get food to eat and clothes to wear you go around doing whatever you want, standing up for some nonsense satanic philosophies. Are you not saying all of this because you're fed and clothed daily and attend one of the—if not the most expensive of universities in this country? Are you not speaking this way because you were born and bred in the four walls of a family where the fingers of poverty cannot reach you—prod you? If you were hawking Gala and bottled water in the streets of Lagos or Kaduna, would you be talking all this nonsense?" As he talks his flabby jowls shake like akamu, his robust stomach expanding and constricting.

The professor unfolds his handkerchief, wipes his forehead, and sits up. "Let's press even further," he says. "You submitted three sample stories. We've read and analyzed them, reviewed them, understood them. The first, "A Man in Love", is about a young boy, an undergraduate student of literature who is deeply involved in an ungodly sexual relationship with a lady, a graduate student who is significantly older than him. If my guess is right, that's you, abi?"

"No. Not me. It's fiction."

"Fictional autobiography?"

"I can't say. It's just a story."

"But there's a heavy dose of verisimilitude in that story. Are you sure that's not you?"

I look the professor in the eyes. "Sir, it's just a story. Please."

"Okay. The second story, "A Home for Desire", is also about a young student of literature who, cut away from fornication and social life, resolves to quenching his sexual urges by masturbating in the secrecy of his room. He, this character, stands close to you like a second skin."

Frowning, I cannot hide my annoyance. "Sir, I draw my stories from facts and imagination. I expect most of my readers will understand this and not try to crosscheck my stories with my own personal life."

The professor continues. "Those two stories are, from the outset, troubling in themselves. In the course of the first reading, we thought we would be able to endure, that was until we read the third story, "Love Story", written in sublime English. It is an awful story, furnished with such excruciating details."

I am silent, fingers crossed, head lowered. I feel drowsy, tired, tired to the bones. I have sacrificially spent the bulk of the day explaining difficult literary terms to, first, a group of Post-UTME candidates, then to a middle-aged Ph.D student who wants to retake his GCE. I am tired and not ready for all this.

Professor Johnson selects two sheets from the sheaf and slides it across the table.

"Read," he says. "Read your 'Love Story'. Listen to yourself." He pushes the papers forward and one sheet falls to the floor.

I don't need to read the story; I know it by heart. Nonetheless I cannot look away from the lines, the dark prints done in Bembo and Goudy fonts. The words of my courage, as it were. I pick up the paper, rub my eyes, begin:

> *"'In class, every morning, my lover passes me by without greeting or saying a word to me. Instead, he goes over to a gaggle of our classmates and hugs the girls tight, one after another, then exchanges slap handshakes with the guys. He is a cool, handsome guy. He is the best I've ever seen. His honey-brown skin smooth and spotless; his teeth as white as, well... snow; his dark hair, overly oiled, a halo around his head, like the hair of an African woman! I stand staring at him, mesmerised by his pink lips. I stand with a prick of jealousy in my heart, hoping he might find out how much I love him. I stand there with my love for him buried deep within me, because to unravel it is death."'*

"For semantic purposes, I have highlighted here in my copy, 'because to unravel it is death,'" the professor says, cutting in. "You will explain that later, of course, in case you have any defense. Continue on from *On Thursday afternoons*. Third paragraph."

I scan the sheet, skip to—

> *"On Thursday afternoons my lover plays keyboard at the Chapel. I go there to see him play, to fill my ears with lovely music. When the notes climb high and melodious, when he closes his eyes and lets his fingers dance swiftly over the keys as the song leader drags 'ogene dooooh' in song worship, I try to imagine my lover seeing me in the darkness of his head. I imagine him seeing that God, sitting on high, is love. And I do hope he remembers that I am created in the likeness of God, that I am love as well, that my kind of love should be acceptable. An all-conquering offering, a sacrifice for the sins of the nation."'*

"Did you hear that?" the fat man interjects. "'An all-conquering offering.' Is there any other all-conquering offering than Christ Jesus? Blasphemy!" he yells. Then with an evil smile spreading across his lips like a blob of oil spreading in a pan, he says, "You can't get away with this, boy. Not while I'm still the prosecutor here."

It dawns on me. These are the men I have been facing: the professor and the prosecutor, the plosives, and the police! I grip the paper tight.

"Read on, boy," the professor beams. "Next paragraph."

Reluctantly, with a tongue as heavy as iron, I continue:

"'I do not listen to music often, but I love to listen to "My Kind of Love" by Emeli Sandé. I like it not because of how it is sung, not for the lilt in Sandé's voice, but for the underlying message it carries, the fact that love can be represented in shades, in fact misrepresented. Love is a deeply personal thing. We should love in our own personal and special way, not guided by rules of nature or religion or tradition. Remember Ziggy Marley: Love is my religion/I don't condemn, I don't convert/Bring all the lovers to the fold/'Cause no one is gonna lose their soul."'

The professor chuckles lightly. "I think I like your style. Your story carries me along like a baby in safe arms." The professor's smiling face suddenly takes on a serious demeanor. "The remainder of your love story, as it appears, is sketchy," he says. "There is a run-through addition to the main plot, a sub-plot that gives quite enough about the protagonist's relationship with a girl. Here it says:

"'I have been dating a girl for many months now and I don't like how it has been going lately. Most evenings, when it is gloomy and I need someone to talk to I call her over the phone and say sweet words to her. Sometimes I read her a poem and laugh at her dry jokes. But most times I refuse to pick her calls. Most times talking to her is talking to wood. Instead of being emotional and touching, as it happens to most guys, my heart, I have observed, is impassive, impassive and unyielding. It appears to me that I'm made up that way: unyielding to the opposite sex—fixed, set, like concrete. I do not know how to tell her that she is not my lover, that what I feel for her is as cold and as waxy as sleeping red oil. Yet I go on with the norm, I drag to get along. Someday I will turn the other way round and, like a pig waddling through murky waters, go against the currents. Every day I pray for strength to say the things I cannot say, to scream loud and clear and then await death if that would be my portion.'"

Sitting back in his chair the professor asks, "Now what does this excerpt suggest to us, boy?"

Silence.

"Did you infer anything?"

I shrug.

"Then what is it? Speak."

"Not that I—I cannot speak," I stutter, "but I cannot make you understand. I cannot make anyone understand what is happening inside me. I cannot even explain it to myself."

"Let me help you out then," says the professor. "Since you're that incapacitated, allow me. You see, the narrator, we eventually discover, is a guy after all. A guy. Like you. But how can that be? From the outset, the narrator, who we perfectly assumed to be a girl, has been speaking about an admiration for a male classmate, until suddenly out of the blue it is said that the narrator—we need not evade the pronoun "he" now—it is said that he, the narrator, is in a relationship with a girl, as is natural, although he feels nothing for the girl, not even the slightest ease. Do you follow to this point? So, in our opinion, this makes the story—your story—entirely weird. I mean what kind of story is this? Do you have any defense?"

Do I have any defense? Defense against what? Defense against the Dark Arts? When did stories become objects of scrutiny that needed to be defended as suspects are defended in court?

Finally, I speak. "It's a love story, sir. Like other love stories. But quite unique. That is my defense."

With his face creased in a deep frown the prosecutor fusses in his seat, making the leather crackle. He tilts sideways until he is comfortably seated. "You mean this is a proper love story? Like Romeo and Juliet, eh?"

"Yes, a proper love story, sir. But, evidently, not like Romeo and Juliet. Like I said, it is unique."

"And what makes it unique?"

"The fact that it is a love story."

"What do you mean? Are you saying that all love stories—stories about a guy in love with another guy, as is the case with your story—are you saying all of them are unique?"

"You don't get me. In clear terms, I am saying that my own story, not all love stories, is unique. Because it is weird, because you've never seen anything like it, that makes it unique."

"And proper?"

"Yes, and proper."

"Shut up, it is not proper," the prosecutor snaps. "It is not a proper story! It is a—I need not use that awful word, but I can't help but use it at this moment—it is a gay story. Homosexual stuff!"

There is silence, prolonged, subjugating the tension in the air.

Words pass in murmurs. A nod of the head, a long perusal of another copy of the story. From where I am seated, a few inches removed from the table, I can see the prosecutor copying from my stories, hunting for words, carnal words. Is the man annotating the report? Is he taking me by my words, the words on paper, rather than the words of my explanations?

After what seems like a long time, the prosecutor signs at the bottom of the paper, slides it into a file that says VERDICT and looks up with a proud face. Gleefully he inserts the tip of his pen into its cap, puts it in his breast pocket, setting his horn-rimmed glasses down on the table. Then he sits back in a way that makes his short, almost non-existent neck crease into folds, like the ring-like segments on an earthworm's body, coming out puffy at the top of his soaked collar.

The professor glances at the papers, then, gesticulating with his long, veinous hands, he demands, "Now explain what you mean by *because to unravel it is death and an all-conquering offering*."

"There's nothing much to say," I begin. "Homosexuality"—I am surprised at how easily I use the word—"homosexuality is not welcomed here in this country. To confess this kind of love in this stifling country of ours, to unravel it, is death. In the same vein, writing about this kind of love and the persecutions that follow, being a writer of such a motion, paddling against the currents, is what I describe as being the all-conquering offering, the sacrifice for the sins of the nation. What nation? Our nation. What sins? The killings in the streets."

"So what are you saying now?" the prosecutor interrupts. "What are you purporting yourself to be now?"

"A voice," I contemplate before continuing. "A voice in the desert. Like the voice of John the Baptist talking about the coming of Christ."

Suddenly the prosecutor leans across the table and unfurls his arm, the flat of his palm catching my face, hard and surprising.

The professor rises. "Careful, Pastor," he says. "Please, sit." He turns to me and says, "It is over now. Do you have anything else to say?" He takes his seat.

I press a palm against my burning cheek. "Yes. What I have to say is that who someone chooses to love should not be anybody else's business. It is not a university authority matter. It is not a government matter. It is not a police matter. It is not your concern! Okay?!" Tears blur my vision, but I have said it all. My mind is now clear. My limbs start to relax.

The prosecutor, clearly pissed, hisses in vexation. "Mad fellow," he says dismissively, saliva gathering at the corners of his mouth. With a quick move of his hand, he presses a button under the table.

In the next moment, the guards from outside the door rush in. They look dangerous; they look like trouble.

"I have written the verdict," says the prosecutor, holding up a file. "Please take this convict to confinement."

"Convict?" I jolt out of my seat.

"Yes. You will be transported to confinement," explains the professor. "You will be in solitary, without food and water perhaps, until you are released by a higher authority—a written order from the chancellor will do—or until you give up these premonitions of yours and repent of your ways."

A heavy hand grips my shoulder. I feel I might piss in my trousers.

"You have to repent," the prosecutor affirms. "You know the Scriptures. You know that everything you've said here is wrong, heretic. You must repent. Else..."

The guards are now standing on both sides of me, with dangerous, hard eyes.

"I—I don't understand," I stutter. "I thought we were having a debate?"

The prosecutor waves a hand at me, waving my words away, waving me quiet.

"Please, take him away."

I look to the professor for help. The thin man is seated, composed in his chair, arms folded across his chest, looking sullen rather than victorious.

The heavy hand drags me up by my shoulder. A speck of pain shoots through my left scapula. I wriggle free, straighten my shirt.

"I will follow you, peacefully," I say. "You don't have to be rough with me. I will cooperate."

But, with a sudden, startling gesture, the guards each grab my trousers at the waist and, lifting me off the ground, drag me away, towards a waiting van.

About the author:

Boluwatife Oyediran is a Nigerian visual artist and an MFA in Painting candidate at the Rhode Island School of Design, USA.